Sign of the Seed

A Veteran Police Officer's Confrontation With Faith

Don Deputy

First Edition Design Publishing
Sarasota Florida USA

Sign of the Seed
Copyright ©2022 Don Deputy

ISBN 978-1506-910-68-0 HCJ
ISBN 978-1506-910-69-7 PBK
ISBN 978-1506-910-70-3 EBK
ISBN 978-1506-910-71-0 LG PRT PBK
ISBN 978-1506-910-82-6 MT

LCCN 2022920164

September 2022

Published and Distributed by
First Edition Design Publishing, Inc.
P.O. Box 17646, Sarasota, FL 34276-3217
www.firsteditiondesignpublishing.com

Sign of the Seed is dedicated to all the brave women and men who courageously serve as law enforcement officers. In particular, this novel is dedicated to the memory of a friend and fallen officer, Craig Herbert, end of watch on March 6, 2005.

The author would like to acknowledge the invaluable assistance of Tina Reid, Janet Simpson, and Alison Whitmarsh for much-needed encouragement and guidance leading to the completion of *Sign of the Seed.*

CHAPTER 1

A reliable donut, is that too much to ask? Mel had been dropping by Detwiler's Delicious Donuts on the way to roll call for years. Tonight, the apple fritter was too doughy, with not enough apple bits or glaze to make it interesting. He liked his apple fritters crispy, sweet, and loaded with delicious bits of apple. While tonight's sack failed at each measure, he ate them anyway. A reliable donut was all he wanted tonight, along with a cup of black coffee and an uneventful shift. He always thought the thing about policemen and donuts was true, at least it was for him.

Most of the old-time late-shift police officers he had worked with not only enjoyed a good donut but loved the greasy food from neighborhood all-night diners. That thought reminded him of his old man, who later in his life complained when he thought White Castle changed their hamburger recipe, causing their famous gut-bombs to be less greasy than before.

Detwiler's Delicious Donuts had been around a long time, longer than Mel had been on the job. Amos Detwiler, the founder, was considered a fine Amish baker during his tenure as the proprietor. He had provided the city's best donuts and cakes along with a morning social spot for the Amish of the area as well as anyone desiring a satisfying authentic Amish pastry, coffee, and conversation. Amos worked the donut dough until rheumatoid arthritis curled his fingers enough to prevent him from kneading the dough or making change for purchases. Jacob Detwiler, Amos's only son, never returned from Rumspringa, the Amish rite of passage. As a result, when Amos retired, he sold Detwiler's to an accountant from New York and, well, there you have it.

Mel often arrived at late shift roll call with a sack of apple fritters, sometimes sharing, sometimes not. He was anxious for Lt. Weber to finish the roll call read. Roll call would usually consist of a pre-shift informational briefing, often including topics such as locations where recent crimes had been committed, any citizen's complaints, such as vehicles speeding through residential neighborhoods, and a review of the previous shift's incident reports and activity. Tonight, a short training video describing the latest blood-borne pathogen was included. If you asked Mel, he would say roll call should never last longer than a two-donut snack. He wanted to get out of the roll call room and start working on a second cup of coffee. Fortunately, Lt. Weber was mercifully brief tonight, and of course, Monday nights were usually slow.

Typically, Sunday nights were the slowest night of the week. Then each following night would get busier and busier, leading up to Saturday night when you could usually count on everything breaking loose. By Saturday night, driving down Washington Street at midnight was like playing bumper cars with drunk drivers. Tonight, a Monday, should be slow except for two things. One, it was just starting to sleet onto the already fallen snow causing the streets to get slicker. And two, they were now in the middle of what he sarcastically called the annual Christmas robbery season. For as long as he had been a policeman, there had always been a significant uptick in quick-stop market and gas station robberies starting Thanksgiving weekend and continuing through Christmas. What he didn't understand was why. It wasn't as if these robbers were doing stick-ups to get money to purchase Christmas gifts.

Mel also couldn't understand, with most people in today's economy using plastic or payment apps for purchases, was it worth the risk? Considering that once a cashier had a hundred dollars in the register, a cash drop into the store safe was usually required. It just didn't seem there was much profit in doing hold-ups anymore. Going to jail over a hundred bucks didn't make any sense, and who was to know if the cashier or some customer was a crazy concealed carry nut with a hero complex. A slow night, that's what he wanted.

Lt. Weber briefly discussed a few recent incident reports, then finished roll call by summarizing an assault report taken after an incident at the Burger Boy Sandwich Shop on State Road 76. Weber explained that a customer from the drive-up window discovered the plain cheeseburger he ordered turned out to be a not-so-plain cheeseburger, loaded with the usual, but unwanted, condiments. The disgruntled customer, later identified as Mack Reynolds, entered the store to complain, which led to an argument with the cashier. After one too many less-than-casual insults to his intelligence, the cashier jumped over the customer service counter after the now-surprised customer, landing a solid right-hand punch square to the customer's left cheek.

After patiently listening to the case summary, late shift officer Thaddeus Morrell remarked, "Good thing that knuckle sandwich wasn't supersized!"

Officer Cory Hubbard stood up to leave roll call and added, "That's one Big Mac attack that didn't go down well."

CHAPTER 2

An hour into the shift, the City of Templeton police dispatcher broadcast over the police radio, "Templeton cars 30 and 62. Car 30 and car 62, check a domestic, 5436 S. Payton Avenue. Apartment number four, the basement apartment, loud domestic dispute. Call came from a neighbor," assigning Officers Adam Simpson and Mel Williams to the domestic.

Adam, a young rookie Templeton police officer, was on late shift being trained by Officer Parker Finchum. Adam was driving and handling all the radio calls while Parker was watching and advising when necessary. Adam stopped in front of the residence, and Mel was waiting for them, having parked his patrol car across the end of the driveway blocking anyone's fast exit.

All three walked through the freshly fallen snow which covered the sidewalk on the north side of the old, dilapidated two-story house, split into four small apartments. Using his flashlight, Adam located a door with the number four posted next to it. Overflowing trash cans occupied a cracked concrete slab next to the basement exterior door, which looked about as secure as a Bernie Madoff investment account.

As Adam knocked on the door and announced, "Police," the officers could hear arguing from inside the apartment. A woman yelled in an exasperated-sounding voice, "See, they're here. I told you someone would call the police," followed by the sound of feet stomping up rickety old stairs. The door creaked open wide and the officers were greeted by a nearly six-foot-tall, curvy middle-aged woman who was wearing a tight-fitting maroon dress that was designed to entice the male viewer. Her long curly hair was pinned up around the top of her head, and the hoops of her earrings seemed large enough to train champion show dogs. She aggressively waved her left hand at the officers in a come-a-long fashion, directing them to follow her as she said, "Come on down here and *talk* to this guy," emphasizing the word talk. The three officers carefully walked single file down the bare wooden stairs and entered the one-room basement apartment.

The apartment was sparsely furnished, lit only by a small lamp on a table in the corner and a bare sixty-watt light bulb hanging from the ceiling. Mel walked over to a middle-aged man sitting in a wheelchair next to a small drop-leaf dining table positioned against a basement wall. While Mel quietly talked to the guy for several minutes, Adam and Parker directed the woman to the opposite side of the room. She used exaggerated hand gestures while loudly describing how after she returned home from work, her boyfriend began accusing her of everything from having an affair to spending all their money.

As she was rattling on about all his abuses, mental and physical, Adam glanced over to Mel, who was leaning over close while listening to the guy, then speaking softly back to him. The guy was wearing an old gray sweater and dirty blue jeans. The way his right pants leg was draped over his lap made it obvious why he was in the wheelchair. He had spittle on his face where the woman had spit on him, and the homemade tattoos covering his left forearm suggested he might have had too much time on his hands. Adam noticed tears in the guy's eyes as he pulled his shirt up to show Mel something on his stomach. The guy then used the loose pant leg to wipe the spit off his face and tears from his eyes.

Adam's attention turned back to the woman who was continuing her tirade and asked her, "Are you injured?" In response, she held her hands, one on top of the other, palms pressed flat across her heart while she said with what sounded like mock passion, "Yeah, Mister Policeman, he hurt me really bad, AND he takes all my money!" ·

"Where do you work?" asked Adam.

"The club, Olivia's Gentleman's Club," she replied, then paused briefly, placing her palms against her hips, fingers forward, as she leaned to one side in a dramatic pose and added as if to explain, "I'm an exotic dancer." With a frown, she turned and pointed at the guy in the wheelchair, saying, "And he keeps accusing me of being with those guys, but I hadn't been."

Adam then overheard Mel, who was squatting down next to the wheelchair, face to face with the guy, in a soft, sympathetic voice, ask, "Do you know how to stop an argument?" After a silent moment, as the guy just stared at Mel with sad, helpless eyes, Mel continued with just one word, spoken gently with obvious concern and compassion, "Listen."

To that, the woman, who must have been eavesdropping, bellowed, "Yaaah baby, *LISTEN!*" She then grabbed her tiny pink sequined purse, tossed her long black coat over her arm, and stormed up the stairs in a dramatic huff. After she slammed the door shut behind her, Parker told the guy to call the police if she returned and caused any problems.

As the three officers walked to their squad cars, they watched the tall woman trying her best to make a triumphant march out of the neighborhood, strutting in high heels not well suited for the slick, wet sheet of snow that covered the city sidewalk. Adam turned to Mel and, with a question in his voice, asked, "That guy, in a wheelchair, living in a dirty basement? That one-legged, spit-wiping boyfriend of a stripper lives in a basement? There wasn't a handrail. I even had to be careful not to fall going up and down those decrepit old stairs."

"Yeah, well," Mel explained, "you see lots of stuff out here." Continuing without any display of emotion, "The guy told me they'd been together off and on again for a little while. Oddly enough, he told me he still loves her. He's a veteran and lost his leg to an IED in the war in Afghanistan. It also tore up his stomach. He showed me where, during their argument, she ripped out the tube to his colostomy bag attached to the side of his stomach. He reattached it before we arrived. He says she makes her money as a dancer at Olivia's but spends it all on cigarettes, junk food, and who knows what else. She also takes some of his military disability pay, leaving him little money to pay for these fashionable accommodations they share," Mel said as he turned and pointed to the shabby door in mock appreciation of the dark, damp, and dingy basement apartment the officers had just left.

"Why doesn't he have a prosthetic leg?" Parker asked.

"He does. I saw one leaning up in a corner. When I pointed to it and asked him about it, he told me it was too uncomfortable and painful to use," Mel replied.

"Those stairs are steep. How does he get up and down?" asked Adam.

Mel replied, "You know, I was wondering that too, so I asked him. He said she never helps him up and down the stairs. He would move the wheelchair close to the stairs and then scoot his butt onto the first stair-step. He would then fold up his wheelchair and move it one step at a time in front of him while using his arm strength to pull himself up or down each stair step while in a sitting position. Then using his one leg, which was covered in shrapnel scars, he would push up or slide down depending on which direction he was moving. He said it was slow going but had no complaints."

Mel paused a second and watched the exotic dancer pull the long dark coat over her shoulders as she was moving down the street, then added, "He may not know much about how to pick women, but in my opinion, that guy, he's the real deal."

wheel chair not with chare.

CHAPTER 3

Officer Jeramy Doodeman was at the Templeton Police station completing paperwork on a theft report while Officer Carl Zimmerman was sitting at the next desk finishing an accident report from the previous night. Suddenly, Templeton Officer Teresa O'Brian's voice interrupted the calm, blasting over the officers' radio microphones in an excited yet professionally controlled voice, "In pursuit, car 41 in pursuit, eastbound 30th Street approaching Gillespie Park Road. Red Dodge Caravan at a high rate of speed." Teresa worked a tactical shift overlapping evening and night shifts and had a knack for finding stolen cars. Hearing the broadcast, all officers still at the police station began to run to their patrol cars.

Department regulations limit two patrol cars to follow the initiating police car in a vehicle pursuit. This didn't prevent other patrol cars from driving parallel to the pursuit, putting them in place to intercept the suspect car if it made a sudden turn. Officers could also try to advance in front of the pursuit to stop civilian traffic at intersections permitting the pursuit to pass safely. They also could get into position to set up a tire deflation device in front of the pursued vehicle.

As Jeramy and Carl raced to the roll call room exit door, Jeramy fumbled, trying to unclip his patrol car keys from his duty belt, dropping them to the floor. He scooped the keys off the floor as Carl cracked a smile in his direction and scooted past him getting into his police car first. Jeramy followed Carl's squad car out of the police parking lot, red lights flashing, sirens blaring, and tires spinning, trying to get traction in the fresh snow.

The pursuit changed direction and circled back, allowing Jeramy and Carl to intersect the chase at 64th Street and Gillespie Park Road. Carl was still in front of Jeramy and positioned his car at 64th Street, where he pushed a dashboard button that remotely opened the police car's trunk lid. He jumped from his vehicle and retrieved the tire deflation device that, when deployed properly, would extend a spike-laden strip across an entire lane of traffic. Jeramy parked fifty feet behind Carl's police car and watched him prepare the device for use. Jeramy was thinking had he not dropped his keys, he would be the one involved in the action, preparing to use the stop sticks, not Carl.

It had only been seconds when Jeramy, who was still sitting in his car, first heard, then saw, the red Dodge Caravan careening toward them with Teresa in pursuit. As trained, Carl stood behind his patrol car, using it as a shield from the oncoming pursuit. Watching the cars approach, he waited for the right time before tossing the spike-covered strip into the Caravan's travel lane. Immediately after the Caravan rolled over the spikes, Carl would need to quickly use an attached rope to retract the strip to prevent Teresa's police car from also rolling over the spikes.

Jeramy watched Carl heave the device into the street, then suddenly, the Caravan swerved, trying to avoid the spikes. Because of its speed and the slick road conditions, the Caravan went into an uncontrolled skid sideways, crashing into the front of Carl's patrol car. The impact looked and sounded like an explosion, complete with fiberglass car body parts hurled into the air and then scattered all around the snowy street. The force from the colliding minivan violently pushed Carl's patrol car back, striking him and trapping him underneath.

In the excitement of the pursuit, Jeramy and Carl both left their sirens on. That, along with the bright red and blue flashing emergency lights mixed with the smoke and radiator steam, created a surreal setting among the residential neighborhood's brightly lit Christmas lights and yard decorations. When Jeramy got to Carl, he immediately knew it was very bad.

Car chase into police ch.ll

CHAPTER 4

Police funerals are steeped in tradition and honor, and in that respect, Carl's was no different. Carl's funeral was different in that he was the first Templeton police officer to die in the line of duty.

Templeton was formed as a small unincorporated town 40 years prior, and the police department grew as the town matured into a city. From the original town marshal and one deputy, the department expanded to 72 sworn officers by the time of Carl's death. Unfortunately, it seemed every couple of years, a Templeton officer got hurt on duty. Sometimes in a traffic accident, responding to an incident, other times while apprehending a resisting criminal, or as in Cory's case, injured in a training accident. Cory's incident was notable because he accidentally shot himself in the foot during semiannual handgun qualifying at the pistol range and thus entered into an unwanted chapter of department history. Regardless, no Templeton officer was prepared for the ordeal of an on-duty death.

Policemen can be good at supporting each other in times of tragedy. Officers arrived for Carl's funeral from police departments all over the nation, one or two from each of the country's coasts and many in between, to honor Carl at his funeral. The viewing took hours, which no doubt took its toll on Carl's pretty wife and two young daughters. How were they to know just five days prior this would be their fate?

The line for viewing the flag-draped coffin snaked around the inside of the church, stretching out the main door and into the parking lot. Jeramy always thought open-casket funerals were morbid, and he was pleased this was a closed-coffin funeral. Most of the people in the line tried to say something meaningful to Carl's wife but really, what was there to say? When it was Jeramy's turn, he had no words. Instead gave her a gentle hug. He thought it cruel to put this fine young family through all the pomp and circumstance typical of a traditional police funeral, which served the surviving officers and the police department more than the deceased's family. The funeral began after the viewing ended. Among others, the police chief spoke, the mayor spoke, and the Lt. Governor made an appearance, giving a brief word of encouragement. Even though some of the speakers had never met Carl, all had kind words describing his heroism, good character, and devotion to his job.

Templeton Police Department Chaplain Bill Gossett was the last to speak. The funeral was held in the church Carl attended. Chaplain Gossett, who had also been Carl's pastor, spoke with conviction that while Carl's body was no longer with us, because of his strong faith, Carl's soul was now with Jesus.

Jeramy had heard this all before at other funerals. He had little experience with this type of churchy talk other than his attendance at weddings and funerals, what he called the beginnings and the endings. His mother made him go to Sunday school when he was young, but he figured nothing from that stuck. Chaplain Gossett also spoke of Carl's strong faith in God, heroism, and fine character. He mentioned that Carl had been involved in the Coats for Kids program, an effort to collect donations of used children's coats to distribute to the children of needy families during the cold Indiana winter months. Next, he described how Carl volunteered the last Saturday morning of every month at the Salvation Army food pantry. Funny, Jeramy thought, you can work with a guy for years and spend time at a coffee shop talking endlessly about nothing, yet Carl never mentioned such things. Yeah, sure, he always thought Carl was a good guy, but it turned out Carl really was a good guy. As Jeramy walked out of the church through the cold wind to his police car, he stopped and looked back, noticing the tall church steeple through the light snow, pointing toward the heavens.

Jeramy joined the longest funeral procession he had ever driven, winding its way six miles to the cemetery where Carl would be buried. Being a Templeton police officer, Jeramy was in uniform and part of the grave-site ceremony. All officers stood at attention and in formation as the casket was carried to its final resting place, where the chaplain spoke again, committing Carl to eternity. From a hill next to the cemetery, a lone bagpiper could be heard mournfully playing *Amazing Grace*. Jeramy didn't know what grace had to do with it. Carl was a fine young man with a family who needed him. It just didn't seem right. If there was a God in Heaven, why would he allow such a senseless death?

Light snow continued to fall on that cold and windy Indiana day. Jeramy considered it an honor to be part of Carl's service but didn't want this day ever to be repeated. He never told anyone about dropping his keys in the squad room in front of Carl. He often thought about the deadly consequences and wondered, what if he had not dropped his keys, this could have been his funeral, and that thought scared him. He was uncomfortable thinking about the unknown of death.

Funeral and shot in foot.

CHAPTER 5

Glancing in the rearview mirror as he sped away from Piero's Pizza Pies, Piper could see an irate young man run from the entrance of the building. The man was furiously yelling as he tossed a take-out box aside, spilling the fresh pizza onto the sidewalk, then pointed aggressively in Piper's direction. Piper found it amusing. The idiot left his car unlocked and running, then went inside to pick up a pizza. What did he expect a thief like Piper to do, ignore an open invitation to steal the car? Adjusting his body into the seat and getting comfortable, he looked around at the inside of the Chevrolet Malibu and figured it would do.

Stole running car at pizza shop

CHAPTER 6

Police work is a twenty-four-hour-a-day, seven-days-a-week occupation. While the Templeton Police Department was involved in conducting Carl's viewing and funeral services, neighboring police departments arranged to handle all calls for police service within the Templeton jurisdiction. So, life went on while Carl's did not. Except for the sadness caused by the loss of Carl, the next shift after the funeral was business as usual.

It did seem to help when the Chief hung a nicely framed portrait of Carl's last department formal photo in the lobby a week later. Things began to normalize relatively quickly. There was no other choice. The officers had an important job to do.

Charles enjoyed being a police dispatcher, and everyone called him Chuckles. He had a sharp dry wit, but nickname aside, none of the officers could recall ever seeing him smile, much less chuckle. His career started over 25 years prior as a uniform police officer. It didn't take him long to realize, with his fragile temper, as well as the type of police activity in Templeton, that he was likely to do serious damage to some ne'er-do-well who was not quite deserving that level of punishment. That was Charles, and he was smart enough to figure it out for himself. After this self-realization, his request for a transfer to late shift as a police dispatcher was quickly granted.

In today's strict police hiring process, Charles might have been quickly eliminated during the physical and psychological testing done in today's selection process for a police officer. He remembered his initial department physical, long ago, which was required before any prospective police officer was admitted into the police pension plan. During the eye exam portion of the physical, Charles was doing his best to read the letters on the chart. He carefully leaned over a line taped to the floor, which provided the proper distance between him and the eye exam chart, straining to read the letters on the chart. Meanwhile, the doctor, a cigarette dangling from his yellowed lips, stood next to him, leaning over the same taped line, adjusting his glasses, also straining to better see the letters on the very same eye chart. At the time, it was legal to smoke indoors, but Charles didn't expect it from a doctor during a medical exam. Back in the day, you applied for the job and if the police department administrators liked you, you were in, regardless of whatever a nearsighted, nicotine-addicted physician might have to say.

Because of Charles's experience on the street, he became a good, if not unique, dispatcher. He was savoring the thought of getting home and enjoying a cold brew when he took a call at 2 a.m. from a resident on Clinton Drive. The caller wanted to anonymously report a loud family domestic dispute in the mobile home next door.

Charles dispatched Jeramy and the rookie officer, Adam, who was in training with Parker. Parker appreciated being a field training officer or FTO for short. Being an FTO allowed him and his trainees to jump other officer's assignments, getting involved in more activity. The older officers didn't mind because the officer being trained would be responsible for any resulting paperwork. Parker and his current rookie officer got along well because he insisted on the job being done right, and Adam wanted to learn to do the job correctly.

Adam drove the squad car to the trailer on Clinton Street. As trained, he parked on the street, blocking the end of the driveway with his squad car. Adam and Parker only had to wait a few seconds for their backup, Jeramy, to arrive. Parker and Adam approached the front door while Jeramy walked through the snow to the back corner of the trailer to watch the rear for anyone trying to escape out the back. As the officers approached, they could hear loud arguing inside the mobile home.

Adam knocked on the front door. After about a minute, an older woman opened the door and seemed surprised to see police officers on her front porch. Adam thought she appeared to be close to 80 years old, but when he later used her ID to check for arrest warrants, he discovered she was only 65. He guessed, with her deep face and neck wrinkles, the thin gray hair pulled back into a stringy ponytail, how the dirty old house dress hung on her emaciated frame, and the brown cigarillo hanging loosely from her thin pale lips, anyone could have guessed her to be much older than her actual age.

As Adam and Parker began to talk to the woman, Jeramy walked to the front door and entered the trailer. The living room was illuminated only by an old floor lamp in a corner. The lampshade may have been white at some point, but now it was a dirty yellowish color.

Jeramy approached a young man who was standing behind the old woman and guided him into the adjoining kitchen. The guy was tall, drug-addicted skinny, and the homemade tattoos on his neck screamed bad judgment. He was disheveled, yes, but Jeramy's attention was drawn to the left side of his forehead, where a large lump was developing. Brownish goo was in his hair and on his forehead around the lump. Jeramy pointed to his forehead and said, "Dude, you look like the devil's piñata. What happened?" The guy acted surprised as he rubbed his fingers over the lump and said his Gran hit him.

Between the two combatants, the story came out that the guy lived with his grandmother. He was a pill popper, and his grandmother a whiskey drunk. Grandson had been routinely stealing grandmother's pain pills. Instead of just sitting him down and politely talking to him, like civilized family members should do, grandmother, a devoted snuff user, whacked her grandson over the head with a twenty-four-ounce canning jar. She used the jar as a large spittoon, explaining the lump and the source of the brown goo. It was clear Gran didn't empty the jar often, causing the chew juice to jell up.

Amid this family chaos, Jeramy looked around the ratty old trailer. It was a shotgun-style mobile home with two tiny bedrooms and a bathroom they shared. One thing they didn't share was the housekeeping duties. The place was a mess, with empty beer cans and whiskey bottles scattered around while the smell of stale cigarette smoke hanging in the air was suffocating. Ashtrays in the room were full of cigarette ash and butts. Under the lamp, next to a decrepit-looking recliner, was a square-shaped end table. The only thing on the end table was a large round ashtray. At first glance, the ashtray reminded him of an old-fashioned Thompson machine gun. The kind with a round ammo wheel in the center because the ashtray had about 20 unlit brown cigarittos lined up evenly around the outside edge. Filter ends all pointing out for what Jeramy figured was rapid-action smoking. The furniture was dirty and worn, arranged only for the convenient viewing of an old television.

As Jeramy walked around the inside of the trailer, he noticed the rug had an old, spongy, dirty dampness he could almost feel through his thick duty boots. Furthermore, the wood subflooring creaked as he walked and, in places, felt dangerously weak. Looking around the kitchen, he wasn't sure how many days' worth of dirty plates and silverware were in the petri dish of a kitchen sink, but it smelled so bad it could gag a maggot. Plates with partially eaten meals were left on the table, and Jeramy had no idea what caused the dark specks on the wall but hoped it wasn't black mold.

He looked around the small living room, thinking what a disgusting mess surrounded these people and this place. Silently he asked himself why anyone would want to live this way. Looking around, he noticed there wasn't anything hanging on the walls. There were no watercolor paintings, no family photos, no wall decorations, no velvet painting of Elvis, not even an ugly tapestry of dogs sitting at a table playing cards. There was absolutely nothing these people valued enough to proudly display in their home, except for a medium-sized crucifix hanging neatly from a hook on a living room wall. Jeramy stared at the crucifix, wondering what it was doing in a place like this. Was this the only thing these people valued enough to place prominently on their walls?

Only wall decorations crucifix in drug home

CHAPTER 7

Templeton's third shift roll call was scheduled to begin at 2200 hours, or 10:00 p.m., in civilian speak. The room had two large conference tables pushed together and about a dozen mismatched beat-up old office chairs scattered about the tables. The armrests to the office chairs had been removed so the uniform officers could sit more comfortably while wearing their duty belts. Otherwise, every time an officer would attempt to get out of the chairs, he would have to wrestle with all his attached gear, including the pistol, to get up and over the armrests. The walls were covered with large bulletin boards displaying everything from wanted posters, criminal intelligence bulletins, internal memos, police equipment brochures, and the occasional letter from a citizen. A large screen television was mounted on a side wall and was supposed to be used for training. Before roll call, the late shift officers usually used it to watch a local news station. There was also a large standing cabinet that contained all the forms the officers needed because you can't run a police department without a slew of different forms. The roll call room was situated just inside the building's back door, which opened into the police parking lot.

The Templeton Police Department officers worked a schedule typical of many police departments; six working days followed by three days off, with each workday consisting of eight and one-half hours. Second shift began at 2:00 p.m. and ended at 10:30 p.m., overlapping third shift by half an hour. This gave the third shift officers time to conduct roll call before having to take calls for police service. During roll call, Lt. Weber assigned the officers to patrol districts, read any new information from the roll board and handled any other detail shuffled down to him from the department command staff. He would then allow his officers time for discussion. Roll call often morphed into a freewheeling gab session of exaggerated old war stories, good-natured ribbing, or gossip concerning the newest waitress at Dio's Pancake Palace.

During tonight's roll call, Weber was reading the prior shift's activity when he came to a police report concerning a residential burglary. The burglary occurred sometime during the previous weekend, which was unusual because residence burglaries typically occur Monday through Friday during the day while most people were at work. On the other hand, businesses were usually burglarized at night, when people were at home.

Many people incorrectly believed homes were normally burglarized at night. A residence burglar doesn't want to confront the homeowner inside the future victim's house. This is why he waits until the homeowner has left for work before breaking in. Residential nighttime cat burglaries rarely happen because there's too much risk of being caught. A residence burglary on the weekend suggests a different type of suspect. Maybe someone that the homeowner knew or someone who knew the victim would be away from home. Weber read off some brief details of the incident, the address, and that the point of entry was a rear patio door that had been forced open. According to the police report, it didn't appear as if anything was missing. However, a large saltwater fish tank had been smashed, leaving expensive dead fish all over the ruined carpet. The victim reported he thought an ex-girlfriend was responsible.

Weber should have seen it coming, like throwing an underhand slow-pitched softball to a major league slugger. Thaddeus often played the part of the department jokester even though he didn't look the part. He had sharp facial features and a thin yet muscular build. His uniform, unlike many policemen, was always well-fitted, clean, and sharp looking. Weber, who was starting to bald, was envious of Thaddeus' neatly trimmed, thick, full head of hair, barbered so regularly it always appeared to be the same length. Thaddeus started it off with, "This case seems a little *fishy* to me."

Cory followed up with, "I think the girlfriend is *gillty*."

Back to Thaddeus, "Only the *scales* of justice will know for sure."

Not to be bested, Cory responded, "Think she'll *clam* up?"

The volley bounced back and forth like a senior's division championship pickleball game. Humor had always been a welcome part of late shift roll call, and Weber was pleased joking around had returned so soon after Carl's death. In mock disgust, he threw his hands up while walking out of the roll call room as the background banter continued.

Back to Thaddeus, "Naw, the detectives will never clear this one. They always let the big ones get away."

Cory countered, "Oh, no, I bet they clear this one up *snappy*."

Thaddeus again, "What *bait* should they use to catch the suspect?"

Using the palm of his hand, Cory slapped the center of his forehead and exclaimed, "This *scampi* happening."

Thaddeus again, "I bet the detectives will buy her alibi *hook, line, and sinker*."

Cory leaned back in his chair and crossed his arms as if getting comfortable, then finished the exchange with, "Ahhh, nothing like a good fish story."

Bad puns

CHAPTER 8

A few hours after roll call Charles received a call from the Imperil Liquor store located in the Lakewood strip mall reporting a robbery had just occurred at the store. Instead of assigning officers to major crimes that were in progress, like most dispatchers, Charles would often broadcast the incident, quickly announcing the necessary details and warnings the responding officers needed, such as the type of incident, suspect and suspect vehicle descriptions, and if weapons were seen or suggested. He then waited for officers who might be close to the incident to respond.

In this case, the perpetrator was a white male driving an older blue Chevrolet Malibu. Late shift in Templeton had some younger, more aggressive officers, so there was never a problem getting a response to such a dispatch. Of course, Parker and Adam responded and were the first to arrive, securing the scene until their backup, Weber, also arrived. Teresa and Jeramy cruised the area searching for the suspect's vehicle.

After the robbery suspect ran from the store and out of sight, the clerk ran to the front door, closed it, turning the deadbolt to the locked position to prevent the suspect, for whatever reason, from re-entering the store. This was when the clerk saw a light blue Chevrolet Malibu speed away down a side street.

After hearing the clerk describe the robbery, Weber, thinking the incident sounded like a string of robberies that had been occurring in neighboring jurisdictions, requested a detective be called to process the crime scene. It would be important to do a thorough investigation because, as most officers know, and Mel always stressed, hold-up men, like drug dealers, rarely stop their criminal activities until they either get caught or die. Charles sent a message to Detective Scott Pierson's cell phone with brief details about the incident along with the location, knowing Pierson would not welcome this 1:00 a.m. notification.

Detective Pierson did not like being on call. Most of Templeton's detectives worked a Monday through Friday day-shift schedule, which required one of the eight to handle after-hours and weekend call-outs. The Templeton Police Department had eight detectives. As a result, each one was on call one week out of every eight, and this was Pierson's week.

For Pierson, the upside was the compensatory time off he accumulated. He often used this comp time to take three-day camping and fishing weekends, which, since his divorce, is what he found he enjoyed most. While on call, he kept a set of clothes hung on a hook inside his bedroom closet door, expecting at least once each week of call-out duty to get that middle-of-the-night call. When that happened, he would dress like a fireman when a nighttime fire alarm went off.

After Pierson arrived at the liquor store, he briefly talked to the clerk. He asked to watch the store surveillance video hoping to obtain a still shot of the suspect. Unfortunately, because of the camera angle, the only views of the suspect were of the back of his head. The grainy images from the cheap video system showed the hold-up man wearing a dark-colored hoodie. His right hand was in a pocket as if he was hiding a pistol while using his left hand to point at the clerk demanding cash.

Generally, people don't realize the purpose of most video surveillance cameras mounted inside stores which deal primarily in cash, isn't to help identify robbery suspects. The cameras are often aimed straight at the clerk to keep store employees honest. Why this camera was positioned differently was unusual, but without good photographic evidence, it was back to old-fashioned police work.

Pierson retrieved his latent fingerprint kit from the trunk of his unmarked police car and began dusting for latent prints. For show, he would dust the entire customer service counter for fingerprints. Because hundreds of different people's greasy fingerprints each day smeared across the top of the counter, the odds were against getting any identifiable prints. As a result, he usually ended up with unidentifiable fingerprint smudges as well as fingerprints overlaid on top of each other, which made them impossible to identify.

Pierson learned that if you didn't dust for fingerprints on surfaces such as this customer service counter, victims would think you weren't putting enough effort into the investigation. To avoid unwarranted citizen complaints, he always dusted anywhere a suspect might have handled something. Even when knowing there was little chance of recovering identifiable fingerprints. He held to the simple yet good advice Mel gave him when he was a rookie, if you could get in trouble for doing something, don't do it. But with a stern look, he added that if you could get in trouble for not doing something, then don't be lazy and go ahead and get it done. In such instances, Pierson figured he might be second-guessed if he didn't dust for latent prints on the customer service counter. As a result, he always made an attempt.

Pierson used his fingerprint feather duster and an ample amount of latent print dust to process the entire surface of the counter, occasionally stopping to examine his progress. As he expected, the counter was covered with fingerprints overlaid on top of each other, making them unusable. But the glass exit door was a different story.

In the past, he'd had great success lifting good fingerprints from glass entrance and exit doors. For some reason, unlike the store's restrooms, the glass doors of quick-stop stores were usually exceptionally clean. He thought this anomaly must result from some type of corporate management directive. Regardless, the glass on exit doors were usually where he got the best robbery suspect latent fingerprints. Putting himself in the robber's shoes, he reasoned having just committed a robbery, your adrenaline is pumping, and you're in a hurry and almost in a panic to escape the scene. As you run from the store, you probably have a pistol or cash in your right hand, as a result, you throw your left hand at the exit door push bar. Being in a hurry and possibly distracted as you look around, running to the exit, you miss the push bar and slap your open left palm and fingers onto that smooth, clean glass door, leaving behind five fresh fingerprints and one flat palm print. For a detective, it doesn't get much better than that. To Pierson's delight, tonight, that's precisely what he lifted off the inside of the glass door.

Door Finger prints
on stone door

CHAPTER 9

Everyone called him Mel, even though that wasn't his real name. In fact, his name wasn't even Melvin. His actual name, given at birth by his father, a political history buff with an interest in the eccentric, was Millard. Named for the former president of the United States, Millard Fillmore.

Mel's father's favorite saying came from President Fillmore, "May God save our country, for it is evident the people will not." When Mel later learned more about Millard Fillmore, it became evident why he held a soft spot in the old man's heart. Not only was his dad a history buff, but he also had a twisted sense of humor. Fillmore was, of all things, the "unlucky" thirteenth president of the United States but was never actually elected to the presidency.

As vice president to President Zachary Taylor, Fillmore succeeded Taylor as president when Taylor died in office. For some reason, Mel's dad had a low opinion of Taylor and told Mel that President Taylor died from a bad stomachache. Mel later learned he died due to a fatal case of gastroenteritis. Fillmore had been born into poverty and, as a young man, had been desperate to learn, resorting to stealing books to educate himself. It seemed he enjoyed education so much later in life he married one of his former teachers. When he didn't get re-elected president after his only term, he later unsuccessfully ran for president as a candidate for the newly formed political party appropriately named the Know Nothing Party. Yes, Millard Fillmore certainly was the kind of guy the old man could get behind. Of course, he never liked the name Millard, and from a young age, he became known as Mel.

On late shift, things usually slowed down around 3:00 a.m. By the time the officers got any required paperwork done, it was 5:00 a.m., which was when Mel and Cory usually met at Dio's Pancake Palace for one last cup of coffee and maybe some breakfast. The sign outside read, "Dio's Pancake Palace, Where Everything is Dio-*licous!*" A bit of an overstatement, but if you stayed away from the sometimes overcooked and slightly greasy county fried steak, the menu was better than acceptable. Of course, for the local policemen, the coffee was always free, and the meals were half-priced. Having a marked police car in the parking lot not only discouraged robberies but, according to Dio, travelers figured if the police ate there, the food must be good. Cory knew better. The police ate there for the half-priced pancake breakfast.

Carolyn was a long-time waitress at Dio's. Some waitresses, like policemen, preferred to work late shift, and Carolyn had worked late shift at Dio's ever since Cory could remember. It seemed to him that she had a bit of a crush on Mel, who, in turn, seemed to be flattered by the attention. Previously, Cory had asked Mel about Carolyn's apparent interest in him. With a sly smile, Mel responded, "Slightly chubby fifty-six-year-old men were in pretty big demand these days." Adding, "Just maybe, women of a certain age considered him a clunker hunker."

How odd, thought Cory, to see a possible budding romance between a couple in their fifties. Of course, what did he know about romance? He, in his mid-thirties, married over ten years now with two kids and a dad bod he wasn't proud of. For him, romance seemed to be a thing of the past. He often joked that after he got a vasectomy and was now shooting blanks, someone closed the shooting range. But as it often happened, both officers were called away from their coffee to investigate an early morning traffic accident.

CHAPTER 10

Gil didn't like mean drunks like his Gran. But he was thankful for clumsy drunks with poor finger dexterity that, once they left a bar, struggled to fish their car keys out from their pockets and in the process unknowingly spill change on the parking lot. He didn't drive, not only because his driver's license was suspended, but he'd never owned a car. Gran had a car until he wrecked it driving to the drug store to get a refill on her pain meds. Prior to that, he had often driven his Gran to various places. It made him crazy the way she had always complained about his driving. By his way of thinking the old bat might as well have sat in the back seat because that's where it seemed she was trying to drive from.

His nightly routine, even in cold winter weather, was to start by either walking or riding his bicycle in the middle of the night to a quiet residential neighborhood where he would rattle the doors of a few parked cars hoping to find loose change or cash tucked in the ashtray or cup holder of an unlocked car. Maybe he would get lucky and find a wallet.

In fact, this was how he swiped the bike he was using, leaning up against a porch in the middle of the night. It was a 26-inch Schwinn nine-speed, tricked out with a thumb activated bicycle bell and a wire basket attached to the front.

One time he found a semi-automatic pistol in the glove box of an unlocked parked car. He quickly traded it for ten bucks along with something new he had never tried before. Something that looked like a marijuana cigarette but called "wet." After he smoked the wet, he was so out of his head messed up he couldn't find his way home.

He later discovered wet was made by soaking marijuana in formaldehyde, then rolling it into cigarette papers or jamming it inside a hollowed-out cigar, called a blunt. When he heard how it was made, he wondered what lunatic would think to soak a marijuana cigarette in formaldehyde? He decided that it must have been some dope fiend funeral director who was getting a stiff ready for viewing, dropped his doobie in the formaldehyde, but not wanting to waste it, smoked it anyway, creating a completely new way to fry your noggin.

Sometimes during the summer, on a weekend night and after a full day of yard work, a tired homeowner might accidentally leave his garage door open all night. This was a big mistake because during his nighttime thievery, Gil always found something small worth pilfering from those open suburban garages. Hand tools were especially easy to pawn because most hand tools didn't have serial numbers or identifying marks stamped on them. Small hand-held power tools were also easy to pawn because no one keeps a record of their serial numbers making them impossible to claim if located at a pawn shop.

Some nights Gil's take was better than others, but there was always the bar parking lots. In Indiana, last call for drinks is 3:00 a.m., with closing time at 3:30 a.m. The bar parking lots usually emptied by 4:00 a.m. Luckily, there were several bars within an easy bike ride of Gran's trailer. Strip bars were the best pickings. Their customers always arrived with a wad of one-dollar bills to tuck into the dancers G strings because everyone knows strippers don't make change. After a few drinks, the drunks finally leave the bar, making their way into the dark, poorly lit parking lot. Any leftover one-dollar bills, along with loose change buried deep within their pocket might fly out and onto the pavement as they drunkenly tried to pull out their car keys.

On a good night, Gil might find a ten or a twenty-dollar bill in one of those parking lots. He had to watch his step in the back lot of Olivia's Gentleman's Club because there was nothing gentlemanly going on back there. In fact, he heard the back lot was called "The Crack Whore Café," because of all the crack needles and candy wrappers the dancers left scattered about. A good thing about Olivia's parking lot was the chain link fence bordering three sides which conveniently caught most stray paper money a windy night might try to blow away.

Of course, there were aluminum cans he scrounged from the neighborhood, throwing them into the basket of his bike. At home he stored them in one of several empty 55-gallon drums sitting behind Gran's trailer. Years ago, Gil's grandpa had worked as a dishwasher for a now long-closed diner in Templeton. Part of his job was to empty the restaurant's grease traps into 55-gallon drums. The thing that wasn't part of his job was occasionally rolling empty 55-gallon drums home then selling as burn barrels.

After a night of scavenging and thievery, he would hunt down some dope fiend selling dexies. Of course, most of his downers came from Gran's stash of pain pills, but he also had to have his uppers because, well, you know, life had to have a balance. Gran didn't need those pills anyway as she was medicating herself well enough on cheap beer and Dog Legg Whiskey. When Gran wasn't chewing tobacco, she was smoking those stinking brown cigarittos. When she wasn't chewing or smoking, she was drinking beer or whiskey, or both mixed together. Good thing for him the pain pills were on mail-order auto-refill, because she would never remember to refill them on her own. On this night, it was almost daybreak before he rode his bike back to Gran's.

Riding his bike in the cold December snow and slush was not easy, but it was faster than walking. The basket fastened to the handlebars was perfect for a roadside scavenger such as himself. He could use the night's take of aluminum cans to cover up anything in the bicycle basket he may have stolen along the way. As he was approaching the entrance to his trailer park, he passed the construction site of a new subdivision called Rose Garden Villas, hardly noticing the retention pond being dug out of the ground toward the back of the property next to a grove of trees. Riding his bike he noticed the new construction of the middle-class cookie-cutter box houses being built. Lucky for him because that meant someday, close to home, there might be more unlocked cars to rummage through. That was Gil, always looking on the bright side of things.

CHAPTER 11

From watching the television news, it seemed there was a lot of evil in the world, but Jeramy wasn't so sure. Yes, he knew there was plenty of bad behavior to go around, but he felt most people were good and honest. Jeramy agreed with Mel, who often claimed 5% of the people caused 95% of the problems, and if the judicial system kept that 5% in jail, crime rates would have to go down. Mel was convinced people in the U.S. weren't serious about fighting crime. He often explained during roll call that it was simple, if we as a country were serious about reducing crime, we would put criminals in jail and keep them there. Continuing this rant, he would explain that jail isn't supposed to be comfortable. It's supposed to be punishment, which would also serve to protect society during the time the criminal is incarcerated. As a result, crime rates would have to plummet, at least according to Mel's theory.

Mel's idea of what an appropriate amount of time a criminal should be in jail might not be in sync with today's progressive thinkers. He had heard all the arguments suggesting incarceration wasn't the most effective way to prevent recidivism. However, in all his years as a policeman, he had never met a thief, hold-up man, or wife-beater who changed his ways because of some government social program. Criminals were people, and most people responded to proper motivation. Which for criminals would be jail sentences appropriate to the crime.

Don't talk to Mel about jail overcrowding because his pat response was to build more jails. He would explain, "We build more roads when they get too crowded. Why not jails?" To Mel, crime was just one big societal pothole needing to be fixed. He explained it would be less expensive for society to keep lawbreakers in prison than to constantly have to deal with their public havoc.

Not letting a good tirade end too soon, he frequently suggested that many neighborhoods became economically depressed because of increased crime in those areas. "Whoever heard of property values going up in crime-ravished neighborhoods where gangs run wild?" he would coyly ask. He would then ask who would invest in new businesses, such as a grocery store or hardware store, in such crime-ridden areas, much less buy a house and put their kids in the local schools.

Insurance rates go up because of crime. Families are torn apart because of domestic violence, which in turn causes an economic burden on society to care for those victims. Mel agreed that when criminals go to prison, it could have a negative financial impact on their families in the short run. But in the long run, those families were better off with the relational felon in lock-up. To reward a crook by releasing him from jail early for good time is crazy, he complained. If the criminal had been good in the first place instead of committing the crime that sent him to prison, he wouldn't have to concern himself with an early release. According to Mel, it was, "simple, treat them like kids. When they're bad, off to the corner they go."

Mel's rantings caused Jeramy to wonder about the old saying, spare the rod, spoil the child. It was probably the same with adults. Where did he remember hearing that phrase? Perhaps Sunday School as a kid? He was surprised after all those youthful Sunday mornings, something must have sunk in after all. Jeramy thought most people were good, and he was often proved correct during the Christmas season around the police department.

Most December days leading up to Christmas, one or more citizens, a representative from a local company, or another city employee would often leave goodies such as cookies or candies at the Templeton Police Department for the officers to share. The thought was always nice, but with each offering left, the chief's secretary would set the treat in the roll call room next to a note naming the person or organization that provided it. This way, each officer could choose which treats they felt safe to enjoy. Some officers like Cory would eat just about anything brought in. Others were more choosey, as with Mabel the cat lady's coconut cream cookies.

In years past, Stanley, the owner of Sedgwick Wrecker Company, who had the towing contract for the Templeton Police Department, would deliver a couple of cases of whiskey to be distributed among the officers. This Christmas gift was meant to serve as a thank you for the business generated from all the vehicle tows resulting from police services, such as auto accidents, drunk driving arrests, and any other vehicles towed at the request of the Templeton Police Department. Today that type of gift would be unacceptable. As a result, the Sedgwick Wrecker Company now shows its appreciation by making a generous contribution to the City of Templeton Fraternal Order of Police's Shop With A Cop Program. Templeton Police officers used donations like this to take disadvantaged kids Christmas shopping a few weeks before Christmas. This year wasn't going to be the same because Carl had been the coordinator of the Shop With A Cop Program.

During Carl's tenure as the local FOP's coordinator of the Shop With A Cop Program, he enlarged the number of the disadvantaged served to include children who had been victims of crimes or who had been injured in accidents within the Templeton jurisdiction. Carl always thought of these kids as the department's extended "family." Jeramy considered taking this job over for Carl but wasn't sure he wanted the responsibility, mainly because fundraising was part of the coordinator's job. Jeramy had seen Carl at work raising funds and was amazed at how smooth he was. He always ended his pitch with a genuine smile suggesting, "No one ever got in trouble for being too generous."

CHAPTER 12

Jeramy checked the weather forecast each day before dressing for work, and tonight the forecast was for cold enough temperatures to merit wearing thermal long underwear. He always wondered how much all the police gear he wore on duty weighed, and tonight he decided to find out. While still in his skivvies, he stepped on the bathroom scales, tipping it at a disappointing 181 pounds. Afterward, he pulled on his upper and lower long underwear, then slipped his ballistic vest over his head, fastening it across his chest with hook and loop self-fasteners. The ballistic panels were manufactured from a special type of fiberglass woven into a panel. Separate panels slipped into the front and back of the cloth vest cover, like a pillow inside a pillowcase. The front and back panels of the cloth vest cover were connected by straps that draped over the wearer's shoulders, much like a sandwich board advertisement. Not only was the vest thick and uncomfortable, but it was also hot, causing Jeramy to perspire even in cool weather. After he adjusted the position of the vest, making it more comfortable, he put on a pullover long-sleeved black mock turtleneck over the vest, then slipped into his uniform shirt.

In cold weather, Templeton officers had a choice between wearing a clip-on black uniform tie or a mock turtleneck shirt, the latter being what Jeramy always chose. The reason for this choice was most officers universally disliked the traditional clip-on tie. The uniform tie is a clip-on because a regular tie worn around an officer's neck could be dangerous if a suspect resisting arrest grabbed the officer's tie and tried to choke him with it. Just as critical in deciding which tie to choose, according to Cory, was that no officer had ever been known to have accidentally dragged a mock turtleneck through his pancake syrup while dining at Dio's. So, at least for him, the choice was easy.

Because of department regulations, the uniform shirt was full of metal buttons, collar brass, a nameplate, a years of service pin, and a police badge that always felt too heavy for the shirt's fabric. All of these had to be removed before laundering and then reassembled on the shirt before the next wearing. In a struggle, the badge was usually the first thing the resisting person grabbed hold of, often ripping it from the shirt. An ink pen, small notepads, and any small police-related reference material that would easily fit were placed into either or both breast pockets of the uniform shirt. Jeramy then pulled his uniform pants on and threaded a regular black belt through the belt loops.

Next, he slipped on his boots that laced up over the ankles. An officer had to keep those ankles secure because you never knew from night to night where you were stepping and into what. Finally, Jeramy wrapped his duty belt around his waist and fastened it tightly. His duty belt held the holstered pistol, two extra ammo clips, a taser, and a small pouch containing latex gloves, which were used when handling evidence or performing first aid.

Also attached to the duty belt is a handcuff case that accommodates at least one pair of handcuffs. Jeramy noticed Parker, always rough and ready, carried three pairs of handcuffs. Parker's handcuff case was designed to carry two pairs, and he draped a third over his duty belt next to the handcuff case. This practice may seem extreme, but there were times when an officer might use two pairs of handcuffs when arresting a large man. In cases such as that, the officer extended the length the cuffs could cover by connecting two pairs of handcuffs together, making the combination longer.

In Templeton, it wasn't unusual to arrest more than one person at a time, thus possibly requiring the use of three or more pairs of handcuffs. Parker was fond of saying handcuffs were a lot like toilet paper, something you just couldn't have too much of. Cuff'em and stuff'em, was his motto. But then Parker had the same opinion concerning ammo and carried twenty extra rounds in an additional extended-capacity ammo magazine he tucked into a back pocket.

After pulling his police radio from a battery charger, Jeramy slipped it into a fitted leather radio holster also connected to his duty belt. Each officer carried a portable police radio, but in years past, the portable radio had been as heavy as a masonry brick. Today's portable radio has a sturdy hard plastic case and is much lighter.

After sliding a small can of pepper spray into another fitted leather holster, he was ready to attach the belt keepers. Belt keepers are small leather straps that wrap around the duty belt and the regular pants belt. Once the two ends of the belt keeper are snapped together, the duty belt is held tight against the regular belt, keeping it from slipping down. Each officer usually used two or three belt keepers. If you were a tad overweight like Jeramy, the regular pants belt had to be fastened tightly around the waist to keep the equipment-laden duty belt from sliding down, requiring constant readjustment. Some belt keepers have a ring attached which is used to slip a flashlight into, adding even more weight. Another type of belt keeper has a clasp to attach a key ring for easy access, much like the one he had trouble with the night Carl died.

Lastly, he attached his bodycam to his shirt and connected the police radio's wireless remote speaker to his uniform shirt epaulet, which completed his uniform ensemble.

Jeramy refused to wear the department-issued eight-point hat, not just because it looked like something a 1950s cab driver or old-time milkman might wear, but because it messed up his thinning hair. Finished with the nightly dressing routine, he stepped onto the scale, which displayed 202 pounds. He was not surprised the police gear weighed 21 pounds, but that didn't include the flashlight he carried on late shift nor the winter car coat he kept in his squad car. No wonder he often had a backache at the end of the shift.

CHAPTER 13

At roll call, Lt. Weber read off the list of crimes reported since their previous shift, covering the usual assortment of residential burglaries and vehicle thefts mixed with a few domestic incidents. In addition, there were reports of several minor thefts from vehicles in the Spring Hill neighborhood. This launched Mel into a five-minute diatribe laced with mild obscenities about people who left their cars unlocked, causing officers more work writing police reports as a result of the larcenies. He finished the outburst with his sarcastic sounding but heartfelt and often repeated, "If it weren't for victims, this would be a great job."

Weber, trying to get back on track, began to read a report from his clipboard. "Seems there was a burglary at the Boy Scout Campground storage building over the weekend. The caretaker said twelve bows, three dozen arrows, and two pellet guns were stolen."

No sooner had those words been spoken when Cory scrambled out of his seat, feet shoulder width apart, hand on the grip of his holstered pistol, and in a semi-crouched position of pretend readiness for action, excitedly asked, "Lieutenant, should we circle the wagons?"

Weber, seeing that roll call was now officially out of control once again, folded up his notebook to leave. As he walked out of the room, he could hear Thaddeus mocking both Cory and Mel by singing a song he affectionately called the "Pancreas Song."

There was no end to the ribbing Cory received since he accidentally shot himself in the foot, nearly severing his big toe, while doing semi-annual handgun qualifications at the pistol range a few years ago. Still, Weber couldn't understand why Thaddeus had to make fun of the pancreatic infection that put Mel off work for three weeks the previous summer.

As he walked away, Weber patiently tried to ignore Thaddeus, who was singing his Pancreas Song loudly and off-key to the tune of *O Christmas Tree.*

O Pancreas, O Pancreas,
Why do you hurt him so, oh?
O Pancreas, O Pancreas,
At least it's not his toe, oh.
We know it hurts,
It hurts a lot,
But not as much
As being shot
O Pancreas, O Pancreas,
Why do you hurt him so, oh?

Jeramy laughed out loud as he listened to Thaddeus's silly parody of *O Christmas Tree.* He thought back to his Sunday school days, remembering the song's third stanza announcing the birth of Jesus. He chuckled again when it occurred to him that Thaddeus twisted up a song memorializing Jesus' birth with Mel's suffering pancreas and Cory's poor mangled foot.

Cory interrupted Jeramy's thoughts by informing Thaddeus, "Hey, buddy. I found the perfect Christmas present for you at a bookstore today."

"Oh yeah?" Thaddeus questioned.

"Yeah," Cory replied, "a book called *An Idiot's Guide to Criminal Investigation.*"

"Really?" Thaddeus asked. He tilted his head back and pressed his forefinger to his chin and, with fake surprised interest, retorted, "That's a coincidence because I also got you a book as a Christmas present, *Gun Safety for Dummies.*"

Weber ended roll call by adding, "Cory, the only gun you'll ever be proficient with is a super soaker!"

Other than a complaint about a loud party and a report of a runaway, it was a slow night on patrol. Jeramy was face-in-his-plate dead tired. He usually was a good daytime sleeper, but this was his first day back to work after three days off. He got up that morning at 9:00 a.m. intending to grab a nap before he went to work at 10:00 p.m. Unfortunately, he didn't get around to that essential late afternoon snooze. He had drank two cups of coffee since roll call, but the only effect they had was to activate his bladder, and still, he could hardly hold his eyes open. It didn't help he had the heater turned up in his police car to combat the cold wind outside, making the car's interior toasty warm.

Jeramy stopped his police car for what seemed like a long red light at 10th Street and Perkins Road. His eyelids were getting heavy, and he was fighting the urge to close his eyes, even for a second. As he waited for the red light to turn green, he drowsily watched the windshield wipers rhythmically move back and forth, keeping the lightly falling snow from accumulating on his windshield as his mind gently drifted. The next thing he knew, he was startled awake and stunned, momentarily unaware of where he was or what he was doing. While trying to regain his wits, he was thankful his foot was still firmly planted on the brake pedal. Looking up and out the windshield, he was surprised the stop light he last remembered being red was now green. But for how long?

Still a little disoriented, he wondered how long he'd been there and how many times the light had changed. He quickly glanced around, getting his bearings. He was surprised to notice cars were carefully creeping around his stationary marked police car and through the intersection as if on tiptoes trying not to disturb his sleep. He didn't know how long he was snoozing at that stoplight but sensed it was way too long. Taking a deep breath, he rolled down the car window letting in the cold air before driving away, trying to appear as if nothing out of the ordinary had happened.

Jeramy thought most people who worked during the day took their eight hours of nighttime sleep for granted, then decided a short walk in the crisp night air might wake him up. He drove to the Templeton Plaza on State Road 76 to walk the sidewalk along the storefronts. He would note this in his daily activity log as a security check. Yes, he thought, that would look good on his activity log, a security check.

The Templeton Plaza was an older strip center in mild disrepair. Tenants included a grocery store, a drug store, Enzo's Barber Shop, and the Shoe Show. At night, all the store names lit up over each respective store in bright neon letters. For the last several months, the S in Shoe was burned out of the Shoe Show neon sign, which must have confused many a midnight motorist.

Jeramy wasn't far from his squad car when, at about 4:00 a.m., Charles dispatched information on a robbery that had just occurred at the Easy Stop on State Road 76, committed by a white male. Jeramy was close and responded. He was glad Parker and Adam also responded, which would leave them with the paperwork. By the time they arrived on the scene, the suspect was long gone.

Detective Pierson was again called to conduct a preliminary investigation and to process the crime scene. This time, he was unable to find any identifiable fingerprints but did recover a digital file of the surveillance video showing an image of the face of the male who threatened the clerk. The clerk had described the hold-up suspect as a white male, possibly in his mid-twenties, skinny and wearing a black pullover hoodie with something spelled out in red lettering on the front. All of which the store video confirmed. The officers agreed this robbery was probably committed by the same guy who robbed the Imperial Liquor Store a few nights before.

CHAPTER 14

"Those stupid cops will never catch me," thought Piper. He'd been a thief most of his life, breaking into houses, stealing cars, and anything else for a quick buck. He hadn't had a job since he worked for a car wash as a teenager. Having to be at work at a certain place, at a time to work all day, then clock out, all for peanuts? That wasn't the life for him, and he never wanted to have another boss. It was bad enough when he was a kid, his mother telling him what to do.

Piper had run out of the liquor store and jumped into the Chevy Malibu he had stolen from the pizza place. He drove for several minutes, making multiple random turns before pulling into a grocery store parking lot. He settled in among several other cars, hoping not to be noticed. He counted the money from the robbery and was disappointed at the $80 he got. At least it was better than the $68 he got from the Easy Stop store.

Disgusted, he drove away thinking he couldn't risk keeping the Malibu any longer. The cops had to be looking for it by now. He decided to leave the car somewhere in plain sight. He smiled as he considered how dumb the cops were and wondered, after he dumped it, how long it would take them to find it. It didn't matter. He had to get rid of the car before he got caught in it. He not only used it for the robberies, but it also had made a dry, if not comfortable, place to sleep. Homelessness had its perks, but sleeping accommodations wasn't one of them. He would park between a couple of other cars in a lot with bad lighting and hope not to be noticed dozing in the back seat. After using this car in two robberies, which was probably one too many, he didn't want that cop named Parker to catch him anywhere near a stolen car.

Piper thought cops with shaved heads were always the roughest. The last Templeton cop that hassled him was a policeman named Parker, who not only had a shaved head but looked like a weightlifting roid who couldn't wait to blast his taser at some poor guy.

It was cold, and Piper decided that since he was already parked in a good place, he would get some sleep. He didn't have much in the way of possessions. Homeless people didn't need much except an old blanket and long johns. The long johns he shoplifted a few weeks ago made getting through a cold night easier. He planned to catch a few hours of sleep, then abandon the Malibu by parking it somewhere and walking away. It was running low on gas anyway, and tonight he didn't want to deal with siphoning gas from another car. Hopefully, the next car he steals will have a full tank, as this one did.

As Piper fell into a ragged sleep, he dreamed of returning to a beach town somewhere in Florida. In his dream, he hopped on a southbound freight train and jumped off when he started seeing palm trees. In fact, running off to Florida is just what he had done a few years back. He hitchhiked his way south, mostly catching rides from long-haul truckers looking for someone to talk with to pass the time while on the lonely road. He wasn't in Florida long when he got busted for stealing a car. After ten days in jail waiting for trial, the idiot judge released him on his own recognizance, and he did what you might expect, he left the state.

Deep down, Piper thought he might never again leave Indiana and its cold northern winter nights simply because it was familiar. He knew where the food pantries were, the best street corners to beg from, and where the homeless shelters were, even if he didn't like to stay in them. The local shelters had too many rules, such as no alcohol, no drugs, and some required you to take a shower before they would allow you to stay. He didn't so much mind taking a shower, which was usually a welcomed treat. He just didn't like being told what to do. Some shelters required a medical evaluation to be completed, and others made you listen to a preacher give a sermon, what career homeless people called ear-banging, before dinner was served. He did appreciate that, before he left, he often got a new set of donated clothes from the larger shelters.

Piper had no family to speak of. He ran away from home after the old man beat him one too many times. A year or so later, he heard his mother passed away, and not long after, his dad died from cirrhosis of the liver.

His dad had worked for VendMate Food Service Company, which primarily supplied prepackaged food and snack items sold from vending machines located mostly in break rooms inside factories and businesses within the Templeton area. A major perk of this job was that he got to bring home sandwiches, donuts, and anything that didn't sell before its expiration date. All expired packaged snacks or sandwiches the VendMate employees didn't take home or eat in their break room were thrown in the company dumpster in the back lot.

After Piper ran away from home, it wasn't long before he got hungry. Thinking of his old man, he headed to the VendMate Food Service Company dumpster to dive for some prepackaged deli sandwiches with recent expiration dates. No one would call the discarded food gourmet, but it did fill his stomach. Anyway, those old warrants for his arrest in Florida were probably still active, but he could still dream about those warm sandy beaches.

CHAPTER 15

Lt. Weber usually arrived for work fifteen minutes early to prepare for roll call. His dad had always stressed that anyone who got to work on time was really fifteen minutes late. Weber used the extra time to check his office email and employee mail slot for any messages or department communications. He also checked the shared supervisor's desk for any notes left behind by the prior shift, then reviewed the recently submitted incident reports for information to share with his officers. He enjoyed reading these reports and made a habit of discussing the highlights during roll call. Weber was different from other supervisors because he tried to supervise using praise rather than criticism. After all, there was so much disapproval and outright ridicule directed at the police in the news lately. His officers deserved to be given credit for the good work they routinely did. He also appreciated humor during roll call, which Thaddeus and Cory were only too happy to supply.

Tonight, he started roll call with another complaint about Pauline the Patio Princess. All the officers knew about Pauline, and none of the male officers would respond to her residence without a backup as a witness. Better yet, a female officer backup as a witness and all bodycams rolling.

The Patio Princess was a worn-out 1970s hippy leftover mental case. It did no good taking her to the hospital on an Emergency Detention Mental Writ because she wasn't crazy enough for the shrinks to keep her, and she didn't appear dangerous to herself or anyone else. If they did keep her, where would they put her? The county mental hospital closed years ago, and with no health insurance to cover psychological disorders, there was nowhere to take her for treatment.

Weber began with, "It seems day-shift was sent to the Patio Princess' house to investigate a prowler." Day or night, Pauline would frequently call the police about nonexistent prowlers. "I was told on good authority when the officers arrived at her home on Bickle Circle that when she answered her door she was wearing only a short waist-length tie-dye tee shirt and flip-flop sandals decorated with plastic sunflower petals, and in this freezing winter weather!" Weber announced.

This was not unexpected. She got her nickname, the Patio Princess because in the summer, she had a habit of sunbathing topless on her back patio. Never mind that her house was on a zero-lot line with no privacy fencing. Most of the neighbors ignored her, considering her eccentric. Still, a few of the mothers with curious teenage boys would occasionally make the call to the police department when the Patio Princess made one of her au naturale appearances. Of course, when questioned about such behavior, Pauline innocently said she was unaware anyone could see her. When her neighbors weren't calling the police on her, she was calling the police about prowlers, which no one else ever noticed nor the police could ever find. What made it particularly uncomfortable for the responding officers was that she was a 95-pound, 67-year-old, blue-haired badge bunny. Her face was so wrinkled from constant cigarette smoking that it was beginning to look like a well-worn Templeton city map. Not to mention the wart on the end of her nose that was hard to ignore. Weber ended the discussion by stating the obvious, "Of course, day shift couldn't find the prowler or any evidence of one."

Weber continued by reading a day shift arrest report concerning a guy who got caught shoplifting at the local Goodwill store. Sergeant Mark Robinson leaned back in his chair while folding his arms and, in a sarcastic voice, commented, "That's dumber than stealing from my place."

Mark's ex-wife problems were epic, even for policemen, who were often divorced. He had been married and divorced three times and was currently living in a free apartment in exchange for working security for the apartment complex. Considering his current financial circumstances, he couldn't afford to live anywhere but in that free apartment. As he explained, he lost at least half his assets every time he got divorced. He figured that, presently, he was down to about one-eighth of his original pre-marital assets, which now consisted of an old Chevy pick-up truck, garage sale furniture, and bad taste in women. According to Mark, when he divorced wife number three, her attorney asked for everything, but at that point, he didn't have everything left to give. He was grateful for the police job, the paycheck being the only steady thing in his life.

Mark was better at dating than he was at marrying, and it seemed his marriages were all like a bad game of Scrabble where none of the letters worked well together. Thaddeus chimed in, "If you hadn't had to pay all those hard-working divorce lawyers, maybe you could afford to shop at that Goodwill. Goodness gracious Mark, somebody needs to suspend your license to marry!"

Mark shot back, "Well, at least I didn't marry someone like the Patio Princess. Although that wart on her nose does remind me of ex-number two."

Thaddeus couldn't resist asking, "Why's that? Did ex-number two have a nasty old wart on her nose too?"

"Naw," Mark smirked, dismissing the idea, then added with a knowing smile, "but she sure was a witch."

Teresa put in her two cents worth by adding, "Yeah, well, I think you and ex-number two both made the same dumb relationship mistake. You married each other!"

Weber, arms in the air and waving his hands back and forth, trying to regain the room's attention, interrupted, "Hey, over here folks, we still have a job to do. Listen, it looks like I'm not getting anything done tonight, but before you head out, make sure you enter your weekly stats into StatCom. And by the way, it's been a busy holiday season for us so far, so keep your heads low. It looks like the Christmas robbery season is now in full swing. Oh, and I have an envelope here for donations. We hope to collect enough money to buy Carl's kids some decent Christmas gifts, maybe tickets for a ball game downtown or something nice like that."

The mention of Carl's kids got Jeramy thinking about what a good dad Carl was. Even though Carl worked late shift and a part-time security job to help pay the bills, he always made time to coach his kid's teams. It couldn't have been easy when you were trying to squeeze in a couple of hours of sleep here, there, and whenever you could. Jeramy was in his thirties and had never married or had kids. Who knows, maybe someday?

CHAPTER 16

After roll call, Parker and Adam walked to Parker's squad car to prepare for the shift. Templeton, like many police departments, issued take-home police cars to officers after their probationary first year was completed. Parker didn't always have a rookie with him, so he usually had his squad car set up for his solitary use. Of course, the police car had all the accessories that any ordinary civilian's car would and all the modifications the standard police package adds to the vehicle. The emergency lights and siren mounted outside were operated from control panels connected to a console installed between the two front bucket seats.

A computer stand was also fastened to the floor between the front seats, with a laptop securely attached. Parker normally had a duty bag spread out on the passenger seat. It contained a filing system for assorted necessary police forms along with pens, pencils, notebooks, and traffic ticket books to use when the e-ticket function of the laptop was malfunctioning, which seemed to be a regular occurrence.

A compact thermal computer printer used to print e-tickets was connected to the back of the console. A vertical shotgun rack was mounted next to the printer. Unfortunately, it took an experienced contortionist to turn around, unlock the shotgun rack and somehow pull it up and over the back of the passenger's seat headrest without an accidental discharge, blowing out the side window.

Parker's police car was equipped with front and rear radar units allowing him to monitor vehicular traffic speeds from both directions. The front-facing dash-mounted control unit for the radar was situated next to the car's spotlight. Unfortunately, the way the spotlight was mounted to the car's frame, it partially obscured the driver's left view out of the windshield.

With most cars, in general, getting smaller, the driving compartment of a modern police car resembled a jerry-rigged cockpit of a jet airplane, but with less space. All this doesn't take into consideration the bulky police uniform an officer must wear. The driver's interior area barely had enough room for a cup holder for that all-important 3:00 a.m. cup of java. Then you had to find a place to put your flashlight for convenient access, being a late shift officer's most used piece of equipment.

It's a wonder more police officers aren't killed in automobile accidents. Fortunately, in those cases where an officer is involved in a severe car crash, the ballistic vest most uniform officers are required to wear often prevents chest trauma injuries. All this, and we haven't even opened the squad car's trunk. Parker's trunk contained a crime scene preservation kit, a first aid kit, an Automated External Defibrillator or AED for short, flares, rain gear, a tire deflation device, a fire extinguisher, and a small box of teddy bears for distressed kids. The stuffed animals were courtesy of Carl, who came up with the idea and worked to get them donated by the local Lion's Club.

It was a tight fit for just one officer, much less two officers, such as tonight when a rookie with all his gear rode along. In that event, everything Parker typically used from his front passenger seat had to be moved to the back seat. For a few days after completing the police academy, Adam rode in the squad car's passenger seat, only observing. After those first few days, Parker allowed Adam to handle all the radio traffic for their car between the dispatcher and other patrol cars. After a few more days, Parker added the operation of the computer laptop duties to Adam.

Parker had to admit Adam was a fast learner, catching on quickly to most aspects of the job. At this point in his training, Adam had been driving the squad car for a few weeks, handling radio traffic and laptop duties by himself while Parker watched and instructed. Adam quickly realized driving a squad car while responding to an emergency can be intimidating.

Parker confidently considered himself a proven veteran of squad car driving. He often bragged he could drive ninety miles an hour through a narrow orange coned-covered construction zone with his emergency lights flashing and siren loudly blaring. Operating the squad car's laptop with his right hand and the gas pedal to the floor with his right foot. At the same time, he used the top of his left knee to guide the steering wheel while daintily eating a powdered donut with his left hand. Accomplishing this feat without scattering any powder remnants onto his dark blue uniform. Tonight, Parker squeezed into the passenger side of the squad car and handed the car keys to Adam, who was sitting in the driver's seat and challenged Adam saying, "Let's see what kind of trouble we can find tonight."

Some officers were content to ride around their entire shift taking routine calls for police assistance and writing occasional traffic tickets, but little else. Not Parker, who was proactive. He would patrol the business district looking for burglaries or thefts in progress. He would also drive up and down State Road 76, watching for traffic offenders, and in particular, drunk drivers. As part of his regular patrol, he would often drive through the parking lot, then go inside one of the quick-stop shops or gas stations to get a cup of coffee. The coffee was usually free because the employees of these places were always happy to see a squad car parked in front of the store.

Because of the recent robberies, Parker asked Adam to drive to the Easy Stop on State Road 76, so they could be seen and demonstrate a police presence in the area. They entered the store, and after greeting the cashier, they each poured a cup of coffee.

As was his habit, Parker stood and talked to the cashier for a few minutes as he sipped the hot brew. He absentmindedly picked up an individually wrapped beef stick from a display rack next to the cashier, intended to prompt impulse purchases. He casually started to read the ingredients from the back of the package when he came across one that read *mechanically separated chicken.* Cartoon images raced through Parker's brain, attempting to understand what exactly a mechanically separated chicken was and how would that taste differently from a manually separated chicken? He also wondered why the manufacturer felt the need to explain in detail how the chicken was separated. Anyway, what was chicken doing in a beef stick? He had never eaten a cheeseburger with packaging listing ingredients indicating it had been made from *mechanically separated cows.* His thoughts drifted as more cartoon images floating around in his brain were now working overtime imagining what the machine would look like that would mechanically separate a cow. This mind-bending conundrum was interrupted when he looked up and noticed a beat-up old black pickup truck traveling slowly, eastbound on State Road 76, passing the Easy Stop. The vehicle itself wasn't unusual, but the reddish-colored substance splashed all over the driver's side door was. Immediately, he knew Adam's next training exercise was about to commence. Parker dropped his coffee in the trash can by the exit door, thanked the cashier, and hustled Adam out of the store. He pointed to the pickup truck and told Adam, "Jump in the car and let's follow that truck."

Adam drove the police car to within several car lengths behind the pickup truck. As they followed it, even the rookie could figure from the erratic driving that the driver was probably intoxicated. As most drunks do, the driver randomly sped up, then slowed down. While the truck wasn't exactly weaving from lane to lane, it was using the entire width of the lane it was traveling in. An odd thing about drunk drivers is they rarely notice a police car following them. Parker instructed Adam to continue to follow the truck, waiting for the driver to commit a traffic offense which would give the officers a stopping charge allowing a legal reason for the officers to stop the vehicle. As the officers watched, the pickup truck very slowly turned left onto Morgan Avenue without using any turn signals, giving the officers the needed stopping offense.

Adam activated his emergency lights, signaling the pickup truck to pull over. After a few seconds of following the vehicle with only their emergency lights on without the driver noticing, Adam turned on the squad car's siren. It still took an entire city block for the driver to notice the police car behind him and pull toward the side of the road. The truck stopped at an awkward angle, only partially leaving the travel portion of the road. Adam stopped the squad car about twenty feet behind but several feet to the left of the vehicle's center. This positioning of the police car would help protect Adam from passing traffic as he stood next to the driver's door conducting the traffic investigation. At Parker's instruction, Adam had already used his police radio to ask for assistance with a driver failing to stop. Mel immediately responded that he was close and would assist.

Adam got busy using his academy training, entering the truck's license plate number into the squad's laptop. The laptop's internet connection seemed slow tonight, so he had to wait longer than usual before getting a response. After receiving a notification that the truck was not stolen or wanted, the vehicle registration popped up on the screen, indicating it was registered to David Leonard. Adam quickly checked Leonard for any outstanding arrest warrants, finding none.

Adam and Parker got out of their squad car and carefully approached the stopped vehicle. In the police academy, recruits were warned traffic stops were one of the most dangerous of all police activities. They were instructed to watch the driver when approaching the vehicle and, when close enough, tap the trunk lid making sure it was closed. The instructor stressed officers had been attacked by suspects hiding inside the trunks of stopped cars. While a rarity, it was still one more thing an officer should check. Also, if possible, officers should look through the back window into the back seat, checking for anyone hiding there.

This being a pickup truck, Adam glanced into the bed as he walked by, amazed at all the trash and beer cans it contained. He got to the driver's side door and stood behind it as he was about to address the driver. Positioning himself this way prevented the driver from quickly swinging his side door open, trying to knock the officer down. In addition, with this type of stance, the driver would have to lean far to his left while turning around to see the officer, making it difficult to start an attack. Adam didn't have to be a gastroenterologist to identify the reddish substance splashed on the side of the driver's door as fresh vomit.

Parker stationed himself at the rear passenger side of the truck so that he could see the driver. This positioning allowed him to monitor the driver's actions while keeping Parker out of any possible crossfire should the driver attack.

Later, while Adam was writing the arrest report on this incident, he figured it took about two or three minutes from the time the truck stopped to the time he got to the driver's side door. Looking through the open driver's window, he could see that the occupant was passed out, foot still on the brake, vehicle in drive, and key in the ignition with the motor running.

Parker had been right. This was going to be a good training exercise. He slid on a pair of latex gloves and directed Adam to do the same. Against all police training, but then what else could be done, he opened the driver's side door and carefully reached into the still-running pickup truck and turned the ignition off. He would put the pickup in park after he got the driver out. Parker instructed Adam to get a trash bag and the vomit box out of the trunk of the squad car.

With a question in his voice, Adam responded with, "Vomit box?"

"Just get the empty cardboard box from the trunk, and don't forget the trash bag," was Parker's response.

Mel arrived, noticed the disgusting splatter on the driver's door, and smiled as he saw Adam return with a box and a trash bag from the trunk of Parker's squad car. Mel had seen this routine before. Some things you just didn't learn at the police academy.

Parker watched the driver, who was hunched over, forehead resting on the steering wheel, as Adam returned with the trash bag and box. "Never wake'em up before you are prepared," Parker instructed Adam while using his military-grade folding knife to cut a slit into the center portion of the bottom of the trash bag. Next, Parker gingerly set the box on the driver's lap. "Now it's time for sleeping beauty to wake up, except we're not gonna kiss this mess."

Parker shook the driver's left shoulder with no luck. Previously, Mel had told Parker that back in the day, the old-timers used smelling salts in situations such as this. Like a lot of other effective policing techniques, this one got discontinued by the brass because of a complaint filed by a citizen after an allergic reaction. "Like drinking alcohol until you passed out made allergies better?" was Mel's sarcastic reaction to the policy change.

Parker continued to shake the driver's shoulder with little effect. Adam was surprised when Parker quit shaking the driver, then pinched and twisted hard on the drunk's left ear lobe, causing the driver to stir. Stir it up was a better way to describe it because the driver sat straight up like a startled deer, deeply gulped some air, then violently spewed projectile vomit all over the inside of the windshield, the dashboard, and the steering wheel. Much of it dripped into the well-placed vomit box. Success of sorts.

Once he finished expelling the contents of his stomach, the driver calmly turned his head sideways toward Parker and, in heavily slurred speech, asked, "Kin I help you ossifiers?"

It is hard to explain how Adam, Parker, and Mel got the driver, later identified as David Leonard, out of the pickup truck. By this time, you couldn't consider Leonard mobile. Fortunately, all their pushing and pulling on the drunk's dead weight was made easier now the truck seat was liberally greased with his regurgitation.

Once out of the pickup truck, a wobbly Leonard tried to balance himself while leaning against the truck. Even so, Adam had to hold him steady. Parker stepped directly in front of Leonard and slipped the trash bag over his head like an ugly black dress. Leonard's head protruded out the hole Parker had cut in the bottom of the bag like a turtle's head popping out from its shell. "Perfect fit. Now you're ready for the ball," Parker said with a smirk. He then explained to Adam that if they had to transport Leonard to jail in the back seat of their car, the trash bag would limit the amount of vomit debris they would have to clean from the squad car.

As Leonard was leaning against the pickup truck, Adam asked if he would take a breath test for intoxication. After a few seconds of what seemed like serious thought, with a thick-sounding tongue, Leonard replied, "I think I am too drunk to take a breazalizard."

Lt. Weber drove up during this exchange and, without getting out of his patrol car, looked at David Leonard, the trash bag, then the vomit box and decided Leonard was beyond drunk and probably in the process of alcohol poisoning. As a precaution, he called for an ambulance to transport Leonard to the County Hospital lock-up, where prisoners were transported when needing medical assistance.

Because arrestees could not be transported in an ambulance without an officer present, Adam would have to ride with Leonard. Still, he didn't want to spend any more time with the drunk than necessary. Even wearing the trash bag, Leonard still had vomit on his face, and some had dribbled down onto the trash bag. Looking at Leonard, Adam couldn't figure out how vomit got into his hair, but the worse part was the smell. This was Adam's first experience with a person so extremely intoxicated. Before this, he had no idea that the smell of vomit consisting of partially digested food and lots of liquor was so utterly repulsive.

Parker would follow the ambulance to the hospital in his squad car. Once at the hospital, the officers would prepare all the proper documents required for requesting a blood draw to be taken from Leonard to be tested for his level of intoxication. They would also complete the arrest paperwork, leaving copies at the hospital lock-up. Next, they would drive a copy of that same paperwork to the county jail lock-up, where Leonard would be transferred once the doctor deemed him sober enough to be released from the hospital. Afterward, they would drive to the police department to finish the incident report, the arrest report, the tow sheet report, the probable cause affidavit, and a charging affidavit which would later be filed at the county prosecutor's office.

The frustrating part was that a drunk driver had to literally kill someone before getting sentenced to any real jail time. Even more frustrating to Parker was all the time spent working on this incident would keep the two officers from other police work. But first things first, Parker asked Adam to conduct a pat down of Leonard to ensure he had no weapons or contraband on his person. Meanwhile, Mel did an inventory search of the pickup truck.

While waiting for the ambulance to arrive, Adam took off the latex gloves and put on a pair of turtle skin gloves. These gloves were designed to protect the wearer from needle sticks or cuts from any sharp object an arrestee may be concealing. After making sure the gloves were on tight, he conducted the standard pat down, searching under the trash bag and doing his best to minimize contact with the vomit. He unfastened Leonard's belt and pulled it loose. Before placing the belt into a plastic bag used to store all the arrestee's personal property, he bent over and ran it through the wet snow removing much of the vomit covering it. While Leonard was leaning against his truck, Adam reached into each of Leonard's pants pockets, pulling out the contents, which included keys, loose change, and an assortment of scratch-off lottery tickets, then dropped it all into the same plastic bag containing the belt. Department policy dictated arrestee's shoes be taken off and searched. Leonard was too drunk to get his shoes off by himself, and there was nowhere to sit him down. Once the ambulance arrived, Adam sat Leonard on the stretcher and removed his shoes. He reached inside Leonard's left shoe and pulled out a big rolled-up, stinky wad of cash, which after being counted and inventoried, totaled $620.

Surprised to find the stash, Parker asked Leonard why he had the money in his shoe. Leonard appeared to think it over, then said, "That's tip money I'm hiding from my wife."

"Tip money? Where do you work?" asked Adam.

Leonard replied, "I'm a bartender at Louie's Escape on Lane Road,"

Adam whistled low, then commented to no one in particular, "Wow, how would ya like to walk on a lump like that all day long?"

While staring at the cash Parker held in his hand, Mel slowly and deliberately replied, "I think I'd love it!" After a short pause while deep in thought, then as if surprised, Mel stood up straight, pointed at Leonard, and blurted out, "Hold on a minute! Wait one second! If this guy gets convicted of drunk driving and his driver's license gets suspended, with the typical exception of only driving to and from work. Does that mean the only place he can drive is to a bar?"

CHAPTER 17

Gil was riding his bicycle through a couple of bar parking lots when he noticed some cops hassling a guy leaning against a pickup truck. He didn't want to draw their attention but was curious why the guy was wearing a weird-looking black plastic dress. Of course, mumbling to himself, "no telling what you'll see coming out of a bar at this time of night around here. Wearing a dress like that, the dude deserves to get locked up."

Gil was tired tonight, so he took another dexie. Earlier, at about 1:00 p.m., he woke up as Gran was yelling at the television. She was watching a rerun of *I Love Lucy* and Ricky was mad at Lucy, saying in his heavy Spanish accent that she had some "splainin" to do. When Lucy gave him a silly look and responded with "Eh?" Gran clumsily propped herself up in her chair and angrily yelled directly at the Lucy inside the television, "He said some explaining, ... explaining...you got some explaining to do! Lucy, are you deaf or stupid or sumfin? Dumb, I tell you. You're dumb!" Uneasily standing while feverishly pointing her crooked little forefinger at the television while she impatiently but slowly spelled out loud so that someone as obviously stupid as Lucy could clearly understand, "Your dumb, D - U - M, dumb!"

During this tirade, Gran lost her balance and pitched forward on the floor, which is what happens when you drink too much Dog Legg Whiskey mixed with cheap beer. Gil would have tried to sleep through the noise, but once Gran hit the floor after she'd been drinking, which frequently happened lately, she usually couldn't get up by herself. She knew Gil was hiding in the back bedroom trying to sleep, so she yelled for him to come and help her and continued to yell until he finally came to her rescue.

After pulling her up by one arm and plopping her back into the ratty old chair, he figured there was no point in returning to bed.

Not only was Gran a mean drunk, but she was also a clumsy drunk, and he was getting tired of picking her up off the floor. Lately, it seemed she was getting drunker earlier in the day. Cranky from losing sleep, he cheered up some, thinking back to last night watching the guy with the crazy-looking black dress get arrested. Now that was funny. It always made him feel better to see someone else get hassled by the cops.

Gil had never been in much trouble, mostly minor stuff such as misdemeanor possession of marijuana, petty theft, and public intoxication. Not enough to keep him in lock-up long. He didn't like jail one bit. The jailers wake you up at 6:00 a.m. for breakfast that wasn't worth eating. The cell blocks were made of cement which seemed to be designed to radiate the cold. The jailhouse prisoner uniforms were loose, and in the Indiana winters, the short sleeves of the prisoner uniforms did little to keep you warm. It didn't help he was so skinny, with no meat on his bones to help keep him warm.

The jail had a television in the community room, but that's where the gang bangers hung out, and Gil didn't want anything to do with gang bangers. Even the cops treated him better than those thugs. In fact, the cops had never beaten him, but the gang bangers had beaten him badly on more than one occasion. While the cops had not always been very understanding toward him, the gang members in this town were downright brutal. It was best to stay clear of them, in jail or out. At least they didn't scream at Lucy on the television in the community room. Gran, that old bitty, could get under your skin faster than flesh-eating bacteria. How could he concentrate on his nighttime scrounging for money if she wouldn't let him sleep?

After getting Gran repositioned in her chair, she was quickly once again engrossed in Lucy's explanation to Ricky about the money he felt was misspent on a new dress. Gil slinked out of the mobile home, jumped on his bike, and made his way toward the local bar parking lots hoping for some daytime luck. In no time at all, he noticed a one-dollar bill at the edge of Olivia's Gentlemen's Club front parking lot. With a little more luck scavenging, he might be able to buy a package of cigarettes.

CHAPTER 18

Today was Jeramy's regular monthly day in court. The county criminal courts had an online calendar that local officers could use to record their preferred dates and times for scheduling criminal trials they would be required to testify. Some officers didn't use the calendar. As a result, when a defendant pled not guilty at his initial hearing, the judge set a random date for trial. These officers ended up with a sort of potluck series of court appearances consisting of different days and times, sometimes at 9 a.m., other times at 1:30 p.m.

As a late shift officer, Jeramy preferred the 1:30 p.m. slot and dates during his workdays, allowing his days off to be completely free of work-related responsibilities. Templeton police officers received a choice of overtime pay or compensatory time off for court appearances. Even so, few officers relished a day in court. Jeramy typically got off work at 6:30 a.m., and on days he had to appear in court, he would sleep until noon, get up for a quick shower, dress, then drive to court. He frequently had to stop at the police department to retrieve trial evidence. When one of his arrests went to trial, and he needed to testify, it often seemed his case wasn't presented to the judge until close to the end of the court session. As a result, it wasn't unusual for his court day not to end until around 5:00 p.m.

Few of his court cases went to trial. Most arrestees worked out a plea agreement before the assigned trial date, saving him from a day in court. Typically, when he did have to appear, once the defense attorney determined all required witnesses and officers had shown up for the trial, he would ask for a continuance. This would allow him to negotiate a favorable plea agreement for his client. Criminal defendants often failed to appear for their court dates, wasting Jeramy's entire afternoon. After court, Jeramy would handle any personal affairs that needed attention. At about 7:30 p.m., he would try to get a few hours of sleep, getting up in time to get dressed and go to work. Sleeping during the day was bad enough, but having such an erratic sleep pattern and still being on top of your game while on patrol all night was hard on many officers.

Court days weren't the only times an officer had to juggle sleeping hours. There were also mandatory training days and days where personal business was scheduled, such as doctor or dentist appointments. Married officers had to contend with weekends spent with in-laws, not to mention summer vacation and holidays when the kids were home during the day while the officer was trying to sleep. Then there is the question of arranging your sleep time on the last day of your six working days. Do you try to stay up all day and sleep a regular nighttime sleep pattern on your three days off? Or do you nap for a few hours the morning of your last shift in your work week, waking in time to enjoy most of the day? Then what do you do on your first day back to work? Do you wake early in the morning like a regular person, then try to nap before going to work? Or do you try to sleep extra late that morning, hoping to get enough sleep to last the whole day and night? On your three days off, do you sleep regular nighttime hours, or do you stay up late at night and sleep late in the morning? Getting good sleep was important for anyone working the late shift, and Jeramy used a white noise machine, room-darkening window shades, and an expensive memory foam mattress, all in an effort to get better sleep. For Jeramy, being single with no kids made getting needed sleep easier.

Jeramy went to the police station to pick up the case file and evidence needed for today's court appearance. The evidence consisted of a small amount of methamphetamine found in a purse of a female he arrested for public intoxication. Rebecca, Templeton Police Department's property room attendant, had temporarily stepped out of the office. While waiting for her to return, he visited with Templeton Police Detective Derek Wilson. The Templeton Police Department's investigations offices and the department's property room were in the basement, and Derek's office was next to the property room. Derek's office was affectionately called Derek's Kitchen. It was equipped with all types of small kitchen appliances, which Derek claimed came in handy on those long nights when he got called out on an investigation. His office had a toaster, a coffee maker, a microwave oven, and a small dorm room-sized refrigerator. Jeramy wasn't sure how many cases got cleared in that kitchen, but he did know that Derek whipped up a mean peanut butter and toast sandwich.

Today Derek was mugging in front of a mirror hung in the corner of his office, trying to put on an unusual looking beaded tie. The tie was made from small colorful beads traditionally found with American Indian jewelry, such as bracelets or necklaces. It was similar to the pre-tied, clip-on ties Jeramy's mother made him wear to church when he was a kid. The difference was this tie had two straps that snapped together in the back. As Jeramy watched, it became clear the tie must have been made using a child's size template because it fastened too tightly around Derek's neck. That, combined with how short the tie was, extending only halfway down Derek's slightly protruding belly, caused Jeramy to snort when he saw the comical sight.

As he looked in the mirror, Derek also thought the tie looked funny but was pleased to have received it. He explained to Jeramy the tie was a gift from a local Native American Indian. Earlier that year, Derek had worked an accidental death investigation involving the Indian's brother. That morning the brother wanted to show his appreciation for Derek's compassion during the investigation by presenting to him the Christmas gift of an authentic hand-made beaded Indian necktie. Derek was genuinely touched by the gift, even if he was amused at the size and many colors of the beads, never wondering why a Native American Indian would wear such a tie in the first place. This was exactly the type of thing Derek thoroughly enjoyed, something unique with a story behind it. He would have to find an appropriate place to hang it in his office. Maybe he would display it next to a decorative gourd sitting on his file cabinet. He found the gourd at a local farmer's market. It was painted to look like an owl, set up long ways, balancing on one end of the gourd and two short sticks stuck into the bottom mimicking bird legs. Of course, with Derek's unusual sense of humor and his love of history, he named the gourd Owl Gourd after the former vice-president. Derek was definitely in the Christmas spirit. As he was comically wearing the tightly fitting and brightly colored beaded Indian tie, he cheerfully ate from a clear baggie that was full of homemade peanut brittle he had just purchased from Chaplain Gossett. The chaplain was selling the candy, homemade by the woman's group at the Templeton First Baptist Church, as a fundraiser to benefit the Shop With A Cop program. He and Jeramy walked toward Rebecca's desk just as she was returning.

Rebecca walked directly up to Derek, pointed a forefinger straight at his chest, showed a silly grin, and then asked excitedly, "Where did you get that?"

Derek impishly smiled but happily started to explain all about the tie, the Native American Indian, and his dead brother.

Rebecca interrupted him mid-sentence and sharply corrected, "No, no, not that! The peanut brittle, where did you get the peanut brittle?"

Once Derek shared some peanut brittle with Rebecca, she relaxed a little, like a drug addict after a fix, then retrieved the evidence for Jeramy. Evidence in hand, Jeramy left the police station. Walking across the street to the courthouse, he felt the holiday spirit as he admired the Christmas lights and decorations wrapped around the old courthouse.

Of course, the female speed freak didn't show up for her court appearance, and a warrant was issued for her arrest. Jeramy figured the warrant would do little good. Maybe she'd get stopped for a traffic violation where the re-arrest warrant would be discovered. Or she might get arrested on a new violation, and the re-arrest warrant would be found during processing. Unless arrested for a serious offense, she will likely be released on her own recognizance pending a trial date in which she would probably not appear again. Jail overcrowding is often cited to justify no bail, low bail, or early prisoner release. Jeramy felt Mel was correct when he explained we should build more jails now and keep criminals locked up until they have served their time with no time off for good behavior. After all, as Mel often claimed, it was bad behavior that got them locked up in the first place. Jeramy gave it some thought and wondered why most people didn't commit crimes. Was it because they gave into their God-given conscience and usually did the right thing?

After leaving court, Jeramy went back to the police department and returned the evidence to the property room. Walking to his car, dead tired from irregular sleep, he noticed a thin man dressed as Santa Claus ringing a Salvation Army bell standing in the slushy snow in front of a drug store. As Jeramy got into his car, he thought that the Santa must be cold ringing that bell all day in the blustery winter weather. He wondered why a guy would take a day to volunteer to ring a Salvation Army bell.

CHAPTER 19

Piper parked the Malibu in the back of a twenty-four-hour Walmart parking lot, where he figured employees parked. Then climbed into the back seat, ready for some much-needed shuteye. He often used this parking lot to sleep when he didn't have a car available to him. Lucky for him, no one ever disturbed or reported him as suspicious. It wasn't long before the sun started to rise, and he thought it was time to move along. Because this was such a good place to sleep, he would never leave a stolen car here.

Piper drove out of the parking lot toward a rundown part of town where he planned to park the Malibu on the street. He would leave it unlocked with the keys in the ignition, hoping a dope fiend would notice, then steal the car. If the cops stopped the dope fiend in the car, he would take the rap. If not, the cops might not find the car until someone thought it looked suspicious and reported it. He parked the car on the side of the road of a residential neighborhood and walked casually from it, his backpack, heavy with all his earthly belongings, slung over his shoulder. He immediately began to look for any unattended car left with its motor running in a driveway while the unsuspecting owner waited inside his house for it to warm up. As cold as it was, he didn't think it would take long to find one. An SUV would be nice because it would have more room in the back to sleep.

CHAPTER 20

Lt. Weber seemed chipper at roll call and started by telling Adam, "The hospital called and complained about Leonard the drunk from last night. They said he made a mess of the hospital holding cell. It seems after he finished emptying his stomach, he dry-heaved the rest of the night, moaning and complaining all the while."

Mel, known for his witty and sage truisms, smiled while adding, "Ya know, I never met a person that ever said, 'I'm glad I had that last beer.'" Adam didn't have much experience with drunks but was sure he would never forget the rancid smell of Leonard covered in alcohol-drenched vomit.

Weber continued, "Guys, it looks like the counterfeiters are back. The Burger Boy on State Road 76 took a counterfeit $20 bill in exchange for a cheeseburger."

Thaddeus couldn't resist, "A counterfeit $20 for a counterfeit cheeseburger? Seems about right to me."

Weber tipped his head slightly and glanced over his reading glasses at Thaddeus with a slight smile before continuing to read from his clipboard. "Let's watch the StorMor Self Storage behind the Templeton Plaza. There were a couple of storage garages that got broken into last night. Also, make sure to look at the surveillance photos from the Easy Stop robbery Detective Pierson posted on the bulletin board." Shuffling through paperwork, looking for the next topic to discuss, he stopped at a memo from Chief Jordan. Weber summarized the memo by stating, "Due to this year's unexpected decline in property tax revenue paid to the city, all department supervisors are expected to monitor future overtime closely."

Unlike some chiefs in the past, Chief Jordan was generally well-liked by the officers. The Chief had worked his way up the promotions ladder from patrolman to chief of police. While the officers respected Chief Jordan, they didn't always hold the town council in the same high esteem. To the officers, it seemed the town council was only interested in pinching pennies, usually the officer's pennies.

No one was surprised when Mel barked, "Well, if you want a police department, you gotta pay for it."

Thaddeus interrupted with his favorite Napoleon Bonaparte quote, "In politics, stupidity is not a handicap."

Weber turned to Sgt. Mark Robinson and asked, "Mark, you got anything?"

"Yeah," Mark solemnly replied, "a mild migraine, a clunker that needs a new transmission, and child support that would cripple a Rockefeller."

Teresa sat patiently listening to the officers, waiting for them to finish, then asked, "Are we going to yuck it up here all night, or are we going to get to work?" She then stood up and marched out of the roll call room as a challenge for the other officers to follow.

At 11:20 p.m., Jeramy responded to Charles's gruff voice over the police radio sending him and Teresa to an auto accident, "Check a 10-50 PI at 5200 Mill Road in the S curve, possible entrapment, fire rescue, and ambulance enroute." In the past, all police departments didn't use the same radio codes. As a result, most departments scrapped the familiar Ten Codes years ago when the Feds strongly suggested plain English be used instead, while communicating over the police. Because new radio technology made it easy for different police departments to communicate with each other, this new directive made those transmissions between agencies less confusing.

Charles was old school, preferring the Ten Codes, and continued to use them regardless of what nonsense the FBI would try to push onto local police departments. He thought Ten Codes were descriptive and concise, something dispatchers and patrolmen both appreciated. He felt he shouldn't take up valuable radio airtime using whole sentences when a simple Ten Code would suffice. He reasoned you never knew when an officer might need that radio space to call for assistance at the very same moment a police dispatcher might be droning on about a barking dog complaint. In fact, using the Ten Codes might have saved Charles's life years before when he was still in uniform. He stopped a car for a minor traffic violation, and before leaving his police car to approach the violator's car, he gave the dispatcher his location along with the license plate number of the violator's car. He then approached the vehicle, but as he was asking the driver for his driver's license, he heard the dispatcher address him over the police radio in a questioning tone of voice, "10-67?" Charles had never heard the code 10-67 used before.

During his time at the police academy, he was required to memorize all 100 of the different Ten Codes but had forgotten what the rarely used 10-67 meant. Charles radioed the dispatcher to stand by, excused himself from the driver, and returned to his squad car. As he had been trained, while moving away from the stopped car, he walked almost backward, never completely turning his back on the driver of the stopped car. Once inside his car, he checked his list of Ten Codes and their meanings and scanned for 10-67. According to the list, 10-67 meant, "Clear for Message." Not quite knowing what that phrase meant, and while still seated in his squad car, he responded over his police radio, "Clear for message." The dispatcher replied that the vehicle owner was wanted for armed rape and other officers were enroute to Charles's location to assist him. Charles appreciated Ten Codes even more after he arrested the driver, searched the car, and found a stolen pistol in the car's console. How else would a dispatcher be able to inform an officer that the person he was interacting with at that very moment, within earshot of the officer's police radio, was a crazy person without saying the person was 10-96, the Ten Code for a mental case?

On occasion, Charles did unconsciously use plain English. One night, it got him in trouble when he sent Mel to Cotton Street and State Road 76 to check a "flake in the middle of the road." When the chief later questioned his choice of words, Charles explained that the word flake was a descriptive plain English word. He explained this reasoning in the casual, non-expressive tone of voice in which he usually talked, which is how he had earned the nickname, Chuckles because, well, he never did. The officers on the shift never complained when Charles used Ten Codes, and they all knew that a 10-50 PI was a traffic accident involving personal injury. Jeramy arrived on the scene and jumped from his car as Teresa arrived. He ran to the Jeep Wrangler, which was lying on its passenger side, while Teresa pulled her first aid kit from her squad car's trunk. Debris consisting of smashed Jeep body parts and the contents from the vehicle's passenger area, including empty beer cans, were spread all over the street for about 300 feet, indicating the jeep had rolled more than once. To Jeramy, it appeared to be a single-vehicle accident where that vehicle traveled too fast in the slick snow as it approached the S curve. As Jeramy reached the Jeep, he saw the driver climbing out the driver's side door, which was now facing up. He helped the driver out and onto the ground while Teresa attended to the guy in the passenger seat.

The soft top of the Jeep had been completely torn away, making it easy for Teresa to get to the passenger. Quickly assessing the situation, she noticed the passenger appeared to be unconscious. His right hand, severed just above the wrist, was bleeding badly. Teresa pulled a tactical tourniquet from her first aid kit and began to apply it to his lower right forearm. She wrapped it around the forearm like an inflatable blood pressure cuff, then twisted a handle to tighten the tourniquet, applying pressure until the bleeding stopped. She then folded the handle down, which secured the tourniquet in place with the proper amount of pressure applied to the limb.

"Advise fire rescue this is a serious PI," Teresa informed Charles over her police radio. Confident she had the blood flow stopped, she began checking the passenger for other injuries and was relieved when she heard the siren of the Templeton Fire Department's rescue squad as it approached the scene. One fireman ran toward the Jeep with a large first aid kit while a second fireman pulled a backboard from the truck.

Mark arrived, assigned the accident report to Jeramy, and told Thaddeus to direct what little traffic there was around the accident scene. After Mark requested a wrecker and started photographing the scene, a fireman approached, asking, "Where's the hand?"

Caught off guard, Mark responded with, "Huh?" Then it struck him. The guy's severed hand, where is it? He answered, "I dunno, we gotta find it!" Springing into action, Mark ordered Jeramy and Thaddeus to start a search of the area beginning in the street just before the debris field began. Then addressing Teresa and instructing her to, "Get to the Easy Stop Store and get a bag of ice."

Teresa raced, emergency lights and siren, to the Easy Stop, where she ran inside and grabbed a bag of ice, yelling to the store clerk that she would return later to pay. As she left the store, she noticed a stack of small blue buckets displayed next to some cleaning items and decided to grab one. She thought if they found the hand, they could use the bucket to carry it and the ice while transporting it to the hospital. Supplies in hand, she sped back to the accident scene.

The medics quickly loaded the injured man into the ambulance and left for the hospital as Jeramy and Thaddeus began the search for the missing right hand. Mark was glad to have Thaddeus on the scene because he seemed able to find things, whether a drunk driver on a slow night or the tiniest piece of fragmented evidence at a crime scene. It wasn't long before Thaddeus found the hand, just off the berm of the road about twenty feet from where the jeep stopped. It was covered in snow, dirt, and vegetation that the Jeep dug up as it tumbled to a halt. Later, they figured that while the Jeep was rolling over, the passenger must have used his right hand to hold onto the roll bar, cleanly severing the hand below the wrist when the roll bar impacted the pavement during the violent rollover.

Thaddeus may have found the hand, but he wasn't about to touch it. Mark, not the squeamish type, quickly took a few photos of the hand before putting on latex gloves. He gently picked up the hand by the thumb and placed it into the small blue bucket. After spreading ice over the hand, Mark handed the bucket to Teresa, saying, "To the hospital, fast!" Teresa jumped in her squad car but immediately wondered where to place the bucket so it would not fall and spill the hand and ice while driving to the hospital. She carefully balanced the small bucket between her legs before spinning the squad car's tires, getting traction in the slick snow as she began the race to the hospital.

Teresa was just a few minutes from the hospital when Charles contacted her by radio, "Disregard the hospital. The medical personnel advised they will not be able to reattach."

Frustrated, Teresa responded on her police radio, "Clear, but I've got a hand between my legs and don't know what to do with it."

Mark calmly contacted Teresa over the police radio and, without a hint of a smirk, instructed her to, "Take it to the hospital emergency room anyway. Let them deal with it." Which she did, then quietly returned to her regular patrol duties.

Jeramy was disappointed this was Parker and Adam's day off because this accident was the type of incident the rookie would have been assigned as part of his training. As it was, he was looking at a couple of hours of computerized paperwork involving completing the accident report and drawing the accident scene diagram. Both tasks required mind-numbing amounts of specific detail, which had to be entered into the accident reporting system.

Officer Teresa O'Brian's family originated from Ireland. She had feisty Irish red hair and a temperament that seemed soothed only by her dry, sharp wit. She may have been short and petite, but she wasn't afraid of working hard and hated it when she missed something, such as a business burglary in her assigned area during her working hours.

Usually, an hour or so before going off duty at 4:00 a.m., she would patrol the business areas of her assigned district, checking windows and back doors. She didn't want to be embarrassed if day shift officers had to take a business burglary report in her assigned area later in the morning. She drove through the Hidden Creek housing edition between moving from business to business. She noticed an older blue Malibu parked on the street. It looked suspicious because it wasn't parked in front of a house, and to her, it just didn't look right. It occurred to her that a blue Malibu was used in the Imperial Liquor Store robbery. She checked the registration plate on the Malibu using the squad car laptop and immediately was gratified with a response informing her the license plate had been reported stolen. Teresa approached the car finding it unlocked and the keys in the ignition. Checking the car by vehicle identification number, a number stamped on the vehicle frame during the manufacturing process, she discovered the car had also been reported stolen.

Thinking this might be the vehicle used in the liquor store robbery and being an experienced evidence technician, she grabbed her fingerprint kit from her trunk and got to work. While waiting for a tow truck to arrive to tow the Malibu to the police impound lot, she dusted for prints on the inside glass of the driver's side door and the rear-view mirror glass. She wasn't an expert at reading fingerprints but was hopeful the prints she lifted from the car were identifiable.

As she was putting the print kit back in her trunk, she looked down and noticed the bottom of her left pants leg was singed, probably from stepping too close to a traffic flare placed in the street at the Jeep accident scene earlier in the shift. She didn't care much about the pants but hoped she hadn't ruined the Cuddle Duds she was wearing underneath as thermal underwear. Those Cuddle Duds were about the only thing that made her feel feminine while working in such a masculine-dominated environment.

CHAPTER 21

As Mel entered Dio's Pancake Palace, Carolyn had a cup of coffee ready for him, placing it at the spot on the table where he usually sat. This table was located in the back of the restaurant, and he sat with his back to the wall facing the entrance. He, like a lot of old-time policemen, when in public places, had a habit of seating themselves so they could see the front door and watch for trouble. Relaxing, he thought, for some reason, the coffee always tasted better at a diner, and this morning it tasted very good. Mel enjoyed coffee. It wasn't just the jolt of caffeine. He also enjoyed the taste and the social enjoyment of coffee, as with Cory during their time spent at Dio's. He also enjoyed his coffee at home while resting, contemplating the total experience, pleasure, and smell of a simple cup of joe.

Mel was sipping his coffee, thinking how nice it was that Carolyn almost always had a cup ready at his regular seat as he arrived at his usual time when Cory interrupted the calm by plopping down in the seat across from him. Cory began talking mid-thought, "Christmas season, wow! The wife has me running in circles again this year. Lots of kids' activities at school and all the Christmas shopping, putting up the tree, and don't forget the annual Christmas march." Noticing Mel's puzzled expression, without skipping a beat, Cory began to explain. "Starting the Saturday before Christmas, we do lunch at my wife's aunt's house with all her extended family. Next is dinner Sunday evening with all the neighbors. Then Christmas Eve is dinner and a gift exchange with my side of the family. We do our little immediate family Christmas at home with the kiddos on Christmas morning. That is after I spent half the day assembling whatever was purchased as gifts. Last year I had to put a mess of tiny decals on a Hot Wheels racetrack. It took forever, and yup, there were 105 decals. I counted them. Then

Christmas evening dinner, including another gift exchange with my in-laws. No wonder I'm getting so fat. And sleep? Forget about it because I work six days straight leading up to Christmas Eve, not to mention the part-time I'm working as a guard at the Templeton First National Bank afternoons that entire week. Lucky thing I am off over Christmas."

"Oh, and did I tell you already, I gotta redo the Christmas lights I hung outside our house? Today, one of my kids told me I didn't put them up tight enough, causing the string of lights to droop. Now they say our place looks creepy at night, like a haunted house! And you know what," leaning back in his seat, hands folded on his stomach and almost out of breath at this point in the long and disjointed ramble describing this year's Christmas ordeal, he added, "sometimes I think it just might be."

Mel enjoyed hearing Cory rattle on about his family life. As miserable as Cory sometimes made it sound, he missed the family life. His wife passed away a few years ago after suffering for years from the treatments for breast cancer which eventually took her life. His kids were grown with lives of their own. By no means was he unhappy, but he did miss the family times he once had. The two sat and enjoyed their breakfast and conversation. Cory was almost finished with his biscuits and gravy when Mel was called away to take a vandalism report.

CHAPTER 22

It was hard for Piper to believe that after prowling around all morning, he couldn't find a car left running and ready for him to steal in this freezing weather. He checked a few gas stations, a grocery store, and the local post office, but to his disappointment, no parked cars were left running while their owners dashed inside to conduct last-minute business.

He figured with no money, no cash, no place to sleep, and nothing in his backpack left to sell, it was time to get back to work. He didn't want to risk doing a hold-up, not without an escape car, so he figured he'd do a break-in, which would be easy enough. He wandered through a few middle-class neighborhoods where it appeared everyone had already left for work. He figured even with the backpack, he didn't look too suspicious. He kept his long stringy hair tucked under a baseball hat, and other than his clothes being slightly dirty and rumpled, he looked like any other young skinny twenty-something guy.

Piper rarely burglarized multi-level houses. Most valuables were hidden in master bedrooms, often located on the upper level of a two-story home. He didn't want anything to do with the upper floors of houses. How would he escape if the resident returned home as he was plundering a second-story bedroom?

As Piper walked around, he found a one-story house with no cars in the driveway. It was surrounded by tall bushes and other overgrown vegetation close to the house. After stashing his backpack between some bushes, he walked to the front door.

His residence burglary routine was always the same. As he approached the front door, he would look around for any surveillance video cameras or video doorbells. Finding none, he would knock on the front door. If someone answered, he planned to ask for Brian. Of course, the reply would be that no Brian lived there. With that, Piper would shrug his shoulders and say he must have the wrong address, then walk away looking for another target. But if there was no answer to the front door, he would walk around to the back door and knock. Honestly, if someone answered the back door, he didn't know what he would say, but he wanted to ensure that no one was in the house before kicking in the back door. If he got no answer at the back door and after a quick look around to make sure there were no witnesses, he would kick in the door.

Using the sole of his foot, he would aim to strike the door as close to the lock as possible, hoping to break the inner door frame, allowing the door to swing open. If he accidentally knocked the door completely down, it would be obvious to anyone within eyesight that there was a problem. Once inside the house, he would close the back door, and no one would be the wiser that he was inside.

With no answer at either door, Piper kicked the back door open. He was startled when something furry scooted past his feet, and then he saw a big gray cat dash out the back door just before he pushed it shut. He didn't care about the cat but glanced out the rear window to make sure no one was watching.

He never wasted time in the kitchen or the living room because nobody hid valuables there. Instead, he went straight for the master bedroom. He quickly stripped a pillowcase from a pillow and went to work, trying to minimize time spent inside the home. After a check under the mattress, then under the bed, he moved to the dresser drawers. He opened the bottom drawer first and rifled through it, looking for anything small and possibly valuable. Heck, he wasn't a gemologist, so he grabbed any jewelry that might look to be worth a buck and tossed it into the pillowcase. Later he would let his fence Rex, figure it out. Piper then moved up through the dresser drawers, leaving the ones he had already searched open while searching the ones above them. No point wasting time closing drawers. After all, he wasn't the freaking maid.

Feeling around deep inside one drawer, he felt something unusual. A quick look inside revealed a roll of cash, which he quickly dumped into the pillowcase. After scanning the top of the dresser, he noticed a small jewelry box and shoved it, unopened, into the pillowcase along with some random coins he scooped up off the top of the dresser. He moved to the nightstand and, in the top drawer, was gratified to find a Glock model 32 semi-automatic pistol lying neatly on top of a stack of magazines. Piper didn't know diddly about handguns, but he knew this pistol would be easy to sell.

He found a checkbook in the next drawer, opened it, and removed the very last check before returning it to the drawer. It would be months before the homeowner would notice that particular check missing, allowing plenty of time for it to be forged and passed. In the master bedroom closet, he ripped open several old shoe boxes. After finding only old photos inside, he tossed each and its contents into a pile on the floor.

He noticed an old coffee can on a shelf in the closet. Picking it up, it felt too heavy to contain only coffee, and he immediately knew it had to contain something valuable. Without opening it, he tossed the can into the pillowcase. It seemed to Piper most people were stupid. They would hide money and valuables in coffee cans, cigar boxes, or other similar containers, then, oddly enough, put those containers in their master bedroom closet, where they looked completely out of place. You might as well put a sticker with the words *"Steal Me"* on the coffee can. Piper never understood why people didn't hide their valuables in something like a cereal box, then place it in a kitchen cabinet where such a box belonged. In all his years as a thief, he had never looked inside a kitchen cabinet for something to steal.

While in the master bathroom, Piper looked for jewelry and took all the prescription medication he could find, no matter what it was. He was no more a pharmacist than a gemologist, so he took all the meds he could find. Rex's specialty was prescription narcotics, and he would know if any of them had street value.

By this time, Piper had been in the house for five to ten minutes and his internal clock was screaming it was time to leave. He threw the pillowcase containing the loot over his shoulder like Santa's toy bag and walked quickly to the back door. Once outside, he hid in the bushes where his backpack was hidden, then crammed the pillowcase inside the backpack, slung it over his shoulder, and casually walked away.

Piper preferred doing stick-ups and getting cash rather than stealing stuff he had to sell. When he had to resort to burglaries, Rex was a reliable source to fence the loot. Piper figured Rex only gave him five to ten percent of the street value for the stuff, but that was the going rate when selling stolen property to a fence, so he saw no reason to complain. He didn't believe Rex's real name was Rex any more than Rex knew what Piper's real name was. Hustlers had to be careful. Snitches were everywhere.

Piper was born Patrick Sandpiper, but as a young kid, not wanting to be known as Patrick or even Pat, he took the nickname of Piper. He didn't want to hold this stuff too long and wasn't about to take any of it to a pawn shop. The legit pawn shops took stuff legally, getting a thumbprint from the seller and recording information from the seller's ID. This was not an option for Piper, not with his criminal history. On the other hand, the pawn shops that were not legit were just too dicey to trust. He met Rex while in the County Jail and trusted him, or at least trusted him as much as you can trust a dope-dealing ex-con with a side business fencing stolen goods. Piper didn't have many choices and didn't want to take a chance doing a stick-up without a get-a-way car.

CHAPTER 23

It was almost 6:00 a.m., still dark and close to the end of Jeramy's shift, when he noticed a vehicle with no taillights in traffic in front of him. He didn't necessarily look for minor traffic violations but didn't ignore the obvious ones. He was able to move through traffic, positioning his police car behind the one with no taillights, then activated his emergency lights as a signal for the vehicle to pull over, which it did.

Before getting out of his police car to approach the driver, he entered the car's license plate number into his laptop. As he did, he noticed a chrome emblem made of two intersecting arcs resembling the outline of a fish next to the license plate. Jeramy knew this emblem had a religious connotation but was unsure what it meant. He approached the driver's door just as the driver was lowering his window. He asked the male driver if he knew why he was being stopped, then asked for his driver's license. Jeramy returned to his police car and used his laptop to verify the driver's license and vehicle registration, determining both were active and the driver had no arrest warrants outstanding.

In the later part of his shift, Jeramy often gave traffic violators a break on minor offenses, anyway, the driver may have been telling the truth when he said he didn't know his taillights were out. He gave the driver a verbal warning and instructed him to have the taillights fixed immediately. After all, how many people check their taillights to make sure they're working?

Jeramy was curious about the fish emblem. He had seen it on other cars but didn't know what it meant. With only a few minutes remaining on his shift, he pulled into a parking lot and was trying to monitor traffic at the stop light as he pulled out his cell phone to do an internet search on "fish symbol."

The search provided a list of responses with headers such as "Sign of the Fish," "Jesus Fish," and, interesting enough, "Ichthys." Selecting Ichthys, Jeramy discovered this symbol originated as a secret sign used by first-century Christians. He read it symbolized, "fishers of men," a phrase Jesus used to describe his followers. As he continued to scan the article, he found that Ichthys was the Greek name for this ancient symbol of a fish. But why Greek, thought Jeramy. Wasn't Jesus Jewish? It was getting late in the shift, and Jeramy was tired. That question would have to wait.

fish or car

CHAPTER 24

"Lt. Weber called off work tonight, so I'll be handling roll call," announced Mark.

"Oh yeah?" Thaddeus added with a wicked sneer, "I hear he's doing prep work for a colonoscopy tomorrow. Gonna get doped, poked, and scoped!"

"If you knew what's involved in that prep work, you wouldn't be making fun of it," Mark said knowingly. "All right, never mind all that," he continued. "Hey, Mel, that vandalism report you took last night. The one where a gal's car got egged? Well, I got a note from Detective Derek Wilson. He talked to the woman's ex-boyfriend, who copped to it. The guy said she deserved it."

"Ah huh, another poultry perpetrator," Thaddeus added, nodding his head up and down bobblehead style as if this was the tenth such incident this month.

"Thaddeus, that was a *foul* shot," Cory smirked, then grinning, added, "Anyway, if Derek needs any help with the case, maybe Teresa can lend him a hand."

Teresa frowned at Cory. She didn't realize her comment over the police radio about the severed hand came out the way it did until about, oh, one fraction of a nano-second afterward. She knew these lug-heads couldn't resist razzing her. Too bad there wasn't a Ten Code to ask for instructions for what to do with a severed hand instead of the plain English she used.

As callous as it seems, it wasn't usual for police officers to work a serious incident, then joke about it later. Jeramy had been around police work long enough to believe most of this admittedly bad taste in humor was probably not some sort of PTSD nor a defense mechanism used to cope with the madness, mayhem, death, and destruction they often witnessed. No, he felt many police officers just saw so many of life's tragedies that they simply became desensitized.

Jeramy could see they all enjoyed the humor, which helped to relieve the stress, and it wasn't as if Teresa didn't bust the other officer's chops on occasion. But the severed hand incident caused him to wonder. At least for a short while, the emergency room doctors thought the hand could successfully be reattached. If they had, wouldn't that have been amazing? Or better said, miraculous? The human body, the way all its parts work together so perfectly. Not to mention how the body can heal itself is astounding when you stop and seriously give it some thought, a miracle in and of itself.

Interrupting Jeramy's thoughts, Mark added, "Oh, and the clothing allowance checks will be issued in a few days. The clerk-treasurer said the delay involved Town Councilor Harold Simmons, who didn't get around to signing the disbursement vouchers until recently." This brought up some hissing and boos from Cory and Thaddeus. Both had kids and depended on the clothing allowance to finish their family Christmas shopping.

Templeton police officers received two clothing allowance checks yearly to cover the cost of replacing worn or damaged uniforms. Originally, the first was scheduled to be issued on June 30 and the second on December 30. To his credit, several years ago, Chief Jordan convinced the town council to move the disbursement date of the December check from the 30th to the 15th. He knew how tough it was to provide for a family on a policeman's wages, especially around Christmas. The officers didn't have to report to the department an official accounting of how the allowance was spent. Chief Jordan's sentiment was that if an officer chose to use the money for something other than uniforms, so be it. On the other hand, he had always made it clear that uniform maintenance and replacement was the primary reason for the allowance and didn't tolerate officers who neglected to replace worn or damaged uniforms, except during December.

"I also got a note from the Investigations Division," Mark continued. "Reminding us that when completing a burglary or theft report, list the value of each item taken. I know some of you don't like attaching values on reports you think are fraudulent, like you're just making out someone's Christmas Wish List, but we have to have the values for the monthly FBI Uniform Crime Statistics submission. I also know you all aren't certified property appraisers but if the victim doesn't have a value, make your best guess." Mark finished by reading off the officers' patrol assignments and released them from roll call.

CHAPTER 25

"Templeton car 36, at 1729 Clinton Street, assist a woman who has fallen in the bathroom and can't get up. Enter through the unlocked back door. Unsure of any injuries. Ambulance is on the way," Charles calmly spoke as he dispatched Jeramy to the incident. Templeton officers had a two-digit radio number used to identify officers while communicating over the police radio and Jeramy was 36. An incident such as this did not always necessitate two officers to respond. In this instance, Charles thought one was sufficient. The ambulance was sent because of department protocol. An ambulance is sent whenever an officer responds to an incident with possible injury. The officer usually arrived first, checking the scene to make sure it was safe for the ambulance personnel to enter, then the officer would try to determine if an ambulance was necessary before starting any first aid.

Jeramy arrived and immediately recognized the trailer as the same location he had recently investigated a domestic between a grandmother and grandson. Remembering what a mess it was inside, Jeramy put on a pair of latex gloves before getting out of his patrol car. He entered through the back door and was hit with the stale odor of cigarette smoke. He heard a rattling sound coming from the back of the trailer and went to investigate. As he walked through the kitchen area, careful not to step in whatever it was that had been spilled on the floor, he noticed two empty Dog Legg Whiskey bottles on the floor and another in the trash can. As he looked around, he wondered if the dirty dishes on the kitchen counter were the same that he had seen the last time he was in the trailer.

Walking through the kitchen, Jeramy recognized the voice of the wrinkled older woman who had been smoking the cigarillo during his last visit. She impatiently yelled at him, "Hurry up and get me out of here!" Jeramy made his way down the hall of the filthy trailer until he came to the open door of the bathroom. Looking in, he noticed her lying sideways, pinned between the toilet and the tub. Her head was pushed against the wall while her legs stuck out next to the toilet. Her house dress was askew and pulled up to her waist, and she held a cell phone in her left hand. He couldn't help staring at the brown stains on the inside of the toilet bowl and all the old dirty clothes piled up in a bathtub that appeared not to have held water for years. He was momentarily lost in thought, wondering where, or if ever, the occupants of this place took baths when the old lady yelled, "What'er ya waitin fer? GET ME OUT OF HERE!"

Not wanting to move her before assessing her for any injuries, he asked, "Are you okay? Are you hurt anywhere?"

"Are you blind or somefin? NO! I'm not okay! I am stuck here by this dang toilet. Can't you see? GET ME OUT OF HERE!" screamed the old lady.

Careful not to rub his clothes against the grime covering the outside of the tub and toilet, Jeramy leaned over the toilet, putting one hand under her shoulder and the other hand under her legs, then scooted her along the floor next to the tub until she was free from the toilet. He then helped her to her feet. He was surprised at how little she weighed but not at the odor of alcohol coming from her breath.

"You did good. Now you can go," she curtly told Jeramy.

As she was pulling down and straightening her dingy house dress, Jeramy radioed the dispatcher, "Disregard the ambulance, no injuries on a toilet tumbler." Then to the old lady, "Yes ma'am, but where is your grandson?" Jeramy politely asked, ever conscious his every word and action was being recorded on his body cam.

"Who knows, the dullard walks the streets all night and sleeps all day. The slacker refuses to get a job. I quit trying to monitor his comings and goings. I don't know where he goes, and I don't ask. That kid's just one lazy mess. Never around to help an old lady. When he was seventeen, his parents threw him out for stealing their pain pills. If it weren't for me, he'd be living under a bridge or somfin," she answered.

Satisfied she was uninjured, Jeramy told her to have a good day and walked toward the back door. Moving through the living room and after removing the latex gloves, he again noticed the crucifix hanging on her living room wall. Odd, what was it about Catholics and Protestants? One displays a cross with Jesus on the cross, while the other displays just the cross with no Jesus. Continuing this thought, as a child, while in Sunday School, it seemed church had a bunch of rules, lots of dos and don'ts. He shrugged his shoulders and tossed the used gloves into one of several empty fifty-five-gallon drums sitting just outside the backdoor of the trailer.

Jeramy got into his patrol car and, as always, once positioned behind the wheel, readjusted his ballistic vest, making it more comfortable as he sat. It seemed every time he sat down, the vest would ride up, bunching around his chin. As much as he hated wearing the vest, he wouldn't consider working a shift without one, not in today's crazy world. Wearing the ballistic vest was mandatory by Templeton's department regulations. This had something to do with a federal grant used to purchase the vests required they be worn, and Chief Jordan was all about correctly following department regulations.

Jeramy didn't know who came up with the term toilet tumbler, but it accurately described this type of incident. How was it that so many older people fell off the toilet and got wedged between the tub and the toilet? He had heard of a few such incidents where the victim lived alone, couldn't call for help, and died as a result.

Later, Charles told Jeramy that when the old lady called the police, he kept her on the phone, monitoring her situation until Jeramy arrived on the scene, which is how Charles handled all police calls for assistance. In this case, while Jeramy was responding, Charles asked the woman what had happened. She told him she was sitting on the toilet and passing the time while answering nature's call, playing video slots on her cell phone. She told Charles she was unconsciously leaning to one side, trying to influence a spin, when she lost her balance and fell off the toilet. Charles shrugged his shoulders and observed blandly, "It happens."

CHAPTER 26

Piper had left a phone message for Rex but had not heard back from him. He didn't want to hold onto this stolen stuff any longer than he had to. The roll of bills he took in the burglary had been a disappointment. He could never understand why some people would roll up a handful of one and five-dollar bills, then wrap the outside with a $50 bill. Who were they trying to impress? At least the cash would get him some hot food.

Rex was always pleased to get blank checks, and Piper was hoping Rex would pay well for this one. He had to admit Rex could be sly. It had been Rex who instructed him to take only one check from a checkbook and make it the last one in the pad. This would give Rex plenty of time to get the check forged and passed before the victim realized it was missing. Piper found some old coins, a couple of two-dollar bills, some old jewelry, including several old lapel pins wrapped in a hanky, an old pocket watch, and a stack of baseball cards, all inside the coffee can. He could never be sure if this stuff was worth more than what Rex would offer, but what could he do? Of course, he pocketed the change and paper currency.

Piper had been thinking about the pistol and smiled as he thought how comfortably it fit in his hand, nice and smooth and small enough to hide in his pocket. He decided to keep the gun. He had never used a real gun during any stick-ups. Usually, he kept his right hand in a jacket pocket, acting like he had a gun while yelling at the store clerk. That usually scared the cashiers enough they couldn't throw the money at him fast enough. Guns could get a guy in trouble, so he mostly kept away from them. But he was smarter than those other guys.

He could handle this pistol. It might be nice to have something he could defend himself with while on the streets. Yes, he'll keep the gun. He didn't know much about pistols, but what was there to know? Just point and shoot, that's it. He pulled the semi-automatic pistol's slide back just a little, enough to peek inside and see a bullet loaded in the chamber. That's all he needed to know about the Glock. It was late, and Gil hoped Rex would call tomorrow.

CHAPTER 27

Derek wasn't sure how he was supposed to get any work done with all the racket going on. Maintenance men were in the building banging around while replacing burnt-out fluorescent light bulbs, and Rebecca was cursing at the copy machine once again. "Why do you keep running out of paper?" she blurted out. To Detective Derek Wilson, the answer was simple, too much paperwork was required in police work, and that's why the copy machine keeps running out of paper. He was finishing up his investigative report on an arrest of a guy who had vandalized an ex-girlfriend's car. Once he was done with that, he needed to prepare some investigative reports on a forgery. It was going to be a long morning in the office.

Not long after being assigned to the investigations division, Derek found his niche, forgery investigations. This realization had been a good thing because he had never considered himself a very good uniformed police officer.

He hadn't been in uniform long before he realized he wasn't writing as many traffic tickets to women as to men. Many women seemed to have a good excuse for whatever traffic violation they had committed, and some would resort to crying. Whatever the reason, he would often feel sorry for them, letting them go with just a warning.

After one such traffic stop, it occurred to him that he probably was not the only male officer failing at his duty to write traffic citations to female violators. In fact, he thought he was probably one of many. Being fair-minded, he vowed to make up for other male officers' lack of traffic enforcement against the fairer sex. Thinking he might be able even things up a little, he decided from that day forward to never give another woman driver a warning ticket, always an actual citation.

That is, until his next revelation, that he was a regular traffic law violator. He admittedly rolled through stop signs, failed to signal for turns, and habitually drove over the speed limit. As he gave it more thought, it bothered him. He didn't think he would change his driving, so he quit writing moving violations. Why write traffic tickets to people for the very same violations he regularly committed? One violation Derek didn't commit was parking in handicapped parking spots.

So, until he was assigned to the investigations division, he satisfied the informal unwritten police department quota of ten traffic tickets per month by writing handicap parking violations. The nice thing about writing a parking ticket, as opposed to a moving violation, was that, usually, there was no interaction with the driver of the car, which for Derek, made it a perfect solution.

Derek didn't like verbal or physical confrontations, both of which often happened in uniform. He had experienced his fair share of suspects resisting arrest because he looked a little soft. He was on the pudgy side, with a round face framed by outdated wire-rimmed glasses.

While still in uniform and responding to bar fights, it often seemed the instigator of the fight couldn't resist pushing his way through a crowd of burly police officers just to confront Derek, and, well, confrontation just wasn't his thing. In those situations, Derek would hang tight, remembering as a rookie, solid advice from Mel, who suggested if someone wanted to fight the police, we were probably going to have to accommodate them. Derek would usually answer that ring-side bell by deploying his taser or using his trusty pepper spray. Mel, being an old-time cop, had no qualms when necessary, going hands-on with a resisting suspect. Rumor had it back in the day, Mel carried a gigantic six-cell, D-sized battery-operated steel flashlight, big as a horse's leg, he used on such occasions.

Deep down, Derek had concerns about how he would react in a serious situation. He didn't consider himself a coward, but he wasn't so sure he was brave either. The best he could hope for was that he was simply untested. He admired Mel's brash confidence and, without admitting it, wanted to be more like Mel. He wanted to be fearless.

Once Derek's transfer to the Investigations Division came through, the interaction with suspects and even some victims across an interview room table was more of a welcome challenge. He soon learned there was an art to many facets of investigative work, particularly interviews and interrogations.

He quickly learned during interviews or interrogations to allow victims or suspects to talk uninterrupted, letting them ramble as long as they wanted. Some could talk for hours about themselves and things they knew, unintentionally offering up useful tidbits of information that could help bring a criminal case to a successful conclusion. Because of this, Derek never interrupted anyone during an interview. You just never knew what you could lose. As for the less talkative victims or suspects, he found silence was an effective tool. People, in general, were uncomfortable with silence. This is why when a person being interviewed or interrogated went quiet, he often would sit patiently, simply staring emotionless until the subject got antsy and often volunteered something which would have been better left unsaid.

Forgery assignments require more paperwork than most other types of investigations. Derek didn't care much for paperwork, but it did give him more time in his office and less time on the street. His office was comfortable and familiar, even if he did have to listen to Rebecca and her occasional struggles with the ever-troublesome copy machine. It was territory he could control.

Getting back on track, Derek returned to the task of tracing a pair of prescription sunglasses. He was working on a forgery investigation that took place at the Templeton First Bank and Trust. The check in question had been taken in a burglary along with other property a few days before the forgery. The investigation had initially been assigned to Detective Pierson. Because forgeries had become Derek's specialty, he asked Derek to take the investigation of the forged check while he continued to investigate the burglary.

Derek found it amusing that while there was no way you could get away with passing a forged check at a local pawn shop or any one of the numerous liquor stores in Templeton, the local banks were a completely different story. The proprietors of pawn shops and liquor stores were more experienced with the shady side of society. As a result, they were more vigilant and could spot a bad check a mile away. They were even better at spotting a crook, while bank employees were far more trusting.

The suspect in this forgery was slick enough to avoid having his face show up on the bank surveillance cameras when entering the bank, partly because of the sunglasses he was wearing. Fortunately, Derek had other resources in his investigative tool bag. He would like to submit the check to the crime lab for DNA testing, but because of the expense and complexities, the crime lab only wanted to do DNA tests on major criminal cases. Derek considered all felonies to be major cases, but apparently, the crime lab had other ideas and would rarely accept forgery evidence for DNA testing.

What the crime lab would do without complaint was fingerprinting, which they did very well. Many types of paper were good for fingerprinting, check paper being one of them. The crime lab wouldn't usually use fingerprint dust on paper evidence, much like a detective or evidence technician would at crime scenes on solid surfaces. Instead, the crime lab technician used a system of fuming the check, usually using a method called gluing. The check would be placed in a clean, closed glass container, much like a fish tank, but with the top covered. Evidence is placed inside the tank along with an open glue pack, and hopefully, within a few hours, some identifiable suspect fingerprints will be visible. After comparing any identifiable prints to all the elimination prints, which in this case would be from the victim and bank teller, all that would be left should belong to the suspect.

Finding a suspect's latent fingerprints on a stolen check usually isn't enough evidence alone to convince a pedantic county prosecutor to file criminal charges. Derek knew he would have to bring the suspect into the office to obtain handwriting samples to use to compare to the forged document, either by convincing him to do so willingly or compelling him by a court order.

In a strange way, Derek enjoyed the handwriting collection process. The sample collection would consist of having the suspect write specific numbers, dates, or words which had been written on the forged document. To ensure the suspect wasn't trying to disguise his handwriting during the sample collection, he would be required to write these numbers, dates, or words not just once or twice but each hundreds of times.

If the suspect had started the collection session trying to disguise his handwriting, after a few hours of repetitive and tedious writing, he would tire and usually, unintentionally revert to his natural handwriting style, which was what the suspect probably used when forging the questioned document. It was almost as if Derek could make the suspect write until getting so frustrated by the brutally slow torture of all the laborious handwriting that he would give up and confess. And you know what, a lot of times, that's exactly what happened.

It was a challenge Derek enjoyed, mano a mano, one on one, face to face, just him and the suspect, but with one proviso, Derek would guide the action. In this investigation, he got a bonus piece of evidence. As the suspect interacted with the teller, he took off his sunglasses and set them on the counter. He then pulled out a pair of regular glasses from his coat pocket and put them on before signing the back of the check. All this while facing away from the bank cameras. Because the check was drawn on a Templeton First Bank and Trust account, the bank teller simply checked to ensure the account had enough money to cover the check. Satisfied the account balance was adequate, she checked his ID, which of course, turned out to be fraudulent, then handed him $267.00, the amount written on the check, minus the eight-dollar check cashing fee. Accepting the cash, he then turned and walked out of the bank, absentmindedly leaving his sunglasses behind.

Fortunately for Derek, when the bank teller later noticed the sunglasses had been left behind, she put them in the bank's lost and found, not yet knowing the owner was a thief. The victim didn't realize the check had been stolen in the burglary until after it was cashed, triggering a text message to the account holder of a low account balance warning. Derek began the forgery investigation by watching the bank surveillance video and quickly noticed that the suspect had left his sunglasses.

Derek retrieved the sunglasses from the bank's lost and found and dusted the lenses for prints but only pulled up smudges. He didn't know much about optometry, but from his experience, having worn prescription eyeglasses since early elementary school, he knew these were prescription sunglasses.

Next, he visited his personal optometrist, who was pleased to be a helpful part of an actual criminal investigation. His optometrist used a lensometer to determine the exact prescription for the glasses. In addition to that prescription, he also provided Derek with the model of the sunglass frame and the manufacturer's name and contact information. Derek returned to his unmarked police car, smiling as he left the parking lot, happy with his progress on the case.

CHAPTER 28

"Know what it's called when a prisoner takes his own mugshot? Give up? A *cell*fie!" Thaddeus joked to anyone in the roll call room who would listen. As bad as the joke was, he did get a few laughs other than his own. Thaddeus probably enjoyed telling his jokes more than the recipients enjoyed listening to them. He usually laughed the hardest, and with his flailing hand gestures, silly facial expressions, and trademark belly laugh, a person couldn't resist joining in.

Standing behind the podium and looking down at his clipboard Lt. Weber interrupted, "I see an incident report here where day-shift Officer David Henderson fished a guy out of a retention pond in Willow Lakes Estates this morning."

"Seems this guy was leaving his home, going to work I guess, and while driving through the housing edition, he lost traction in the ice and snow. Unfortunately for him, he slid into the retention pond on Reilly Road. Another motorist witnessed the action and called the police, then just kinda helplessly stood around doing nothing until Officer Henderson arrived on the scene."

Weber briefly paused and scanned the rest of the report before continuing, "Henderson was close, but when he arrived on the scene, the car was almost completely submerged. The driver was still in the car, apparently in an air pocket, frantically beating his fists on the back window." Weber smiled, dropped the incident report on the podium, and added, "So, get this, Henderson retrieves his trusty sixteen-pound hickory handled sledgehammer from the trunk of his squad car, trudges chest high into the pond and using the sledgehammer, bashed a passenger side window in. He was able to pull the guy out just as the car slid farther into the water, eventually getting completely sucked into the depths of the retention pond muck." Looking up and pointing toward the late shift officers, he asked, "So, I wonder, how many of you carry a sixteen-pound hickory-handled sledgehammer in your trunk?"

Making fun of all the training required for police officers to carry even the simplest of issued equipment, Thaddeus responded matter of factly, "Not me, sir. I haven't been qualified and certified with that particular make and model of sledgehammer yet."

Cory added, "I betcha he gets the Officer of The Year award for this." Then after a short pause, "And maybe a hardware store sponsorship, complete with a decal with a company logo to put on the side of his police car."

"Anyway," Weber continued, "Our shift got hit last night. There were some thefts from the housing construction sites up at Rose Garden Villa's subdivision. Some copper wire mostly." He thought he heard Teresa trying to suppress a groan as he went on, "Also, last night, it looks like we had another run to that trailer on Clinton Street in Meadow View Estates, where the domestic was not long ago. Says here this time it was a medical run."

Thaddeus jumped in, "Yeah, another toilet tumbler. But I bet it wasn't as messy as that excessive diarrhea medical call I had two weeks ago. Whoeee, that was one stink'en mess. I hear the homeowner had to have one of those bio-hazard cleaning companies come out on that one. I bet that cost a fortune."

Cory nodded his head and added, "That incident sure gives new meaning to *Poop* Deck!"

Weber trudged on, trying to ignore Thaddeus and Cory, "And a few days ago, there was a daytime residence burglary on Red Fox Road in the Fox Garden edition, with forced entry to the rear door. It seems cash, jewelry, baseball cards, and a Glock model 32 were taken. The victim's cat, Tulip, is also missing, probably sneaked out during all the commotion. An interesting note here is that the victim had about $5000 in cash stashed in the pocket of a sports coat jacket hanging in the closet where a lot of the stuff was stolen from, but the suspect missed the cash."

"Whew," Mark commented, "that jacket sure has some deep pockets."

"Yeah, well," Cory interrupted, "I bet by now, Tulip is probably pushing up daisies!"

Later in the shift, Charles's curt voice announced over the police radio, "Templeton 62 and Templeton 36" respond to 8010 Mill Court, 8010 Mill Court, on a possible suicide. Medic enroute."

Parker was riding with Adam, using his own car number, 62, at the time of the dispatch. Even in police responses to incidents where the victim is already dead, protocol dictates an ambulance be sent, just in case. Adam had never responded to a DOA before, much less seen a dead body outside of a funeral home, and was apprehensive while driving to the address.

They arrived at the first-floor one-bedroom apartment just minutes before the ambulance. Adam and Parker trotted to the open front door of the apartment to find Jeramy already standing in the living room talking to a middle-aged woman who was wiping her wet eyes with a tissue. He was amazed at how calm Jeramy was as he spoke to this woman, while just a few feet from the two, in the dining room, visible to all in the living room, a man was hanging by his neck from an electrical cord tied to the mounting fixture where a ceiling fan should have been connected. Behind the hanging body, turned over on its side, was a dining room chair. A partially disassembled ceiling fan sat on the dining room table. In the kitchen sink and on the kitchen counter were brownish-red spatters that appeared to be bloody vomit.

Jeramy turned to Parker and said, "I already checked him. He's gone. This is his sister. She said he had a drug addiction he couldn't kick. She found a suicide note tucked inside a Bible she found on the breakfast bar. Have dispatch contact the chaplain on call and see if he can respond. Detective Pierson is the investigator on call, so I'll contact him, fill him in, and let him know what we have and that we don't we need a detective now, but one needs to plan to attend the autopsy. Before that, I'll take some quick photos before the medics cut him down."

As the woman held the tissue over her mouth in an expression of grief, she watched Jeramy walk quickly to the trunk of his police car and pull his department-issued digital camera from his evidence kit. He snapped photos of the door from the outside, then moved inside, taking photos in each room, including the kitchen, where a Bible was sitting on one end of the breakfast bar. An open pizza box with a half-eaten pizza was sitting on the other end of the breakfast bar. Jeramy photographed the dried bloody vomit which had been splashed on the carpet and on the walls in the bedroom. He took photos in the dining room at different angles of the hanging body, finishing just as the medics walked through the door. Even though all the action was being recorded on his body cam, Jeramy continued to take photos as the medics cut the extension cord halfway between the ceiling and the body, being careful not to affect how the cord was tied in case the knot would be needed as evidence. They gently placed the man on his back on the floor, and after checking his vital signs, the medic gave Adam the order to contact the coroner's office.

In Indiana, it's the obligation of either a medical doctor or the County Coroner's Office to declare a person deceased. In cases of unnatural deaths such as accidental, suicide, or homicide, the County Coroner's Office sends a deputy coroner to the scene before the body is removed to make the death declaration.

Because Adam was responsible for completing the incident report, it was also expected that he and Parker wait for the deputy coroner to arrive. During the wait, Adam started to get information from the woman needed for his incident report.

The woman, Elizabeth Perkins, said she was the deceased's sister. As she talked, the hanging victim's story unfolded. She described her only brother, Lou Perkins, as a sensitive but brilliant man. She looked at Adam as she painfully told him, "He graduated at the top of his pharmacy class and worked several years as a pharmacist for the county hospital. He had three kids and, I guess, a loving wife. It all started when he got hit by a car while riding a bicycle. The accident messed up his back and one of his knees. After surgeries for both injuries, he never could wean himself from the pain medication and got seriously hooked." Elizabeth looked away as if into space and added, "Odd, a pharmacist getting hooked on prescription drugs, isn't it?" After a reflective hesitation, she continued, "He lost his wife and kids to the addiction. Not long after, he got fired and lost his pharmacy license when he got caught stealing oxycontin from the hospital."

She paused, then turned and looked directly into Jeramy's eyes. It appeared as if she was pleading with him as she continued, "It would have been best for him if they had prosecuted him and put him in jail. Maybe then he would've been forced to kick the habit. But, oh no, the hospital didn't want to take the public embarrassment of an apparent lack of inventory control in their pharmacy. Instead, they quietly fired him for what they called his attendance issues which, of course, were directly related to the drug addiction."

Elizabeth stopped as she started to tear up again when Parker asked, "But what about all the bloody vomit."

Elizabeth replied, "Yes, of course. He couldn't keep a job because of the addiction, but he didn't have the money to buy oxycontin on the street. He was delivering pizzas until he got stopped by the police. They towed his car because his driver's license was suspended for driving without insurance. So, what's an addict supposed to do when he can't get his drugs? He gets high drinking cheap mouthwash purchased from a discount store. The generic versions contain about 30% alcohol. I hear it is the cheapest high you can buy."

"But," Adam asked again, "the bloody vomit?"

Elizabeth looked at Adam and with disgust directed at no one added, "You think the human stomach can take all that alcohol and so little food for long? My guess is it ate his stomach lining, and here's the result," she remarked as she pointed toward vomit splashed on a wall. "I've been trying to check on him for weeks, but he wouldn't let me in his apartment. I knew he was being evicted and that he was depressed, but I had no idea he would do this, none whatsoever. He never threatened suicide, not once. When I couldn't reach him on his phone today, I came over to try to check on him. When there was no answer to my knocking on the door, I tried the doorknob, and for once, it was unlocked. I think he left it unlocked on purpose, so no one would have to force the door open to find him. I found this note sticking out of the Bible sitting on the breakfast bar."

She handed Adam a yellow sheet of lined notebook paper. With Parker and Jeramy patiently listening, Adam read aloud, "To my kids and family, I am so sorry. I love you very much, but I can't live like this anymore. Please forgive me. I pray to God that he will forgive me for all I've done and what I am about to do."

As he finished reading the note, Adam was relieved when he looked up and saw Templeton Police Department Chaplain Gossett walk through the apartment door. Gossett got along well with all the Templeton officers, and they appreciated that while he was clearly a devoted pastor, he didn't preach at them. He was a big man, over six feet tall and 225 pounds, mostly solid except for the slight paunch that was starting to develop. He didn't usually act or talk like what you would expect from a preacher, and in fact, if you saw him with a group of officers, you would think he was one as well. Jeramy introduced Chaplain Gossett to Elizabeth, then Gossett directed Elizabeth to the living room sofa, positioned with her back to the dining room.

The two spoke quietly and during that conversation, it seemed to Jeramy, who was watching from the dining room but unable to hear the conversation, that a burden was being lifted from Elizabeth. The chaplain distracted her while the deputy coroner arrived and went about his business of noting the condition of, and any injuries to, the body. The deputy coroner and his helper put the body into a body bag and carried it to a hearse for transportation to the county morgue. Once the coroner finished and Gossett explained to Elizabeth what to expect and how to make funeral arrangements, all the officers left the apartment.

CHAPTER 29

By the time Adam and Parker left the suicide scene, it was getting late in their shift, so they went to Dio's Pancake Palace where they could enjoy the night's last cup of coffee while finishing up their paperwork. Once seated, Parker asked Adam, "Hey, as part of your training, do you want to go to the autopsy on the Perkins guy? The chief likes the rookies to attend at least one autopsy during their training." Adam had never considered going to an autopsy before and thought it might be interesting, so he agreed and planned to meet Detective Pierson the following morning and ride with him to the autopsy.

While Adam and Parker were working on the night's paperwork, Jeramy and Gossett entered Dio's Pancake Palace and sat with them at their table. Jeramy had been hoping to sit at another, more private table with Gossett so he could talk to the chaplain but followed Gossett's lead when he plopped down at the table where Adam and Parker had paperwork spread out. The chaplain looked around the restaurant's interior and said, "The Christmas decorations Dio put up this year sure look nice." He smiled, then teasingly looked at Adam and enthusiastically added, "I love Christmas because, you know, without Christmas, you couldn't have Easter."

For a second, Adam seemed puzzled at the remark, then recovered, turned to Jeramy, and asked, "When you got to the apartment and noticed the guy hanging, why didn't you cut him down?"

Jeramy answered, "When I arrived and met the sister at the door, she pointed inside. I entered and took a good look around, then at him. He looked dead, what with the color of his face and the awkward position of his head. I checked his wrist and neck but couldn't find a pulse at either. In addition, he was stone cold, probably dead for a while."

Parker then explained to Adam, "You see, if we find a body that is obviously dead, we don't move it because we may decide to call the crime lab. On a hanging, it's a judgment call. But if there is any doubt at all, cut the guy down and start first aid."

One thing puzzled Adam, and he asked, "The guy left a suicide note but the sister said that he had never talked about suicide?"

Gossett cut in and with a reflective tone in his voice added, "It seems the quiet ones are the ones who end up killing themselves. Contrary to popular opinion, from my experience, the ones who make a point of threatening suicide, well, it seems they usually never get around to it. I figure a lot of times they're trying to get attention or are trying to motivate some type of behavior from another person. You know, like the times a guy might threaten suicide when his girlfriend dumps him. Usually, he doesn't really want to kill himself. He's just desperate to get his girlfriend back by any means." Gossett sat up, leaned back a little, and continued, "Now that I think about it, I'm not sure if I ever heard a family member or a friend of a suicide victim ever say, 'You know, I thought he might do that.'"

Soon the talk drifted and after some typical police-type small talk, Parker turned to Adam and explained how he thought the incident report narrative should be worded. Jeramy jumped at the semiprivate opportunity to bounce a question off the chaplain and asked, "So, the note Perkins left for his family, asking their forgiveness, it also asked God for His forgiveness for what he was going to do." Jeramy looked directly at Gossett and with a questioning voice asked, "Does God forgive you for something you are planning to do? Even suicide?"

After a sip of his black coffee, Gossett replied, "Well, I certainly can't speak for the Almighty, but didn't Jesus die for all our sins, not just some of them?" He paused as if he was choosing his words carefully, then continued, "I understand some Christian denominations teach that suicide is a sin. That you can't ask for forgiveness for a sin that you are planning to commit. For this reason, they think suicide is an unforgivable sin because you obviously can't ask for forgiveness after the fact." Gossett rearranged himself in his seat for more comfort and leaned forward as he continued, "But, Jesus said that the only unforgivable sin is blasphemy of the Holy Spirit." He smiled as he concluded, "I think I'll go with Jesus on this one."

Gossett noticed Jeramy looked confused, then turned his head, glancing at the ceiling as he continued, "Honestly, Jeramy, some questions, I just don't have answers to, just more questions. But from my earnest study of the Bible, there are very few rules to God's saving grace. The apostle Paul said faith was all you need to be saved but isn't faith a big concept? John the Baptist preached repentance. But when the Jewish leaders asked Jesus what the greatest commandments were, His answer was brief. Love the Lord your God with all your heart and with all your soul and with all your mind, then love your neighbor as you love yourself."

The chaplain paused briefly to let the statement sink in before he continued, "Don't misunderstand, this doesn't give a guy a free pass to commit whatever act the Bible teaches is wrong, and figure you're covered by grace. Oh, no, when you truly have faith, your strong desire is to do God's will. Jesus followed up that statement by saying all His laws and instructions are based on loving God and your neighbors. It's as simple as that." Again, looking directly at Jeramy, Gossett emphasized in a serious tone of voice, "You see, it isn't sin that damns a person to hell." He spread his arms in a broad, inclusive gesture and continued, "We're all sinners," Then, aiming his gaze at Jeramy, he continued, "It's the lack of faith in Jesus and not affirming that He died for our sins that damns a person to hell, and in my humble opinion, after reading the Perkins suicide note, he didn't lack faith."

At that, the chaplain took another long sip of his coffee while waiting for Jeramy to respond. After a pause and as the chaplain peered over his cup of coffee at Jeramy, he added, "You know, Elizabeth Perkins asked that very same question." Jeramy watched Gossett closely as he talked, and the chaplain could tell Jeramy had another question and asked. "So, why the funny look on your face?"

Jeramy slowly responded, "So, what does it take to avoid hell; a special prayer, baptism, confirmation, doing good things, or what?"

The chaplain smiled and said, "Jeramy, as I mentioned, there are very few rules to Christianity, but," emphasizing the word *but*, "there are lots of ways to practice it. Here's a real-life example of what I am trying to explain about faith. Of course, you've read about Jesus' crucifixion?" Jeramy nodded his head as Gossett continued, "He was crucified between two thieves. Even though the Bible says they were thieves, many theologians believe since they were sentenced to die by crucifixion, they were probably either dangerous career criminals or murderous insurrectionists in addition to being thieves." Again, Jeramy nodded his head in understanding as the chaplain continued, "It would be hard to believe either one of those hardened criminals ever," this time emphasizing the word *ever*, "did anything in their lives to merit God's grace, salvation, and a place in Heaven, but that's the very point I am trying to make. You can't earn your way to Heaven."

The chaplain leaned forward, speaking softly but deliberately, "Jesus hung on that cross for six long hours. Do you think the three of them just hung there quietly? Not according to the Bible, which tells us Jesus asked God to forgive His executioners. Imagine that, asking for forgiveness for the same guys who are in the process of killing you. Also, at some point, probably early in the six hours, both criminals mocked Jesus. The soldiers conducting the crucifixions carried on a conversation with Jesus and even gambled among themselves for His robe."

"I am sure we don't have a complete account of the entire interaction and all that went on between everyone involved, but a lot was happening while those three were in the process of dying. What we do know is that during those six hours, one of the criminals being executed had a change of heart and made a confession of faith by asking Jesus to remember him when He came into His kingdom. My guess is somehow he was convinced of Jesus' divinity, maybe through a combination of things. We know word had spread throughout the region concerning Jesus' teaching and miracles, and surely the thief was aware of His notoriety." Gossett paused, thinking for the right words before continuing, "Yes, Jesus was, well, I guess you could say, sorta famous. But He often received a mixed reception as He traveled around. There are accounts of people that loved Him but others that loathed Him. Some thought Him outrageous and called Him crazy, while others called Him Lord. As I see it, Jesus loves each one of us and came into this world to save us. So why wouldn't He spend those last few hours, even while painfully hanging on that cross, talking to the two criminals hanging next to Him, trying to save them from eternal damnation?"

Chaplain Gossett sat back in his seat as if relieved, "Well, one criminal did receive salvation and a promise from Jesus that he would be in paradise with Him that very day. You know, I think the salvation of the thief on the cross goes a long way to show just how simple Christianity is and is an excellent example of God's grace."

Jeramy had something else he wanted to talk to the chaplain about. While he thought he believed in God, he wasn't sure about all the faith stuff. What it really boiled down to was Jeramy, the tough veteran street policeman who wasn't afraid of much of anything, was scared to die.

CHAPTER 30

Even though he knew Rex was sometimes hard to get a hold of, Piper was beginning to wonder why he hadn't heard back from him. Piper was hungry, so he went to a fast food restaurant, paying for his black coffee and breakfast sandwich using a few bills and loose change from the burglary.

He sat in a booth as far from the front doors as possible and was trying to get warm. Staring out the window, he was watching cars slide around in the snow-covered parking lot when he noticed an unmarked police car parked in the lot. The driver, a plain clothes cop, entered the restaurant and walked toward a cashier. Piper could always pick a cop out of a crowd. They just had that look. He was ready to bolt, ever conscious of the pistol buried deep in his backpack.

Being an ex-con, Piper didn't want to get caught with the pistol. The cop ordered food from the same cashier who had served him just a few minutes earlier. Uncomfortable with a cop so close, he quietly wrapped up the uneaten portion of his sandwich and slipped his backpack over his shoulder. Carrying his sandwich and coffee, he walked out the opposite door. He wandered toward a truck stop where hopefully, he could sit inside undisturbed while keeping warm as he finished his sandwich.

Detective Pierson usually brought a cup of coffee to work from home using a spill-proof cup, but he was out of cream and had a hankering for a sausage egg and cheese sandwich. He drove to the closest fast-food restaurant and, wanting to skip the long drive-through line, entered the store, ordered his food, and paid with a $20 bill.

When the cashier handed Pierson his change, he shoved the paper money in his wallet, but as was his custom, he glanced at the coins. He turned one old-looking penny over in his palm with his thumb and forefinger and noticed the wheat design on one side. Disgusted, he thought, "Someone must have been burglarized recently," thinking no one knowingly used old coins like this as payment for purchases. He then put the 1945 wheat penny and the rest of the coins he had received as change in his pants pocket.

He was in a hurry and needed to get to the office to check the paperwork on the suicide the late shift called him about in the middle of the night. He received a message that the deputy coroner didn't get the body to the morgue before 2:00 a.m. As a result of missing this arbitrary deadline, the autopsy would not be performed until the following morning. Even though Pierson wasn't needed at the scene, he would be required to attend the autopsy, just in case the pathologist discovered any surprises.

CHAPTER 31

"Why am I up so early?" wondered Gil. "Couldn't Gran wait until a respectable hour for her cereal and cigarittos?" It must be the cereal keeping her alive cause it sure wasn't the cheap beer and Dog Legg Whiskey.

To Gil, it seemed he always had to run off and get her something. Good thing she never compared the change he would hand back to her with the receipt for the stuff purchased. The old bitty probably couldn't count anyway. Mac's Magic Market didn't always have the brand of cigarittos she preferred, and Gran would howl like a mad woman whenever he came home without those nasty brown cigarittos.

This morning, she smelled bad, worse than usual. Gil figured if someone could bottle her body odor, it would be best named *Ode de Sweat*. The last time he smelled something that foul was when Gran used the clothes dryer too soon after Grandpa sprayed the outside dryer vent with coyote urine in an attempt to keep birds from nesting inside. That smelled so bad, even from a distance, one of the neighbors called the fire department.

He wasn't sure if it was true but had heard Gran had been an Army WAC when she was young. WAC yeah, wacked out was more like it. Good thing she had social security coming in every month. Heck, without that, he might have to get a real job. She'd been pestering him to get his GED and find respectable work, but it wasn't until recently he learned GED didn't stand for Get Er Done but was some kinda of test that was supposed to make it look like you were an actual high school graduate, even when you weren't. He decided he just didn't have time for that.

CHAPTER 32

Mel usually arrived for roll call early. It wasn't unusual to see Parker's car already in the police parking lot. As Mel entered the building through the private police entrance, he noticed Parker standing in the breath test room. A middle-aged, glassy-eyed drunk was sitting in a chair in front of the breath test machine, blowing furiously into a plastic mouthpiece, looking as if his face was about to explode. Mel shot Parker a glance and asked, "What, your stats down? You don't get enough action in your regular eight and half hours that you have to bring one to work with you?"

Parker responded, "This dude almost crashed into me when he ran a red light on my way to roll call. You think I wouldn't stop him?"

Mel had been a certified breath test operator years ago and conducted many breath tests for other departments that were short of test operators. He let his certification expire because he spent too much time testifying in court. That aside, what he enjoyed about watching drunks take a breath test was the effort required of the person being tested to get a good breath sample.

The goal is to get air from the very bottom of the subject's lungs, which provides the most accurate blood alcohol concentration. Somehow the machine knows when it is getting that deep lung air but requires the subject being tested to practically blow his lungs out before the machine signals it has a good breath sample with a loud, "DING."

On the other hand, Parker appreciated being a breath test operator because he didn't have to wait while the dispatcher tried to locate a certified test operator to conduct a breath test on one of his drunk drivers, allowing him to get back on the street quicker. Nor did he have to rely on someone else to appear in court to ensure a conviction.

As Mel entered the roll call room, Mark was holding court in one corner, complaining about his ex-wife number three, who was once again taking him back to court. This time she was suing him over their old Christmas tree and its decorations, which he had donated to Goodwill. According to her, these items were awarded to her in the divorce, and the decorations were valuable antiques.

Apparently acting out a scene in his troubled marriage, Mark was accidentally knocking over chairs in the roll call room as he was stumbling around, walking straight-legged with both arms stretched out in front of him while speaking in an exaggeratedly deep, sullen, and spooky voice, "Frankenstein's bride, that's who she is. I tell ya, she's Frankenstein's bride!"

Cory, who was standing behind Mark, put his forefinger to his chin and tilted his head up slightly, posing as if a well-studied scholar deep in thought while commenting, "Well then, I guess that means you must be Frankenstein himself!"

As Mark continued to hold his arms out in front of him, he made a clumsy, stiff-looking, one-legged turn and with an evil gleam in his eyes, advanced on Cory, arms still rigidly straight out, flailing wildly about in front and in the same spooky voice uttered, "I'll get you for that, I'll get you."

Lt. Weber interrupted with, "OK, let's get started before all of this evening's Christmas parties end and the drunks start trickling out onto the streets." Christmas season holiday parties often produced their share of drunk drivers, even though most civilians thought New Year's Eve was the worst night of the year for drunk drivers. With all of Weber's years in uniform, he didn't completely agree. Yes, with all the Christmas parties, the entire Christmas season was rife with drunk drivers leading up to New Year's Eve, which caused him to wonder just what did drinking yourself silly have to do with Christmas? And July 4th always had its share of drunk drivers because, for some, the drinking started early on the hot summer day. But in Weber's opinion, St. Patrick's Day brought out more drunk drivers than any other day of the year. He wasn't sure why but thought it must have something to do with all the amateurs out having fun wearing the funny green hats while drinking green beer.

Weber started roll call with, "We got a bulletin from the state prison's corrections officers. They've noticed some inmates in the exercise yard training other inmates in defensive tactics, demonstrating how to escape after being shot with a taser. The corrections officers have watched them practice dropping and rolling away, trying to dislodge the taser probes. I have no doubt we will cover more on this during next year's taser recertification."

Mel jokingly interrupted with, "Whatever happened to the days when he who is tased, stays."

After a sideways faux sneer, Weber continued, "And here's an interesting incident from the evening shift. A car vs. deer accident on Steele Ford Road." Weber pushed his reading glasses down a little as he scanned the police report for details before addressing the officers, "It seems a deer got hit by a car and managed to hobble up to, then collapse against a house. According to the incident report filed by Sargent Miller from the evening shift, the call came in from the homeowner. The homeowner told the dispatcher that, while the car's driver was okay, it was obvious the deer had at least one seriously broken leg but was still alive. The dispatcher informed the homeowner he would send an officer to investigate but mentioned the officer would probably have to destroy the deer. The curious homeowner asked just how this destruction would be performed. After the dispatcher informed him department policy required the deer be put down with a firearm, the startled homeowner replied by saying that wasn't going to happen while it was leaning against his house, then hung up. By the time Miller arrived on the scene, the homeowner had wrapped a rope around the deer's neck and dragged it twenty feet from his precious vinyl siding, in the process accidentally strangling the animal to death. Weber looked up from his clipboard and said, "In all my years as a policeman, that's a first."

Mark hunched over a little, wringing his hands and with a touch of sinister sarcasm and while using his best Boris Karloff imitation, added, "I have a little *dear* I would like to strangle!"

Weber finished with, "We're supposed to get more snow tonight, then a very cold streak is headed our way. The street department is out pre-treating the roads. Also, Adam, don't forget that after this shift, you're supposed to meet with Detective Pierson for a trip to the morgue for the autopsy of the suicide victim."

CHAPTER 33

Because Gran woke him up so early, Gil decided to relax, pop a downer, and take the night off. It was just too cold and snowy to go scrounging. He was in the kitchen hoping to find some crackers or anything to snack on when he heard Gran giggling as she yelled for him to come to the front window and "take a look."

Gran was standing in front of the picture window in the living room of their trailer, looking out toward the old mobile home across the street. Gran looked absolutely gleeful as she pointed at the trailer, saying, "Wilford's finally done it this time. I told you he would." And in a loud, confident voice announced, "He's finally burnt that trailer down!"

Gil ran to the window and stared lock-jawed, unable to speak. He could see the flames shooting up to the ceiling through Wilford's back bedroom window. Wilford was standing on the front porch trying to pull something big and white out of the too-small front door. Gil found his voice and said, more to himself than Gran, "What's he doin'? Is that a mattress he's wrestling with? It's on FIRE! That mattress is on FIRE! He's trying to pull the daggum thing out the trailer through the front door while it is on fire, HOLY SMOKES!!!"

"Holy Smokes is right," giggled Gran. "I figure that moron probably fell asleep smokin' again. Yup, smokes is the word, alrighty. Look at dat, his breeches are afire!" she added with a crooked smile any Grinch would appreciate.

Gil, on the other hand, was horrified and had finally realized instead of just staring, he should do something. The problem was he had no real-life experience of actually helping anyone, so he watched helplessly as the situation got worse by the second. Wilford finally pulled the burning mattress out of the front door and was dragging it across the trailer's old rickety porch, which, of course, consisted of highly flammable dry semi-rotted wood. Meanwhile, the flames in the trailer's interior advanced into the living room. Gil gasped as he noticed flames quickly climbing the curtains in the living room and figured at that point the trailer was surely a goner. Gil continued watching as Wilford dragged the still-burning mattress into the front yard when it appeared something from behind got his attention. Maybe it was the crackle of timbers from the shabbily built double-wide mobile home that were quickly being consumed by the fire. Or maybe it was Gladys Jones, the trailer park's official busybody, screaming "HELP, HELP somebody HELP!" while frantically running back and forth in the street in front of the burning trailer like she was the Paul Revere of fire watchers. Whatever it was, the distraction caused Wilford to freeze in place long enough to realize, "Fire, fire, I'm on FIRE!" Wilford screamed. In a panic, he pushed the flaming mattress away from him and against the old mini barn sitting on the lot next door. He then ran in small circles in the side yard, swatting at his behind like a clown in a three-ring circus before he slipped and fell into the snow.

Wilford was flopping around in the snow, trying to put out the fire in his pants as Gran, using a crooked arthritic forefinger, scratched the side of her head and calmly wondered aloud, "I thought it was stop, drop, and roll. Not run, fall, and flop. That Wilford, what a twit, can't even save his own life properly."

While they were busy watching Wilford do his impromptu fire dance, the burning mattress quickly caught the mini-barn on fire, and before you could say, "Call the fire department," the inferno spread from the mini-barn onto the mobile home sitting adjacent to it.

Gil was still standing by the window, frozen in place, watching the ever-growing flaming disaster. He looked toward Gran, who was gazing at the inferno, grasping a half-empty can of beer in her right hand while whimsically holding her left-hand flat against her left cheek as she said in a serenely affectionate voice, "Ain't it purty. I always loved campfires. The only thing that would make this better is a bottle of whiskey and a couple of folding lawn chairs." Turning to face Gil, she reminisced, "Remember when we would tent camp and that time your grand-pappy accidentally set that big ole pine tree on fire down there dat Brown County State Park? Too bad your grand-pappy ain't still around to see this!"

As Gran was ruminating on the virtues of a raging fire, Gil remembered years ago, before his grandfather died and before Gran started to drink way too much, that really, she hadn't been such a bad grandmother after all. It was her idea, on those hot and humid Indiana summer afternoons, to take all those fifty-five-gallon barrels Grandpa dragged home from work and fill'em with water from the garden hose for the grandkids to cool down while wading in them. Gran would proudly call them individual swimming pools. After spray painting each grandkid's name on their designated barrel, you had yourself a regular trailer park natatorium. Add a garden hose and an all-purpose tarp on the slope behind the trailer and you were upgraded to a world-class hillbilly water park. As the fire department rolled to a stop in front of the fire hydrant closest to the burning trailer, Gill wondered if maybe she hadn't been such a bad grandma after all.

CHAPTER 34

Mel was dragging by the time he made it to Dio's Pancake Palace at 5:00 a.m. Cory was already sitting in their booth, fidgeting with the menu. Mel was pleased Carolyn had a cup of coffee waiting for him and raised the cup to his lips as he exclaimed, "Ahh, caffeine, the great equalizer."

"It sure didn't take much time for those trailers to burn to the ground, eh?" Cory asked Mel.

Mel responded, "Yup, never does. They were pretty much gone by the time the hose draggers pulled up." Contrary to what civilians might think when policemen call firemen "hose draggers," it's usually meant as a playful term of endearment. Policemen and firemen usually got along well, what with similar hours and work situations. Privately, Mel always thought most firemen were likely frustrated police wannabes. But then, to be fair, he figured most firemen probably believed many policemen wanted to be firemen. "It was kinda like watching a game of burning trailer dominos. Not sure why they put 'em so close to each other," added Mel.

Carolyn returned with a pleasant smile and asked if they were ready to order.

After Cory, uncharacteristically and unenthusiastically, ordered only a small fruit platter, Mel asked, "What, no pancakes with extra butter or a big pile of biscuits and gravy?"

Cory bravely held his chin up, right arm extended with a fork in hand as he firmly and defiantly replied, "Food is the enemy!" Then a little sheepishly added, "The wife says I need to lose some weight. Anyway, the doc says I might be able to lose that stupid CPAP machine if I'd take some pounds off." He dejectedly added, "You know what my wife calls me when I put that contraption on? Top Gun, yeah, Top Gun!"

Mel smiled as Cory continued, never afraid to discuss personal issues. "Anyway, losing some weight might be a plus because some of my summer uniforms are getting a little tight. I can save some big moola if I can shed a few pounds and squeeze back into them. You know what new uniforms cost?" Two things everyone knew about Cory, one, he was notoriously cheap, and two, he battled off and on with his weight. It didn't help he couldn't kick that nasty red licorice and Slurpee habit, but he justified that situation by concluding, really, everyone had something they weren't proud of.

It wasn't long before Carolyn returned with their food. Cory noticed for the first time, for her age, Carolyn was really kinda pretty, and he guessed as a young woman, she must have turned some heads. Mel gave Carolyn a big smile and a sincere sounding thank you. Cory paused as he looked at the happy couple, then considered what his current life had become and what his future life might look like. Sadly, glanced at his unappetizing fruit platter breakfast and knew for sure life wasn't fair.

CHAPTER 35

Adam was tired and it was cold, both of which dulled his senses, which he felt might be a good thing for his first autopsy attendance. He met Detective Pierson at police headquarters for the short drive to the County Municipal Building, where the pathology lab and morgue were located.

After arriving, they passed through a security checkpoint and took an elevator to the basement. Before entering the morgue, they were required to show their police identification and sign in, as access to the morgue was restricted for obvious reasons. Once inside and walking through a hallway leading to the autopsy room, Adam noticed gurneys lining both sides of the hallway. Each gurney was occupied by a body of a recently deceased person. Adam passed one gurney and noticed the body on top had incisions down each leg, from hip to ankle, which were stitched closed with a fine wire. The puzzling thing about this body was while it was face up, both legs were twisted around so the feet and toes pointed down toward the floor over the end of the gurney.

That seemed unusual enough until he noticed a guy in the hall just past that gurney dressed in a white shirt under a wrinkled sports coat with his tie loosened and askew. He was sitting on the floor, back to the wall, arms down hanging awkwardly, legs stretched straight out uncomfortably in front of him, head hung sideways in an unnatural position, and his face had a greenish tinge. All that aside, his chest was moving in and out, and the gurgling snores emitting from his slightly opened mouth caused Adam to conclude this one was still alive, barely. His sports coat was opened wide enough Adam could see a holstered pistol and badge fastened to his belt. A notebook lying on the guy's lap was open to a page with, "Don't Cut on This One," boldly handwritten in bright red ink.

Continuing down the hall, Adam and Pierson walked through the autopsy room door. Adam was immediately struck with an unusual and unpleasant odor. Could that be formaldehyde he wondered? He wasn't sure, but he saw and smelled things he had never seen or smelled before. Inside the room were five stainless steel rectangular-shaped lab tables that looked more like long shallow sinks, which were equally spaced and lined up along the far wall. Each table had a large, curved faucet on the end near the wall, with the table sloping gently down to the opposite end so any liquid could run down into a drainpipe attached to the floor.

Adam watched as a crime lab technician photographed a body occupying the first table. Once he finished taking photos, the pathologist, a woman dressed in blue surgical scrubs, began visually examining the body. She spoke in a disinterested tone as she described the body and its physical condition to a man, also dressed in surgical scrubs, who was writing on a clipboard. Adam later learned this man was a morgue diener. In addition to assisting the pathologist with notetaking, the diener's job was doing all the large dissections and removal of body organs. Meanwhile, the pathologist's job was to dissect and examine each organ, searching for disease, defect, or injury in order to determine a cause of death. Adam wondered why the diener was wearing sunglasses in a basement room that had no windows, but since graduating from the police academy he had seen lots of things he didn't understand.

As the pathologist described an injury to the head, which she believed to be a gunshot entrance wound, Adam stepped over to Pierson, who was talking to the detective working the investigation involving that body. Adam overheard that detective tell Pierson the incident was a murder/suicide. The suicide victim, which was on the autopsy table, had a self-inflicted gunshot to the head. Adam watched as the diener made a Y-shaped incision, called an evisceration, to the chest and stomach area. The diener then, using a bone saw, cut away a large section of ribs, allowing access to the body's internal organs.

The detective told Pierson, "What a shame, a young dude like this. The rest of his body is in great shape. I really don't understand why, in cases like this, where you have a witness and it's clear what happened, why an autopsy is necessary. This was a fresh kill. I mean, he was still alive when he got to the hospital, brain dead for sure, but his heart was still beating. They could have kept his body alive until his organs could be harvested for later transplants. His kidneys, heart, lungs, and even the guy's corneas could have been used. But nope, we gotta pull the plug and let him croak, then shove him into a cooler until we can cut him up and prove he died from the obvious self-inflicted gunshot. Just plain wasteful."

"Yup," Pierson commiserated, then added, "I understand it's the coroner's job to find the cause of death, which includes eliminating all other ways he could have died, but it's like you said, this one is obvious."

Adam was tired, but as he was watching the diener work, he was trying his best to follow the conversation between the detectives. The diener was dissecting the body, removing each vital organ one by one, then handing them to the pathologist, who then weighed each organ on a scale hanging from the ceiling before setting it on a cutting board and cutting the organ into thin slices like a chef would slice warm bread. She was looking for any abnormality that may be present as she searched for any possible cause of death.

Adam watched as the diener leaned over the body's open chest cavity while removing another internal organ. The diener's hands were inside the body cavity as his wrists rubbed back and forth against the edge of the exposed body cavity while he worked. This movement caused a gold bracelet the diener was wearing under the double gloving of his left hand to creep out from under the glove, catching small bits of flesh from the edge of the body cavity into the tiny loops of the gold bracelet.

An uneasy Adam was still watching when Pierson nudged him over to the next lab table. "Wait a sec," Adam said and turned to the other detective and asked, "Hey, what's the deal with the sick-looking guy sleeping in the hall with the note about not cutting on him?"

"Oh, that's my partner, Anthony," the detective said. "I thought he was coming down with a cold when we started our shift 18 hours ago. We caught this murder/suicide case and as we were working on it, Anthony kept getting sicker and sicker until now I think he's got a bad case of the flu. But the guy won't go home while we are still active and on the clock with this case. He said he wasn't turning down the overtime. He made it through the first autopsy, which was the murder victim of this murder/suicide but was starting to get so sick, I sent him out to the hall when the second autopsy was getting started. After he fell asleep against the wall, I set that note on him. Then I snapped a photo and sent it to our Captain back at the office, thinking he'd appreciate seeing Anthony so hard at work."

"Okay, but what's the deal with the stiff on the gurney that has his feet turned around?" asked Adam.

The diener, who was eavesdropping, jumped in, "That dude was a natural death, but a bone marrow donor. After removing the femur and tibia so the lab can remove the marrow, we sewed his legs back up, but without those bones inside, his legs kinda twisted around." Then, with a snicker, the diener added, "but I doubt he'll notice."

The pathologist, who had her hands wrist deep inside the top of the body's open skull, teasingly asked the rookie, Adam, "You know what they call a murder/suicide here at the morgue?"

Adam gave her a questioning look and the pathologist continued, "No? Give up?" After a slight but strategic pause, she continued, "A double-header! Get it, a doubleheader!"

As if on cue, the diener broke into a spirited rendition of *Take Me out to the Ball Game* as he continued cutting away, casually leaning into the body cavity as if he was under the hood of an old car performing routine maintenance.

Pierson grabbed the stunned Adam by the arm and guided him to the table where their hanging victim's body was positioned.

The pathologist and the diener at that table were looking at the photos taken at the scene when the diener, Jack, said with a smile, "You know, I never understood suicide. I always thought there was something worth living for." Then jokingly added, "If nothing else, pizza."

Then the pathologist, Dr. Natalie Foster, picked up another photo and showed it to the diener. Holding the picture, almost as a challenge, she pointed to an open pizza box sitting on the victim's kitchen counter with the pizza shop's name boldly printed on the box lid. Jack the diener nodded his head as he noted, "Oh, Bernie's Pizzeria. Now I understand."

Dr. Foster began the autopsy by conducting a visual exam of the body while dictating to the note-taking Jack, "There appears to be no external visual injuries to the victim's body other than apparent ligature markings to the neck. More pronounced front to back." Dr. Foster, using her thumb and forefinger, forced the body's slightly open eyes much wider as she leaned over to get a better look before announcing with a satisfied tone of voice, "Petechiae in both eyes."

Adam turned and looked at Pierson quizzically and muttered, "Huh?"

Before Pierson could answer, Dr. Foster, interrupted by explaining, "Petechiae are pinpoint hemorrhages caused by asphyxia. Most commonly found in the eyes." Turning to address Adam directly, she continued, "Very common in strangulation victims." Understanding Adam was a rookie, Dr. Foster felt it necessary to continue explaining, "You see, hanging victims don't always die right away. It can sometimes take several minutes. The only force applied to the victim is his own body weight, which is rarely enough to break the hyoid bone," as she pointed to the upper part of the front of her neck. Dr. Foster resumed the external exam of the head and neck while continuing the explanation, "It can take several minutes before the hanging victim passes out due to lack of blood to the brain. As the body is suspended by the neck on the ligature, the pressure on the jugular veins is restricted, resulting in the subject quickly losing consciousness. It can often cause, as in this case, petechiae of the eyes. I suspect in many instances the whole process could be relatively painless, or at least we can hope."

Adam's full attention now was on the body of the hanging victim, and by the time the diener started cutting, his senses were completely dulled. The diener and the pathologist finished examining the neck area by cutting away the skin to see the muscle and tissue better. Next, they moved on to the evisceration of the body cavity, finishing it before starting the examination of the head. At this point, Adam stepped closer, curious to see what was next. The diener made an incision behind the top of each ear and cut down along the back fold of the ears to the upper back of the neck. He connected those two incisions by cutting across the top of the back of the neck, then pushed the fingers of both of his hands through that connecting incision. He curled his fingers up to grasp the edge of the now loose skin with his thumb and fingers and gently pulled the scalp skin up and over the top of the skull, exposing the bone. He pulled the skin from the skull until it was bunched up on the lower forehead, just above the eyes. As he was pulling the scalp over the skull, Adam could hear the unnerving sound of the tearing of flesh as the scalp was being separated from the skull. During this process, the diener explained to Adam, "You see, we need to get into the skull, so we remove all this skin before we open the skull so it won't be so hard for the mortician to put it all back together so this guy will look nice for viewing. Next, we will cut off the top of the now-exposed skull cap and remove the brain. Then once we're done, we can put the skull cap back on and pull the scalp back over it."

Of course, Adam had never seen anything like this before and watched as Jack reached for an electric autopsy bone-cutting saw and began to cut around the top of the now scalped skull cap, just above the eyes. The examination of the brain would start once the skull cap was removed. As the diener was sawing around the skull cap, Pierson, knowing the white powder that was beginning to float around in the air just above the body's head wasn't ordinary sawdust and took a few steps back. Adam, being the curious rookie, took a step forward and was leaning over the body's scalped head, trying to get a better view, when suddenly the bone saw jammed, sending a small bone fragment flying into the air and hitting Adam on his upper lip. Adam let out a surprised yelp as if he had been jammed with a hot poker as he hopped back, bumping into another body-filled gurney. Pierson smiled and couldn't resist a silent laugh. He knew that while Adam's day had been long and grueling, the young officer had handled himself well.

After the autopsy was complete, Pierson drove Adam back to the Templeton Police Department headquarters. He was in the main office checking with the secretary for messages when through an open door he overheard Adam in the roll call room talking to another probationary officer. In an excited voice, Adam explained, "And when you see the old detective take a step back, you better take a step back too." Pierson thought to himself, another day of training complete.

CHAPTER 36

"Rex, you just gotta give me more for those baseball cards and that jewelry. You know that some of that stuff is real gold. And what about all those pills?" Piper begged Rex, who finally called him, but Piper almost didn't answer his cell phone because he didn't recognize Rex's new burner phone number.

"I told you ten bills are all I can give you for this crap. It wouldn't even be that much if it weren't for the check. Take it or leave it. I got business elsewhere. Oh, and you can keep those pills. I can't sell high blood pressure pills and stool softeners to junkies!" Rex said, then turned and acted like he was walking away from the deal even though he did want that check, and the baseball cards looked valuable. He wasn't an expert on collectibles, but who would put baseball cards into individual rigid plastic cases unless they were worth something?

Piper caved, like he always did, and took the ten dollars Rex offered. Haggling with him over stolen stuff never worked. Rex held all the cards and the money. If Rex had known about the Glock, he would have wanted that too, but Piper thought he would rather have the pistol than the little bit of money Rex would have offered.

Piper kept the pistol in his backpack instead of in his pocket. If he got stopped by the cops, they would probably pat him down but might ignore the backpack. Good thing the library didn't have metal detectors on their doors because he needed to get in there to charge his phone.

Of course, Piper never actually bought a cell phone, nor paid for cell phone service. One day he noticed a "Free Phones" sign next to a pop-up canopy in front of the local barber shop and wandered in. He couldn't believe his luck. The government was giving him a cell phone and cell service. After signing some income verification papers, or lack thereof, and showing his Indiana ID card, within minutes, he walked out with a free cell phone and limited free cell phone service. This did present a problem, which was, he had nowhere to charge the phone. One cold day he wandered into the public library to use the restroom to warm up when he noticed cell phone charging stations at each patron cubicle and the problem was solved. After he got his ten bills from Rex, he walked through the snow heading to the library, all the while thinking it was about time to steal another car.

With business concluded, Rex wanted to make some serious space between him and Piper. He didn't like Piper and didn't like doing business with him. He reasoned the owner of some big store might not like some of his suppliers either but still did business with them anyway. Of course, those suppliers probably didn't steal and rob for a living, or at least he hoped not.

He hated that Piper had his new phone number and hoped that if Piper ever got busted, he wouldn't have that phone on him, but what could he do? After all, Rex's phone number would be listed as a recent contact. The phone he used to call Piper was his burner phone, but Rex still didn't like the idea of a punk like Piper having any of his contact information.

Rex would never let Piper or anyone like him know where he lived or did business. In fact, he did business out of a garage he rented from a retired dentist who dabbled in low-income rental real estate. Why take the risk of any of the morons he did business with following him and finding his home? Nope, he always met his "suppliers" somewhere else, then drove off in his old work van, zig-zagging his way through different streets to his rented garage to dump off the latest haul and store it until he could unload it. It was too risky to keep stolen stuff at home. He strapped an old aluminum extension ladder, stolen, of course, to the top of his van to make it look more ligit in almost any part of town.

Tailgates stolen off the back of pickup trucks have been the money maker lately. Steal'em in the middle of the night, easy, quiet, and quick to remove, not to mention profitable to resell. Rex had contacts at junkyards that were always looking for pickup truck tailgates. He liked dealing with catalytic converters as well. Lots of addicts brought him stolen catalytic converters. All you needed to steal a catalytic converter from a pickup truck or SUV was a battery-operated power saw, the cloak of darkness, and about one minute. Rex had a different salvage yard where he would sell the catalytic converters. You had to know with whom you could safely do business. The law had been coming down hard on most junkyards and recycling companies lately. As a result, these establishments began to obey some state laws ordering them to identify each person selling something by a photo ID and making a computer record of the sale, which would then be electronically sent to the local cops. It was getting tough for a hard-working thief to make money anymore. Fortunately, Rex found there were always some salvage yards and junk dealers working crooked angles to maximize their profits at innocent victims' expense. Contacts, in his business, it's all about contacts.

CHAPTER 37

"Now the chipmunks are burrowing under the concrete slab of my attached garage. I gotta somehow get'em out of there before they cause any more damage," complained Cory. "I think," he continued, "I finally got rid of the moles and voles that were tearing up my backyard. And I know for sure this last summer, I got rid of that big ole snake I told you about. Ran over him with the riding lawn mower." He then stood up straight and while tapping the tip of his forefinger against his chest he bragged, "Yes siree, made four one-foot snakes out of one four-foot snake!"

Everyone was used to Cory complaining about his trouble at what he affectionately called his humble abode situated on five acres at the edge of town. Just last week he complained about his wife's indoor cat. Cory hated that beast, but maybe not as much as it hated him, who once displayed its displeasure with Cory by crapping in one of his tennis shoes.

Then there were the birds that, no matter what he did to try to prevent it, constantly made nests in the pergola on his back porch. He hung rubber snakes and stuffed animals on the edge of the pergola and even put a huge plastic hawk on a table under it to scare the birds away, all with no luck. Every spring the birds just kept building and then rebuilding the nests, even after Cory repeatedly tore them down.

The trouble with the birds didn't stop there. Sometimes in the spring, during nesting season, while on his riding lawn mower cutting grass toward the back of his lot near a grove of trees, the birds would swoop down on him like World War II kamikaze dive bombers in what he thought was an attempt to keep him away from their nests in the trees nearby.

It was the carpenter bees that frustrated him most, and they were destroying the treated wood railing around his back porch. No matter how much he applied stain to the wood and sprayed carpenter bee repellent into the holes they created in the wood, the bees kept coming back. He savored the sweetly satisfying "ping" of revenge he heard when swatting those wood-burrowing pesky insects in midair with the quick swing of an old tennis racquet, slicing up the tiny creatures with the tightly strung racquet strings and a well-timed swing.

Cory, not naturally an outdoorsy type of guy, was getting to know the employees of the local hardware store. He was beginning to enjoy talking with them, then shopping for grass seed, lawn fertilizer, and weed eater cutting cord, along with extended discussions about the merits of different insect sprays, fake hornet's nests designed to scare away the carpenter bees, mothballs to shove down the chipmunk holes, and his go-to product, snake repellent pellets. Yes, Cory was at war with nature, losing the battle, but still gallantly in the fight.

"Cory, you think you got it bad," Mark interrupted, "at least you don't have to divvy up your meager paycheck into child support payments every month to three different nutcase ex-wives."

Thaddeus jumped in, "Mark, maybe to make things less confusing on child support paying days, you oughta make a big foam finger glove for each of those ex-wives. You know, like the ones you see at the ball games that say our team is *#1*," Thaddeus explained, holding up his right hand, forefinger extended as an example. "Except, in your situation, you would have a regular big foam finger glove with the index finger sticking up for your first ex-wife that says *#1*. Then, for your second ex-wife, you could have a foam finger glove with the index finger and middle finger sticking up with *#2* written on it. Lastly, or at least we hope lastly, the same for *#3,* but she would have a three-finger glove that said *#3.*"

Teresa interrupted with a sarcastic, "Oh, I bet that would make the ladies feel really special."

Lt. Weber ended the wife numbering scheme by starting roll call with, "Can we get started now? I got a memo from the chief. He convinced all the local gated communities which use keypad-operated gate openers to designate a special keypad code of 0911. That way we, and the Templeton Fire Department, don't have to keep track of all the different keypad gate codes for all the different communities to make emergency entries." Shuffling through some other papers, he continued, "Also, we got a BOLO," then for Adam's benefit, but smiling in Mel's direction, "or for you rookies like Mel, a *Be on the Look Out*, from the Franklin Police Department. They took a complaint of a white male in his early thirties, driving a gray SUV, trying to lure an eight-year-old little girl waiting at her school bus stop, into his SUV by offering her some Skittles."

Cory, leaning forward and holding his hand up like an impatient grade school student trying to get the teacher's attention, excitedly added, "I'd get in that van for some Skittles!"

"Oh, I bet you're exactly what that perv was looking for," a disgusted Teresa muttered.

Weber finished roll call by giving the late shift officers their patrol assignments and telling them, "The forecast for early morning is a low of a very chilly five degrees. Oh, and I want to thank Cory for taking over for Carl with the Shop with a Cop program. Cory, let us know if we can be of any help."

Leaning back in his chair and rubbing his stomach, Cory replied, "I sure could use some help getting some of those Skittles!"

At about 1:00 a.m., after a slow start to the shift, Charles's deep voice burst out of Jeramy's police radio speaker, "Templeton 15, Templeton 62, 15 and 62, at 6251 Wellington Avenue, 6251 Wellington Avenue, person stabbed as a result of a domestic. Medic has been started."

As a supervisor, Mark often responded to radio dispatch runs as an assisting officer and even more often on incidents assigned to officers still in training. Adam and Parker had already arrived on the scene and were retrieving their first aid kit from the trunk as Mark rolled up.

As all three walked quickly to the front door, Adam noticed five or six smooth flat stones carefully stacked by size, from largest on the bottom to smallest on the top, in the front yard close to the porch. As they were walking, Adam pointed at the stack and asked, "What's that all about? I have seen stacked stones like that before, but not sure of the meaning."

Mark replied with a sarcastic tone of voice, "Some new age thing. I think it's some kind of memorial that's supposed to spread harmony, peace, and good luck. Stuff like that, I think."

At the already-opened front door, they were greeted by a young woman in her twenties. Her arms were folded over her chest as she leaned on one leg against the door frame in an angry-looking stance as she told the officers, "He's in the kitchen by the sink, sulking."

"I'll stay here with her. You guys go check on him," Mark told Adam and Parker.

As the two entered the kitchen, Parker could hear Adam gasp. A male was leaning over the kitchen sink, running water over his left forearm while more than just a little blood mixed with the running water was circling in the sink before flowing down the drain.

The male had a painful grimace on his face, looking away while moving his arm slowly back and forth under the sink's faucet, rinsing blood off his arm. He was careful not to disturb the long, hard plastic professional hairdresser's rat tail comb, which was sticking all the way through his forearm. Two inches of the pointy handle of the comb was sticking out the bottom of his forearm, while the comb head was protruding out the top. Parker grabbed a dish towel hanging on a nearby hook, then looked at the guy's arm, trying to determine how to wrap the injury and stop the bleeding. Even wrapping it with gauze would be tricky, with each end of the comb sticking out opposite sides of the arm. Parker was glad to hear the ambulance's siren as it rolled to a stop in front of the house.

"That whore didn't have to stab me in the arm, not after stabbing me in the heart!" he angrily blurted out to Adam, who in turn gave him a confused look. The guy grimaced in pain as he continued, "I thought something was wrong, you know, between us. When she left her cell phone on the table and went into the bathroom to do her hair, I looked at her text messages. It wasn't so much that things were going wrong between us as much as things were going right with some other guy," he finished. Dejectedly he continued to move his arm back and forth under the running water rinsing the still-trickling blood from his arm.

Mark was listening to the female, getting her side of the story as the medics arrived. He pointed toward the kitchen and the medics rushed past him carrying their bags of medical gear. He was listening to the woman as he was watching the medics wrap the guy's arm with sterile gauze, grotesquely leaving the comb in place, relegating its removal to the emergency room doctors.

"He had no right to throw my cell phone in the toilet. I wasn't doing nothing wrong," the woman emphatically told Mark. Looking into the kitchen while the medics worked on the guy's arm, she continued in an exasperated but convincing voice, "I was just defending myself. What's a lady supposed to do?"

After the medics loaded the injured male into the ambulance, Adam arrested the young woman for battery with injury. While waiting for the jail wagon to pick her up for transportation to the county lock-up, Mark watched her as Parker helped Adam photograph the crime scene. Adam took pictures of the cell phone lying at the bottom of the toilet bowl, then photographed the blood trail leading from the tiny bathroom to the kitchen, then the kitchen sink area. Once finished, the officers closed and locked the front door on their way out of the modest starter home. Walking to their patrol car, Parker stopped and paused to look toward the stone stacking in the front yard as he casually commented, "Guess it wasn't tall enough."

Adam and Parker finished the mountain of paperwork required for a domestic violence arrest, then drove to the hospital to recover the pointy comb the doctors removed from the guy's forearm, knowing it would be needed as evidence in court.

Once back at police headquarters, Parker showed Adam how to properly package the bloody comb for storage in the evidence room. Because there was blood on the comb, it would need to be put into a cardboard container. This would let air pass through, allowing the blood to dry properly without causing mold. Adam labeled the box with the incident number, date, time, and his name. After taping the box secure with tamper-resistant and biohazard-marked evidence tape, he signed his name over the edge of the tape to prove what Rebecca, the property room attendant, liked to call the integrity of the evidence. The theory being, if someone tried to tamper with the box, they would have to break the tape where the officer signed over it, making the disturbance obvious.

CHAPTER 38

One would think Templeton Police Department detectives would know better than to leave their office doors unlocked. There were too many practical jokester policemen around the place to justify otherwise.

A recent example occurred a few days after Halloween when Thaddeus and Cory took a call on a report of a body in a dumpster. On arrival, the body in question turned out to be a life-sized, human-looking, stuffed dummy dressed as a vampire, complete with a Dracula mask. The officers figured someone probably tossed it into the dumpster after an elaborate Halloween party. Seeing an opportunity for a good prank, they quickly devised a plan. Thaddeus drove the dummy to the police department where he and Cory dragged it to the basement where the investigation division offices were located.

Unfortunately for Derek, his office was the only one left unlocked, leaving him to be the unlucky prank victim. Thaddeus and Cory planned to place the dummy sitting upright in Derek's office chair with a coffee cup positioned next to it on the desk.

Once inside Derek's office, Thaddeus could see all the possibilities and revised his plan. He directed Cory to lay the dummy face down, flat on the office floor in front of the desk, with its arms stretched out. While Cory was positioning the dummy on the floor, Thaddeus looked inside Derek's small dorm-sized refrigerator and grabbed a bottle of ketchup. He opened the center desk drawer where Derek kept all his pens, pencils, post-it notes, paper clips, rubber bands, and of course, silverware. Thaddeus pulled out a butter knife and poured ketchup over the center of the back of the dummy, then got down on one knee and with the gusto of an experienced serial killer on a deadly rampage, plunged the butter knife into the center of the glob of ketchup and into the back of the dummy. Fortunately, the ketchup splatter was contained to the dummy's back and off the office carpet. Cory and Thaddeus then slinked away, wishing they could be around when Derek arrived for work that morning. As luck would have it, Rebecca arrived at the office first. She had some paperwork for Derek, so she checked his office door. Finding it unlocked, she opened the door, turned on the light, and let out a blood-curdling scream. Chief Jordan's office was on the ground floor, just above the investigator's offices and he heard the outburst. He responded to find Rebecca standing next to her desk, one hand over her mouth and the other pointing to Derek's open office door. Jordan immediately entered the office and, as he teasingly later told the story, proceeded to pronounce the vampire dummy dead on arrival.

That incident, however, wasn't enough for Derek to learn his door-locking lesson while working amongst such juvenile practical jokers. Today, Rebecca, once again, was the first one in the office. She was inventorying evidence collected from the last three shifts when Derek walked past her desk on the way to his office. A minute or so later, she heard Derek let out a celebratory, "WhooHoo!" Seconds later, he pranced to Rebecca's desk, smiling broadly while holding with both hands what appeared to be a scratch-off lottery ticket directly in front of his face.

"$5,000 smackeroos! What I can't do with that kinda money this time of year!" Derek cheerfully announced. He turned the lottery ticket over to glance at the back and added, "I found this lottery ticket inside a Christmas card left on my desk. I was so excited I didn't notice who it was from. Anyway, I don't play the lottery. How do I cash this baby in?"

Rebecca glanced at Derek with a bored-looking stare, already knowing it was a fake lottery ticket because a matching one had been left on her desk as well. She was more lottery savvy than Derek, immediately recognizing it as a fake. She was only mildly amused as she scratched hers to find she had won $5,000. Reading the back of the card, she discovered that winnings were redeemable from the elusive Tooth Fairy but only on the fifth Saturday of February. After Derek flipped the lottery ticket over and began to read the back, she could see a dramatic change in his face as the realization dawned on him that he was not $5000 smackeroos richer, but just another victim of a tasteless prank.

"Yup," she said, "I know, I got one also. Too bad because I could've used that cash for Christmas too."

Dejectedly he asked, "What kinda of sicko would do this to us?"

Rebecca calmly answered, "Oh, only about any one of the 70 or so Templeton police officers who work around here, that's who." She continued, "By the way, someone from the Sandeford Medical Manufacturing Company left a telephone message for you after you left the office yesterday," as she handed Derek the phone message memo.

Derek visibly perked up and hurried to his office to return the phone call. He wanted to know which retailers or optometrists in the Templeton area sold the Flottur model of the Sandeford brand of eyeglass frames. After a short but pleasant conversation with an inventory specialist, Derek was told the Flottur eyeglass frames were currently manufactured for sale to only one wholesaler, Cerny Wholesale, Inc.

Derek, always curious even about mundane things, asked, "How did your company come up with a name like Flottur?"

The inventory specialist replied, "In the Icelandic language, Flottur means classy, but these frames are one of our less expensive models. If you want nice frames, try the Di Classe."

"Well, while I am at it, what does Di Classe mean?" questioned Derek.

The Sandeford rep replied, "It also means classy, but," in a more excited voice, "that's Italian!"

"I'll keep that in mind," Derek said blandly, ending the conversation.

After a quick internet search for Cerny Wholesale, Derek found a phone number for customer service. He called the number and listened to the recorded message twice, trying to figure out which number to press to talk to a real person. Failing that, he hit the keypad digit number zero, hoping it didn't send him to recorded phone message eternity. After nine rings, and as his habit demanded, he always counted in his head each ring, a pleasant-sounding young woman answered the phone and asked how she could help. Derek identified himself as a police officer from Templeton, Indiana, and explained what he wanted.

While he waited for the woman to find the appropriate office to transfer him to, Derek fidgeted with one of the many challenge coins he collected and displayed on a cabinet next to his desk. Challenge coins are medallions the size of a large coin that displays emblems commemorating an organization or event. These coins recently became popular in police and military circles, and Derek became so fascinated by the World War I challenge coin origin story he became an avid collector.

He had learned that during World War I, a United States Air Squadron lieutenant was very proud of his unit, and he personally arranged to have medallions with the squadron's unique insignia stamped on them and presented to each member. Afterward, a squadron member was shot down over Germany and taken prisoner. During his imprisonment, the Germans took his identification but, oddly, let him keep the tiny leather pouch he wore around his neck, containing only the squadron medallion. The prisoner escaped German custody but, while dressed in civilian clothes, happened upon a French military unit who thought he was a spy. He had no way to prove his identity, but as the French soldiers were preparing to execute him, he showed them the medallion. Fortunately, one of the French soldiers recognized the insignia, saving the soldier's life.

Derek was fidgeting with his favorite coin, a New York City Police Department challenge coin dated 9-11-2001 when a helpful male voice over the phone jolted him back to business by asking, "Can I help you?" Derek briefly explained he was working on a criminal investigation that involved prescription sunglasses. While trying to explain that he wanted to find the retailer that sold the prescription sunglasses, the male over the phone interrupted, "You understand we sell eyeglass frames all over the country, primarily in the Midwest United States area. Finding the retailer that sold that particular frame might be difficult. What city are you calling from?"

Derek responded with, "Templeton, Indiana."

He could hear the tapping of fingers on a keyboard, and a few seconds later, the man reported, "Your lucky day, sir, there is only one retailer that we sell frames to in Templeton, and that's Scott's Optometry at 810 Jefferson Street."

Derek politely thanked the man for the information before disconnecting the call. So far, obtaining information about the sunglasses had been relatively easy, simply because, at this point in the search for the owner of the prescription sunglasses, he had not requested any patient information. Changing the focus from finding the retail seller of the prescription sunglasses to who purchased them from the retailer, posed a privacy problem.

Because the sunglasses were prescription sunglasses, they were considered a medical device and would be covered under HIPAA privacy regulations. The solution to this problem was, of course, more paperwork. Derek prepared the required subpoena for this situation. Once approved by the county prosecutor, the subpoena would compel Scott's Optometry to provide the name, address, and personal identifiers, such as a date of birth or social security number, for any and all persons that Scott's Optometry sold Sandeford Medical Flottur eyeglass frames to, in combination with lenses matching the eyeglass prescription Derek's optometrist provided.

Derek had always wanted prescription sunglasses, but they can be expensive, and his vision insurance wouldn't cover their purchase. He wondered how a guy who had to pass forged checks could afford prescription sunglasses.

CHAPTER 39

"This was crazy waiting for an easy steal," Piper impatiently thought aloud. It was getting colder, and heavy snow had been falling for hours. Instead of waiting to find an easy car to steal, like the last one, which had been left unlocked and running, he decided to steal one the old-fashioned way, with a flathead screwdriver. After a short walk to the local hardware store to snatch a screwdriver, he would be in business.

He needed a big screwdriver to use as leverage to break the car's ignition switch. The size of the screwdriver posed no problem as he shoplifted it. He simply jammed it inside his bulky hoodie sweatshirt and walked out of the store. He had two sweatshirts on underneath the hoodie. Piper learned that being homeless, it was important to layer your clothes properly because you often carried around all your earthly possessions, including an entire wardrobe.

Piper was tired of not having a comfy vehicle to inhabit, but fortunately, he came up with an idea. He had previously been in the county lock-up with a guy who had been a janitor at the Serenity Plus Assisted Senior Living Complex who got busted for stealing jewelry from some residents. Something the guy told him seemed interesting now. He told Piper that, apparently, the old fogeys never wanted to give up their stuff, like the houses they had lived in or the cars they used to drive until they were absolutely forced to.

This guy had mentioned Serenity Plus had a section in one of their parking lots designated for residents who still owned cars but never drove them. Since the families and staff didn't want the senile old geriatrics ever to drive again, the section of the parking lot they chose to park these cars was purposely in a remote area, as far from the living quarters as possible. Out of sight, out of mind, the thinking went. Serenity Plus was too far for Piper to walk, so he used a few bucks he got from the burglary to take a city bus which let him off within a couple of blocks of the nursing home.

It was still snowing when he arrived late in the evening, and he couldn't believe his luck. It was a big complex with lots of parking lots. All he had to do was look for the parking lot farthest from the main doors, and when he did, he noticed 20 or so cars parked closely together, all completely covered with snow.

It looked as if none of the cars had been moved for months and he was convinced no one would miss any one of them anytime soon. He hoped to steal a car and use it longer than the cars he had taken in the past. For this reason, he didn't want to punch the door lock, which from the outside would make the car look suspicious as he was using it. He tried the door handles of three or four cars before he found a Cadillac that was unlocked. Pleased, he got in thinking it would be a great vehicle to use. Using the screwdriver, he gently pried off the hard plastic cap covering the key entry to the ignition. He didn't want to damage the cap because once he started the car, he planned to reattach the cap, then insert an old key into the ignition making it look normal.

Once the ignition cap was out of the way, Piper stuck the screwdriver into the open ignition and turned hard, causing an internal part to break, allowing the ignition to turn and hopefully start the car. He could hear the faint metallic breaking sound as he turned the ignition, but after a brief weak cranking sound of the cold motor trying to turn over, it went silent. He tried turning the ignition again, pumping the gas pedal repeatedly, but this time it produced no noise at all. In frustration he pounded the sides of the steering wheel with both hands, quietly swearing to himself about the crazy old geezer who let the car battery die. He removed the screwdriver from the ignition and replaced the chrome cap. He looked around to ensure no one was watching, then got out of the Cadillac, searching for another unlocked car.

After checking a few more cars, he found an unlocked older tan minivan. After opening the van's driver's door, he was pleased when the dome light lit up, proving the van's battery had some juice. He quickly got in and closed the door, extinguishing the tale-tell light, even though all the snow covering the van probably prevented any light from being visible from outside. Piper repeated the vehicle stealing steps he took with the Cadillac and was rewarded when it fired up after only a couple turns of the screwdriver.

He looked around the car's interior but couldn't find an ice scraper. Where was the ice scraper? Every car in Indiana this time of year had to have an ice scraper inside, didn't they? You couldn't go through an entire winter without one. With no time to keep searching, he jumped out and used his arm to wipe as much loose snow off the van's windshield as he could, but even after rubbing hard, he couldn't remove the thin layer of ice which covered the windshield. He climbed back in, and even though he could hardly see out the frosted windshield, he managed to move the van to another, less obvious part of the parking lot to wait until the defroster heated up and melted the ice.

After moving the minivan and waiting five or ten minutes, the windows started to clear. While waiting, he noticed some footprints in the fresh snow on the sidewalk next to the parking lot. A few minutes later he could see those footprints disappear as new falling snow came down. This caused the worry to diminish that someone might notice the bare spot in the snowy parking lot where the minivan had been parked. A few minutes later, Piper drove out of the Serenity Plus Assisted Senior Living Complex parking lot, smug in the knowledge that he had a vehicle that probably wouldn't be reported stolen anytime soon. He plugged his cell phone into the cigarette lighter and his satisfaction was complete as he noticed the charging icon light up.

CHAPTER 40

"Sooo, my son is selling these magazine subscriptions as a fundraiser for his Junior Scout troop. I was looking through the sales catalog thinking I gotta buy at least one subscription so the little bugger can get his journalism badge or some silly thing like that," Cory told Mel while waiting for roll call to start. "when I see this advertisement for a subscription to a magazine called *Pregnancy* selling for $14 for one year. But, under that, written in bold letters, the advertisement declared for just $19, you get two uninterrupted years of *Pregnancy*. Yeah, right," Cory smirked, "like my wife would just love to have two uninterrupted years of pregnancy!"

Mel missed the family life he once had and enjoyed how Cory often self-depreciatingly joked about his domestic situation.

Exasperated, Cory continued, "With me on this shift, there's no worry about anything like that happening! You know, if the brass could create a worse shift than late shift," he said while pointing his forefinger directly into his chest, "I'd be on it."

Changing the subject and smiling as he turned to the rookie, Adam, pointing down at his right leg, he said, "You know, I'm getting even with that guy that shot me." Adam looked confused as Cory continued, "Yeah, I'm eating his food. I'm spending his money." Then with the timing of a well-rehearsed comedian, he paused strategically before continuing, "But I haven't slept with his wife yet!" Adam, being more serious-minded, had to think a second about what he just heard and then put it all together as Cory finished this often-told comic routine by proudly pounding his chest with one fist and proclaiming, "But, hey folks, I'm the first guy in my family to get shot by the police!"

"Cory, I'd like to start roll call now, or are you waiting for some applause?" Lt. Weber asked while impatiently tapping his clipboard on the podium sitting on the roll call table. Weber began with,

"Thaddeus and Jeramy, I got an email memo that you both are scheduled for your CPR recertification next month. I forwarded the email to each of you so you can put it on your calendars. I also sent a reminder to everyone on the shift to make sure you get next year's vacation requests to me as soon as possible, so I can start plugging them into the coming year's work schedules." Weber went on, "Oh, and I got word from Detective Pierson that Jeff Volmer, the kid driving the stolen van that killed Carl, has a hearing next Thursday at 1:30 p.m. in Municipal Court. I plan to be there and would like as many of you as possible to attend. Hopefully, it'll send a message to the judge showing him how interested we are in this case."

Mel interrupted with, "It might have helped some if at least one of the judges in the five previous car theft cases he'd been arrested for had given him some time in the juvenile center instead of just cutting him loose each time."

Weber, sensing that Mel was done, read off the officers' beat assignments for the shift and finished with, "Before you leave, the patrol supervisors got a memo from the chief who thinks there've been too many accidents on State Road 76 and would like to see more traffic enforcement there."

Parker stood up and announced, "Happy to oblige, Lieutenant," slapped Adam on the back and said, "Well then partner, let's get to work!"

It wasn't 20 minutes into the shift when Charles's gruff voice bellowed over the radio, "Car 36 and car 15, 36 and 15, investigate a domestic, 6301 W. Mitchner. Two men arguing over a video game."

Mark turned his squad car around in a driveway and started to the address while acknowledging the radio run with, "Enroute, I'm close." Cory responded to Charles, acknowledging he was also on the way. Mark drove to the residence intending to wait in front until Cory arrived because it usually wasn't a safe practice to approach any type of domestic alone.

As Mark got close to the house, he could see two guys, he later learned were brothers, in the front yard, nose to nose, locked in a verbal standoff. The bigger one, brother number one, sucker punched brother number two on the side of the head, knocking him flat on his back into the snow.

Seeing this assault, Mark drove his car up over the sidewalk and out of the narrow street, then jumped from his squad car and ran toward the commotion. Brother number one glanced sideways, seeing Mark trotting straight for him, and he took off running away, stomping through the four-inch-high snow to the back of the house. Meanwhile, brother number two, still on his back in the snow, was struggling to get up, looking as if he was doing his best to make an adult-sized snow angel. Not skipping a beat, Mark ran past brother number two, running after brother number one, chasing him into the backyard. During the short foot pursuit, he used his left hand to key his police radio microphone, which was snapped onto his left shoulder epaulet, and yell that he was in a foot pursuit, giving his location and direction of travel.

He was trudging through the heavy snow and was beginning to get winded when brother number one lost traction and fell. Mark jumped on top of him to stop his flight, releasing his radio microphone from his left hand and tossing aside the flashlight that had occupied his right hand. He used his body weight to hold down the struggling brother, face down in the snow. He used his left hand to reach for his handcuffs while pressing his right forearm and body weight down into brother number one's upper back trying to control him.

Almost out of breath, he wondered where Cory was just as someone jumped on his back and heard brother number two scream, "You can't do that to my brother!" Now completely involved, Mark was still trying to hold down the first brother with his right forearm while also trying to fend off the second brother with his left arm.

After chasing brother number one through the heavy snow and now wrestling both crazy brothers, Mark was almost to the point of complete exhaustion. He wished he'd kept himself in better shape when suddenly, MoJo, the brothers' five-year-old mangy pit bull, came charging onto the scene. MoJo latched onto Mark's left boot and, with his powerful jaws, started to pull and jerk, managing to drag the pile of all three wrestlers backward a foot or so in the slick snow.

Amid the increasing chaos, Mark saw Cory's police car drive up and stop in the one-lane alley bordering the brothers' backyard about 100 feet away. The backyard was fenced, but he figured Cory wasn't so overweight he couldn't make it over the fence. Still, it didn't appear that Cory was attempting to get out of his car. He saw Cory turn his head sideways out the car window and look directly at him wearing an impish expression on his face but continue to just sit inside his patrol car. Mark, frustrated, yelled, "Get outta that car and help me!" But to his disbelief, Cory continued to sit in his police car.

In what seemed like minutes, but actually only seconds, Mark continued to wrestle the brother combo while, at the same time, trying to kick the dog away in what must have looked like a Saturday Night Professional Wrestling brawl gone horribly wrong. Then, unbelievably, out of the corner of his eye, he watched Cory simply drive away.

It took a second to realize his backup, Cory, the guy he was depending on to help him out of this mess, his fellow police officer and brother-in-arms was driving off, leaving him there, almost at a point of total exhaustion, to wrestle two psychotic brothers and one deranged pit bull, all alone. He couldn't understand how Cory could abandon him. Watching Cory leave, he felt an odd mixture of fear and anger well up, and for just a second, he lost his concentration. That's when he felt an incredibly sharp pain way up high on the inside of his left thigh, in his most tender and private of personal places, and painfully realized the angry beast had bitten him.

The situation seemed hopeless until a few seconds later when he noticed Cory running from the front yard of the brother's house, along with Thaddeus and the brothers' mother. While Thaddeus and Cory took care of business getting the brothers under control and handcuffed, the cooperative mother tried to corral the half-crazed and slobbering MoJo. Still lying on the ground, Mark checked the damage the dog bite did and was grateful the pain was subsiding. His pants were badly torn, and through the tear, he saw two canine puncture wounds and scratches to his upper inside thigh.

Mark clumsily stood up, trying to keep his weight off his left leg. While brushing snow off his uniform, he angrily protested, "Someone outta throw that crazy beast some tainted meat!"

Thaddeus, who had started to walk one of the handcuffed brothers to a waiting patrol car, paused and looked back, then down at Mark's leg and replied with a wink, "I think you already did!"

Mark, coming to his senses, abruptly turned toward Cory and, using both hands to wildly gesture, accusingly asked, "Why didn't you help me? Why didn't you get your butt out of your car and come help me instead of driving off?"

Cory glumly looked down to avoid eye contact and replied, "I'm really sorry Sarge, but I couldn't get out of the car." He continued, explaining in a deliberate but apologetic voice, "A snowplow, see, it pushed the snow high up on the side of the road up against that fence." Cory pointed at the offending fence and continued, "and the snow musta froze solid there. I couldn't open my car door wide enough to squeeze out."

Trying to change the subject, Cory looked up and over to the brothers' mother, who was still yelling at the pit bull by name while pulling on the dog collar struggling to get even a tiny bit of control over the still raging and barking MoJo, then calmly observed, "Boy, that MoJo, he sure has some bad JuJu."

CHAPTER 41

Gil was tired of going out into the cold nights, scrounging for aluminum cans and any loose change he could find in parking lots and unlocked cars. The take was usually meager for the risk he was taking. Previously he had considered becoming a porch pirate, stealing packages from porches, but he had heard many people had doorbells with a camera, and he didn't want his face showing up on someone's doorbell camera. No, that wouldn't do. He might get caught, and anyway, daytime thievery would seriously interfere with his delicate sleep schedule.

He tried street begging but didn't like standing out in the cold and hated it when occasionally someone would approach and yell at him to get a job. Anyway, there was just too much competition for street begging. How could he compete with Pete the Wino? Pete would do tricks on his 20-inch Stingray bicycle while begging for money on the sidewalk close to the street corner near the Wok 'n Roll Chinese Buffet. He would show off by pulling wheelies with one hand on the handlebars while balancing the bike on its back wheel with the front wheel pointed high into the sky. He would ride that bike like a cowboy, using his free hand to hold a mop bucket out toward the stopped cars hoping for donations. Nope, he couldn't compete with that guy.

He noticed a Christmas card from Aunt Melba that had arrived in the mail that day. Bored, he opened it and found a ten-dollar Walmart gift card inside meant for Gran. It didn't take long for an idea to form in his head. This was the Christmas season, the time of year for giving and more specifically, giving cash and gift cards through the mail. He shoved the Walmart gift card in his pocket, which Gran would never miss, and off he went, walking to the Spring Hill neighborhood to explore some mailboxes.

It was about 2:00 a.m. and Gil figured most homeowners had already brought their mail in for the day. To his surprise, out of the first 20 or so mailboxes he checked, four still had mail inside. Of those four, he found five envelopes he figured contained Christmas cards. He couldn't just stand in the street rifling through envelopes, so he jammed them into his coat pocket, intending to open them later, then moved on to the next street. Only once a car passed by, and when he noticed it coming from a distance, he stepped onto the sidewalk, acting as if he was just on an innocent midnight stroll. Once the car passed, he was back to plundering mailboxes.

His old clothes were getting more than ratty, and it was time for a change. He was hoping he might take in enough cash to get that thrift store wardrobe makeover he so badly needed. After all, it was the season to be merry, and it was kinda nice walking through the neighborhood with a pocket full of colorful Christmas cards while enjoying all the Christmas lights hanging from trees and houses, shimmering in the fresh snow.

As Gil was walking back to Gran's place, he cut through Rose Garden Villas, a new housing edition being built. He had to walk around an empty retention pond which was still in the process of being constructed. Even though he knew nothing about retention pond construction, it appeared it was almost complete, and the construction crew had just finished installing drainage pipes. The pond was located toward the back of the edition, and at this time of night, with no streetlights up yet, it wasn't visible from the nearest road. Some roads had been put in, but construction had started on only a couple of houses in the front of the planned edition, probably model homes, Gil figured. He made his way around to the back of the empty pond and walked up a hill. From the top, he could see Gran's mobile home situated in the back row of the trailer park.

CHAPTER 42

Piper was pleased with the theft of the minivan and decided he would try his luck with another robbery. He knew of an ATM machine by the Templeton Bank, just a block away from Olivia's Gentleman's Club. Typically, an ATM such as this would not be used much at 2:00 a.m. except for the fact that this one was located close to a strip club.

Piper assumed some of the old guys who went to strip clubs would probably run out of cash after too many drinks, but before the bar closed at 3:00 a.m. Of course, the dancers weren't going to take a check in exchange for a lap dance and the bar wasn't about to cash a check written by a drunk. As a result, he figured some of these guys would make their way to the closest cash machine for a quick withdrawal.

Piper stashed the minivan on a side street next to the bank, then hid in the bushes lining the parking lot next to the ATM and patiently waited. During the wait, he wondered why he hadn't thought of this before. After all, he could not only rob the guy while using the bank machine but also steal his car. Giving that more thought, he decided stealing the car wasn't such a good idea after all because the robbery victim would immediately report it stolen. No, he thought, the minivan from Serenity Plus was the vehicle to hang on to for a while. After all, the old codger from the nursing home who owned it may never miss it.

As Piper considered his auto theft options, he noticed a dark gray sedan leave Olivia's Gentleman's Club parking lot. The sedan slowly turned in his direction, then turned into the bank lot parking in front of the ATM, straddling the white lines dividing the parking spaces. A goofy-looking older guy in rumpled clothing got out of the car and walked toward the ATM, stumbling a little while stepping up onto the sidewalk. He stood in front of the machine for what seemed like a couple of minutes trying to pull his ATM card out of his wallet. Piper watched as he dropped his wallet, then almost fall as he reached down to pick it up. The man was finally able to remove the card from his wallet and insert it into the machine. He tapped a few numbers into the keypad, and when the ATM spit out some bills, Piper made his move, jumping from the bushes and rushing toward the now startled guy.

Piper didn't even have to pull his pistol out. He ran up to the man and, with one hand, grabbed the cash, then with his other hand, he pushed the guy away. Cash in hand, Piper turned and ran toward the stolen minivan, leaving the guy to stumble off the curb bordering the parking lot, falling backward and hitting the back of his head on the blacktop parking lot.

A few minutes later, "Templeton 51 and Templeton 52, 51 and 52, respond to the ATM next to the Templeton Bank and Trust, 7601 State Road 76. Person injured in robbery, medic enroute," Charles announced over the police radio.

Cory arrived on the scene and found Wayne Thompson, a retired piano tuner, sitting awkwardly on the curb's edge. Thompson was leaning forward with a cell phone in one hand, still talking to the police dispatcher while holding the back of his head with the other. "Hey buddy, let me look at the back of your head," Cory asked. Thompson pulled his hand away from his head and Cory could smell the strong odor of alcohol as he bent over to shine his flashlight at the back of the man's head. Cory noticed a bloody gash and said, "I think you're gonna need some stitches to fix your noggin. What happened?"

"Well, I dunno," a puzzled Thompson slurred, "I was just making an ATM withdrawal when I got attached."

"Attacked, you mean you got attacked," Cory politely corrected him. "What did the attacker look like?" Cory asked as he was jotting down the information needed to complete the robbery report.

"Young, skinny, white guy, I think," Thompson said.

Cory then asked, "What was he wearing?"

Thompson answered, "I think some kind of black sweatshirt."

As Cory was scribbling the description down on his notepad, he was thinking about the recent robberies at the Imperial Liquor Store and the Easy Stop store.

Thompson looked up and noticed an ambulance stop in the parking lot. He pointed and asked, "What's that for?"

Cory answered, "That bump on the back of your head. I think you need to go to the hospital and get that cut looked at."

Thompson waved his hands back and forth in front of him as he protested, "Oh, no, I don't need to go to no hospital. I'll be okay. Maybe I just need to go home and forget about all this."

Cory pointed to the sedan, which was still running, and asked, "Is that the car you drove up here in?"

Thompson replied with a slow nod of his head, saying, "Yes, sir."

"Well," Cory said, "don't you think you might have been too drunk to drive here in the first place?" After a brief pause intended to allow Thompson to consider his situation, Cory continued, "If you don't go to the hospital to have that bump on your head looked at, I'm going to have you blow into a breath analyzer before I let you drive away. If you fail the breath analyzer, I'm gonna lock you up for drunk driving. *OOOORRRR,*" drawing out the pronunciation of the word "or" like a mid-day game show host offering a contestant the exciting choice of a prize hidden behind one of two doors, he turned and pointed to the waiting ambulance, "instead of the test, you take the ambulance to the hospital and not go to jail." With little deliberation, Thompson gladly accepted the trip to the hospital.

After driving several miles from the ATM, Piper stopped to check his take. "Forty bucks! How long did that old dude think $40 bucks was gonna last at Olivia's?" he thought as he stared at the two $20 bills he held in his hand. Oh well, at least he didn't have to siphon gas again and decided to drive the minivan to a truck stop by the interstate. It was cold and he thought he might enjoy letting the minivan idle all night with the heater on as he slept. He hoped it wouldn't look suspicious if he parked on the side of the lot near where the semi-trucks parked.

CHAPTER 43

When Lt. Weber entered the roll call room, Mel was sitting at the conference table with the other officers, busily eating his second apple fritter and watching the news on the training television. The news reporter was interviewing a politician who wanted to change the state's law concerning stop and frisk, making its use difficult to justify. The politician also complained about police officers in general, using phrases such as abuse of authority, police brutality, official misconduct, and other nonsense.

Weber interrupted Mel's bad mood with, "Let's get the shift started."

Not hiding his irritation at the news coverage, Mel finished his second apple fritter, daintily licked the tips of each of his fingers, removing the last remnants of donut glaze, then disgustedly replied with, "Okay, now I'm ready for another day of persecution and abuse." Clicking off the television and with a sly smile, he added, "But at least it beats working for a living."

Thaddeus grinned and added, "You know Mel, if I wasn't a policeman, I think I would have a good job!"

Glancing back at the television and referring to all the recent news which had been critical of the police, Mel added, "Lieutenant, if I," Mel held both hands up as in air quotes, "identify as a cranky old 1970s policeman, can I still conduct No Knock search warrants?"

Cory burst out, "What's the air quotes for? You are a cranky old policeman!"

Jeramy smiled as Mel gave Cory an evil glare. He enjoyed listening to the roll call banter and knew most of it was all just talk. This group enjoyed their work as police officers and performed their jobs well. He was proud to work with them.

"Hey, before we get started," Mark interrupted, "I was at the medical clinic yesterday on a follow-up visit for the dog bite. While I was in the waiting room, I ran into the guy that got stabbed with the comb. Remember the guy that threw his girlfriend's cell phone in the toilet? He was also there on a follow-up visit so the docs could make sure that the nasty stab wound was healing properly. Guess what he asked me? He asked if he could have the comb back. You know the one that was sticking clear through his arm! Get this," Mark exclaimed while holding his hands apart wide, palms up, in a questioning motion, "he wants it as a souvenir!"

Listening to this while sitting in the roll call room, Cory unconsciously reached down and ran his hand over the gunshot scar on his leg as he said in a serious tone, "You'd think the scar would be enough of a souvenir."

Thaddeus sensed a sliver of an opening and chimed up, "Yup, that kinda case sure is *flush*trating."

Cory turned to Thaddeus and added, "But her story was so full of *crap*."

Back to Thaddeus, "Seems to me like she was just answering nature's *call*."

To everyone's surprise, Weber jumped in, pointing at Thaddeus, and with a sober look, he declared, "Keep this up and *urine* trouble." Smiling, he read off the patrol assignments and released the shift.

Teresa was the first officer to leave the roll call room as she muttered, "Guys, your *potty* talk is nauseating."

CHAPTER 44

The Investigations Division's offices were in the basement. Pierson's office was down a hall past Derek's office. To get to the hallway, he first had to walk through an open work area where Rebecca's desk was situated among a group of file cabinets, worktables, and a large copy machine. Pierson was still unhappy about the middle of the night phone call from Cory describing an ATM robbery and how Cory explained he thought it might be connected to the Imperial Liquor Store and the Easy Stop robberies. Pierson had tried to listen carefully to Cory. His mind was in a sleepy midnight fog, but in the end, he agreed with Cory's assessment.

Pierson sipped the day's first cup of coffee as he walked through Rebecca's work area. She was staring at her computer screen with a bitter look on her face. The keyboard between her elbows, which were resting on the desk, while her hands pressed against each side of her face in an exasperated pose as she said, "Stupid computer and laser printer must be married because they sure aren't communicating!" She stood up as if to address the printer, then abruptly jerked the paper tray out of its slot and roughly shuffled the paper before reinserting the tray back into the printer. Pierson, deciding not to get involved in any office equipment relationship complications, moved stealthily past Rebecca's desk toward his office.

As he passed Derek's office, he noticed Derek leaning into the office refrigerator and grab a small container of orange juice. The juice was obviously intended to complement the two slices of lightly buttered toast, which sat neatly on a plate placed exactly in the center of his desk.

Pierson thought Derek went a little overboard on some things, like decorating his office, particularly at Christmas. As was standard for the entire month of December leading up to the 25th, Derek wore a festive Christmas tie. Today, the tie featured a colorful picture of a snowman standing next to a brightly lit Christmas tree. Pierson paused to glance into Derek's office to see what new Christmas decoration may have recently been added to the décor. After scanning for a few seconds, he spotted it. On a file cabinet, in a corner, a Christmas nutcracker at least twelve inches tall, standing at attention and, yes, wearing a blue police uniform. Plaques and photos were scattered randomly on his office walls, but most puzzling was a nameplate on his desk with the words, "No Refunds" etched onto it instead of his name. Pierson thought Derek needed a refund on that Indian beaded necktie hung on a coat rack. Also hung on the wall, among other things, were a Norman Rockwell reproduction of a painting of a policeman and a small boy sitting on bar stools in front of a soda fountain. On another wall hung a bulletin board displaying a collection of police department uniform shoulder patches. A plaque with only the word *Geronimo* etched boldly in red and a professionally framed page printed from the internet of Ernesto Miranda, accompanied by Miranda's last mugshot, held prominent positions on his office walls.

The Geronimo plaque was truly a curiosity, and some officers thought it was just another example of Derek's many eccentricities. It was common knowledge that a challenge coin collection and particularly this framed Miranda internet information page were among Derek's most treasured possessions. It wasn't so much the internet page, the mugshot, or the professional framing, but much like his challenge coin collection, it was the story behind it. In this case, it was the story of ultimate justice concerning Ernesto Miranda.

Derek was a history buff with police-related history holding a special place in his heart. In Derek's opinion, Ernesto Miranda was a historical figure within the police culture. Ernesto Miranda is the person for whom the infamous Miranda Warnings are named. The Miranda Warnings are what most people know as their "rights" should they ever be arrested. One of those "rights" is the right to have an attorney present while being questioned by a police officer. Another is the right to remain silent.

There are many reasons Derek appreciated the Miranda story, not the least of which is that most people have the wrong idea as to how the Miranda Warnings really work. Many people think a policeman is required to recite the Miranda Warnings to each person they arrest, and if the officer fails to recite these warnings, it's like a Monopoly get-out-of-jail-free card. This is a misconception because a policeman is only required to recite the Miranda warnings when questioning a person who is either under arrest or in police custody while not allowed the freedom to leave. All this aside, Derek enjoyed the story behind Ernesto Miranda and the Miranda warnings.

Miranda was arrested in Phoenix in 1963 for raping an 18-year-old mentally disabled woman. After his arrest and during questioning by the police, he admitted to the rape. At trial, his attorney argued Miranda was never told that he didn't have to talk to the police, even though, at the time, police officers were not yet required to advise a person of such a right. The case worked its way up to the United States Supreme Court, which decided that with only an eighth-grade education, Miranda couldn't understand that it might not have been in his best interest to confess to a crime to the police.

The result of this landmark case, now known as Miranda v. Arizona, was that policemen were required to recite a set of warnings to criminal suspects they were about to question. As in every good infomercial, there is a, *But wait, that's not all,* to this story. After the Supreme Court overturned Ernesto Miranda's initial rape conviction, the case was sent back to the original trial court for a retrial. Because Miranda had not been advised at the time of his arrest that he didn't have to talk to the police, his confession to the rape was not admissible as evidence in his new trial. During the second rape trial, the new jury never heard about Miranda's confession to the police. Because the remaining evidence against him, even without his confession, was so compelling, he was again convicted and sentenced to eleven years in prison.

Like many criminals, after his release from prison, Ernesto continued his life of crime and between crime sprees, spent time in and out of jail. By that time in history, almost every police officer in the United States was carrying a well-worn laminated Miranda Warnings card. Then, one night in 1976, in a less than tragic twist of fate, Ernesto Miranda was stabbed to death in a bar, and guess what? When the police arrived and attempted to interview the suspect in the stabbing, that suspect refused to give a statement, invoking his Miranda privilege to remain silent. Oh yes, Derek loved happy endings to sad stories.

Pierson finally made his way into his office and started working through a stack of incident reports which had recently been assigned to him for investigation. He eventually came to the incident report on the ATM robbery at the Templeton Bank and Trust. After reading through the narrative and glancing at the suspect's description, he again agreed with Cory's assessment that this sounded like the same guy who did the Imperial Liquor and the Easy Stop robberies. Thinking back to his days working in uniform, he remembered Mel was known to say, 'Hold-up men don't usually quit committing robberies until they either get caught and put in jail or until they die." After several years of experience as a detective, he agreed with Mel's assessment.

Pierson made a few notes in the ATM robbery case file, set it aside, then logged into his department computer and began reviewing his email. He opened one from the county coroner's office informing him that the hanging on Mill Court had been ruled a suicide. No surprise there. He printed out the email to place into the case file and to remind him to prepare a Report of Investigation form, closing the case without further investigation. He often thought his job had become too much of a paper chase and sometimes sarcastically wondered if his investigative performance would better be evaluated not by the number of cases he investigated and cleared but by how much each of his case files weighed when completed.

He then moved to an email from the burglary victim on Red Fox Road. The email contained the serial number for the Glock semi-automatic pistol taken during the burglary. He prepared the paperwork necessary to have the weapon, with its make, model, and serial number, entered into the National Crime Information Center, more commonly known as NCIC, a database of stolen property. All officers use NCIC to check recovered or suspicious property to see if it had been reported stolen or was wanted for some other reason.

With the NCIC paperwork complete, he returned to checking his email and was discouraged after reading an email from the prosecutor's office. The email was sent to inform him a trial on a child neglect causing death case had, once again, been continued to another date far into the future. This case had been dragging on for nearly three years, with one continuance being granted after another. The only redeeming fact was the suspect, the mother of the deceased child, was still in jail, serving time on a parole violation from a previous narcotics conviction. At the time of the death investigation, the mother was a heroin addict with a new baby girl. She lived in a squalid apartment, and one night she got high, then, as was her custom, fell asleep in bed with her three-month-old baby next to her. Sometime during the night, too high on heroin to notice what was happening, she rolled over in bed on top of her little baby girl, suffocating the baby to death. When the mother woke up late the following morning, she found her baby girl motionless and cold.

The mother and the deceased baby were still in the apartment when Pierson arrived on the scene. He was an experienced detective and had seen many unusual and disturbing things, but he would never forget the sight of this lifeless baby lying on the bed. The pallid-colored skin of death covered her tiny body. The baby's still soft skull and developing head was round, but because of the compression from its mother's body weight, the head was flat on two sides, much like a wheel. The mother sat in a chair in the corner of the room staring vacantly into space, looking as if she was having difficulty staying awake.

Pierson had no patience for the mother and less for her attorney, who kept the case from trial by requesting continuance after continuance as a delay tactic. He was probably hoping some necessary state's witness would move away or, in some other way, be unable to appear for trial. That's when the defense attorney would demand a dismissal based on the unavailability of a necessary state's witness to testify and be cross-examined. Pierson did his best to understand the attorney was just doing his job, distasteful as it was, but failed in the attempt. This all caused his mind to drift back to something he remembered from English Literature 203 while in college. Something Shakespeare wrote in his play, *Henry VI*, "First we kill all the lawyers." Peeved that one of the few things he remembered from his four expensive and torturous years in college, written by the Bard more than five hundred years ago, still rang true today.

He continued checking recent emails and noticed one from Sgt. Wood, a senior latent fingerprint examiner from the county crime lab, caught his attention. If submitted fingerprints were not matched to anyone, Sgt Wood usually sent a form letter to the investigating officer by snail mail informing him of such. When a latent fingerprint was matched to a suspect, a quicker method of communicating was used, either a phone call or email. After a quick glance at the content of the email, Pierson's mood immediately brightened.

The email explained that Wood had submitted the latent fingerprints recovered from the scene of the Imperial Liquor Store robbery into the FBI's Automated Fingerprint Identification System, or AFIS for short. The submission resulted in a possible match had been made from past or present inmate records. Wood explained in the email that this AFIS notification of a possible fingerprint match was lead information only. He then performed a visual examination, comparing the latent fingerprints lifted from the robbery scene to the inmate fingerprints in the AFIS database, which was considered a possible match. Wood reported that after this examination, he confirmed the fingerprints of a former inmate, Patrick J. Sandpiper of 4455 McCloud Street in Templeton, Indiana, were a positive match to the fingerprints recovered from the robbery scene at the Imperial Liquor Store. It's difficult to explain how an investigator feels when a case starts to fall nicely into place. Satisfaction, yes, but there is more to it than that. But it was beyond his ability to verbalize properly. What he did know was he needed to get to work.

Pierson did a criminal history search on Sandpiper, finding an interesting arrest record. It appeared Sandpiper was a serial shoplifter, had priors for several thefts, a conviction for a residential burglary, another for a business burglary and, imagine that, an arrest for a robbery. In addition, Sandpiper collected a bunch of probation violations along the way. It seems the robbery charge was dismissed because the victim failed to show up for court. In all, Sandpiper had spent less than a year in jail as a result of all his criminal efforts. Pierson also found an outstanding arrest warrant for Sandpiper out of Florida for vehicle theft, but Florida had a policy of not extraditing for non-violent felonies such as this vehicle theft. He leaned back in his office chair and wondered how Sandpiper, who was only 29 years old, managed to rack up such an impressive criminal history in so short of time, and why wasn't he still in jail instead of out committing more crimes?

He pulled Sandpiper's mugshot from the criminal history database and created a computer-generated six-picture photo line-up to show the victims of the Imperial Liquor Store, the Easy Stop robberies, and now, the ATM robbery. He had to be careful to make sure the other pictures included in the photo line-up consisted of males who looked similar to Sandpiper. If the clerk at the Imperial Liquor Store could identify Sandpiper from the photo line-up as the person who robbed him, that along with the fingerprint match, would be enough to file robbery charges against him in that case. If the victims from the Easy Stop and the ATM robberies could also identify Sandpiper, he hoped to tack on those robbery charges as well.

As Pierson picked up the phone to call the Imperial Liquor Store clerk and arrange a meeting, he heard the ding of his computer announcing a new email. Glancing at the computer screen, he noticed a new email from Sgt. Wood. Pierson's smile grew large as he read the email. Wood just got a match on a fingerprint recovered from the rear-view mirror of a stolen blue Malibu that the Templeton Police recently recovered. Much to Pierson's delight, the fingerprint was identified as that of one Patrick J Sandpiper. It was shaping up to be a busy yet productive day.

CHAPTER 45

Derek was in his office reviewing his notes on the forgery of the stolen check passed at the Templeton Bank and Trust. He had received a subpoena issued by the local prosecutor's office commanding Scott's Optometry to provide him with any and all patient information for any customer who had purchased the Flottur model of the Sandeford brand eyeglass frame in combination with the eyeglass prescription of OS – 1.00 – 0.50 x 180 + 2.00 add 0.5 p.d. The optical gibberish was all Greek to Derek, but it was the prescription his personal optometrist had provided to him after examining the suspect's sunglass lenses.

Derek was unfamiliar with Scott's Optometry but hoped for the best as he gathered his case file and made his way to his unmarked police car. He didn't call Scott's Optometry in advance requesting an appointment to talk to them about the case, wanting his visit to be a surprise. What he didn't expect was that he would be a welcome surprise. His personal optometrist was happy to help, but Derek wasn't asking for patient information. After entering Scott's Optometry, he introduced himself to the receptionist and showed her his police identification. He briefly explained the purpose of his visit and presented her with the subpoena. The receptionist, whom he later found out was named Judy, smiled broadly, turned sharply in her swivel chair, and yelled into the open door of a back office, "Hey Dick, come on out here. You're going to want to help with this."

A tall, portly, middle-aged man with neatly combed grey hair and wearing a clean white smock entered the reception area from the back office. He looked at Derek and held his hand out as he introduced himself, "Hello, I am Richard Scott, but you can call me Dick. How can I help you?"

"Dick, this is Detective Wilson. He wants to talk to you about some glasses!" Judy excitedly announced, smiling widely and extremely interested in what was happening.

Dick turned to Derek and replied, "Well, you could make an appointment and..."

Judy abruptly interrupted, "No, no, I'm sorry, Dick. Detective Wilson wants to talk to you about a robbery! Isn't that exciting?"

Derek interrupted, saying, "It was a forgery, not a robbery. But yes, I could use some help." Derek continued by explaining about the forgery, the sunglasses the suspect left behind, and the whole business of tracking the Flottur sunglasses using his optometrist to find Sandeford, then Cerny, and now, here at Scott's Optometry. After his explanation, he handed Dick the subpoena with the request for information.

Dick held the subpoena in front of his face and quizzically read aloud, "Subpoenas Duces Tecum?" Then looking up at Derek, "What the heck does all that mean?"

Derek, honestly not knowing what the term meant, replied with a short, terse, and in his best authoritarian voice he often used to bluff his way through such situations, "It's Latin," as if that was all the explanation that was required.

"Well, okay then. Let's check our computer and do a little search for the Flottur." Dick looked over Judy's shoulder at the computer screen as she was already pecking away at the keyboard searching for all their customers who had purchased the Flottur over the last couple of years.

While checking individual purchase records against eyeglass prescriptions, Judy explained, "That's a very popular eyeglass frame, mostly because it's inexpensive." Derek and Dick patiently waited as Judy continued her search. Derek was impressed with the speed at which Judy navigated through the various computer screens, then, "Ah ha, here it is, Brian Sanders, 6403 Paula Drive, right here in Templeton," she announced with a smile and obvious satisfaction of a job well done. Judy leaned close to the computer screen and continued reading the eyeglass transaction's particulars.

Derek wondered why a guy who could afford to purchase a pair of prescription sunglasses would be committing a forgery and asked Judy, "How did he pay for the sunglasses?"

She turned in her chair and looked at Derek as she teasingly replied, "He didn't, you did," pointing her right forefinger directly into Derek's face.

"Huh?" Derek questioned.

"Medicaid, your hard-earned tax dollars paid for Brian Sanders' sunglasses. That's why he got the Flottur, they're cheap, and Medicaid doesn't pay much for eyeglass frames." With an inquisitive look, she returned her gaze to the computer screen and after a few moments, announced, "Well, this guy's prescription didn't change much over five years. Medicaid patients get only one pair of glasses every five years. My guess is when he found out his prescription didn't change much from his last eye exam, instead of getting a new pair of regular glasses, he decided to spend his Medicaid money," Judy turned and looked at Derek, saying, "I mean our money, to buy the Flottur frames, and had the lenses tinted as dark as Medicaid will allow and still pay for them, which provided himself with a nifty pair of free prescription sunglasses."

Derek gave Judy a funny look as if he didn't quite understand. Judy, picking up on his confusion, added, "Medicaid doesn't pay for prescription sunglasses, but they will pay the cost of the tinting of the lenses, up to a certain point, and that's what it looks like we did with Sanders' glasses."

On the way back to his office, Derek drove by 6403 Paula Drive, the address Brian Sanders gave to Scott's Optometry. It was a four-plex in disrepair, close to a pay-by-the-week shady motel he knew to be occupied mostly by drug addicts and thieves. He wasn't prepared to confront Sanders yet, so he drove to his office to prepare another subpoena, this one ordering Sanders to submit to providing handwriting samples.

Derek returned to his office and conducted a criminal history check on Sanders, finding all the common criminal offenses one would expect from a drug addict: possession of cocaine, theft, shoplifting, and of course, forgery. He began what was to him the routine task of preparing a subpoena to compel handwriting samples from Brian Sanders. There was no point in spending much time looking for Sanders until he could immediately drag him back to the police station for the handwriting samples. Otherwise, he may never be able to find the suspect a second time.

Derek started by organizing his thoughts on paper, jotting down the facts of the case as he knew them using his black Classic Century Cross pen. Years ago, when transferred to the investigations division, the Cross pen was a gift from his father. Showing pride in his son, his father told Derek a good detective should always have a pen, so it might as well be a nice pen. He would often pick up that Cross pen to write and be fondly reminded of his father. One other thing he wished his dad had done for him was to teach him how to tie a dress tie into a Windsor knot. Unfortunately, after his transfer to investigations, that fatherly duty was left to a simple online instructional video.

Derek quickly completed the narrative part of the subpoena, explaining how the forgery suspect's physical description matched that of the detailed physical description recorded on Brian Sanders' latest arrest report. He then described the process of how he determined the sunglasses left at the bank were Sanders' sunglasses. Once completed, he electronically transmitted the paperwork to the county prosecutor's office, hoping to get a quick approval.

CHAPTER 46

Lt. Weber took a sheet of paper from his clipboard and looked in Mark's direction as he announced, "Mark, good news, the Indiana Department of Health says MoJo didn't have rabies." Then he held the paper closer to his face and while squinting, acting like he was continuing to read, "But it says here they're not so sure about your date from last Saturday night."

Mark raised his hands up as if surrendering and cynically responded, "Hey, don't worry, nothing happened." Mark relaxed, leaning forward, and continued, "Anyway. that woman was more complicated than the operating instructions to a digital watch. I had a bad feeling about that gal."

Teresa, being the only woman in roll call at the time, turned her chair toward Mark, giving him a severe stare while explaining, "You couldn't find your feelings with a GPS!"

• Weber tapped his clipboard on the conference table as he often did when trying to regain control of roll call. Then he started with, "The Crime Watch coordinator asked that we watch for gangs spray painting gang signs along the railroad underpasses." Turning to the next page on his clipboard, he continued, "Looks like there was another employee theft at the Burger Boy. The detectives think the evening shift manager ran off with the night deposit and hasn't been heard from since." Weber addressed Adam, the rookie, explaining, "This seems to happen more often than it should. I think some of these fast food managers get paid so poorly and work so many long hours that when they decide to quit, they just walk out, taking the night deposit as a sort of severance pay. Also, it looks like we have a complaint that some homeless people are hanging out behind VendMate again, trashing up the place."

Thaddeus's cell phone started to ring, and he quickly silenced it while looking at the caller ID. Roll call went silent and everyone could hear Thaddeus as he answered the call, trying to say quietly, "I'm in roll call. I'll call you back later, okay?" He then put his phone away and looked up to see everyone staring at him. Thaddeus sheepishly, almost embarrassed, looked around, saying, "What? It was just a phone call. Give me a break, will ya?"

"Okay," Weber said, "I guess we're finished with roll call and all our personal business. Let's get out there and get to work."

After finishing some paperwork, Cory left roll call and noticed Thaddeus sitting in his police car in the police parking lot. He walked up, seeing that Thaddeus had his window cracked open. Standing next to the police car, he could hear Thaddeus talking on his cell phone, saying, "Yes, I see Ernie. How about I come to see you this week and we can talk about it some more then?" After Thaddeus hung up, he looked up and noticed Cory standing outside his driver's window, so he rolled it down the rest of the way.

Cory looked at Thaddeus and, with a question in his voice, asked, "Ernie? Was that Ernie Buford?"

"Yeah," Thaddeus replied, "he's having some problems."

Not understanding, Cory asked, "Problems, what kind of problems would he have? Isn't he in one of those memory care places?"

Thaddeus replied, staring straight ahead over his steering wheel, not looking Cory in the eye, "Yup, it wasn't maybe six or seven years after he retired from the police department his wife died. That's when he started gradually having some memory loss problems and ended up at Serenity Plus Assisted Living."

Thaddeus paused, but Cory nudged him with, "And?"

Thaddeus loosened up some and continued, "You know Carl, he started visiting Ernie. Taking him candy, donuts, and stuff, you know, just being Carl. But you know, being in memory care, Ernie had no idea what happened to Carl." He looked at Cory and continued, "Then, a few days after Carl's accident, I saw a telephone message on Rebecca's desk from Ernie asking for Carl to give him a call. Rebecca took the message because she didn't know what to tell the old guy and asked if I could return the call to see what he wanted. I did, and when Ernie told me that Carl had been visiting him and helping him with some personal stuff, well....," Thaddeus put both hands on the steering wheel and again, looking straight ahead as if he was impatient to leave but continued, "So, I went to see him last week, like Carl would have. It was good seeing him, but not in there, not like that. They have him in a secure area of the building, so that he can't just walk away. It seems that tonight, he had the wild idea his son-in-law is stealing his money. Heck, Cory, there's no money. I talked to his daughter a few days ago and she told me that Ernie's flat broke and has been for a while. The nursing home takes his pension check and most of his social security, leaving him with about a hundred bucks a month that he spends mostly on candy bars and soda pop in the commissary. Whoa, boy, those nursing homes are expensive!"

Cory asked, "Ernie doesn't know what happened to Carl?"

Thaddeus answered, "Naw, and honestly, I haven't had the heart to tell him. I just said he was busy."

Cory smiled while compassionately reaching into the police car and giving Thaddeus a gentle pat on the shoulder before walking away with great respect for Thaddeus and sincere gratitude for having such a good guy for a friend.

CHAPTER 47

Piper was happy to have the minivan. While it was more comfortable than he expected, it was a gas hog. It was just about out of gas, and he was almost out of money. He was still bummed about only getting forty bucks from the old drunk at the ATM, and that didn't go far. The last time he was in the slammer an old-timer told him something interesting about how, years ago, it was easy to steal gas at gas stations. After listening to the old-timer, he wondered why in the world any gas station owner would allow a guy to pump gas into his car before paying for it. Or better said, why would anyone like Piper ever pay for gas he just pumped into his car when he could just drive away without paying?

He only had a few bucks, so tonight, he would have to siphon some gas if he expected to run the minivan's heater to stay warm. He didn't have the supplies he needed to siphon, but after some thinking, Piper came up with an idea, the dollar discount store. The last time he was in a dollar store, he noticed clear plastic tubing in the hardware aisle and thought that might work. While at the store, he also could buy a gallon of distilled water to siphon from a car into the empty gallon water jug. For only two bucks, he could buy all the tools required to keep him warm tonight, and as luck would have it, two dollars was all he had left. He hated to spend it, but it would be hard to shoplift the gallon of water.

He parked the minivan in the dollar store parking lot, and as he entered the store, he noticed the cashier watching him out of the corner of her eye. Piper, being a realist, understood her concern. It was almost closing time, the store was empty except for the two of them, and he didn't look nor smell desirable. But what could she do? On this visit, he planned to actually pay for the merchandise, and that thought made him smirk. What did she think, that he would stick up the lousy place? He doubted the cash register held even the $40 bucks he got from the ATM drunk. It just wasn't worth his time. He quickly found the clear plastic tubing in the hardware aisle, then grabbed a gallon of spring water sitting next to the distilled water. He hesitated as he looked at the gallon container and wondered what the difference was between spring water and distilled water. No matter, he thought as he approached the cash register, he didn't plan on drinking that crap anyway. It wasn't even carbonated.

Not looking Piper in the eyes, the cashier quickly scanned the two items, bagged the tubing, and announced, "That'll be two dollars and fourteen cents." For a second, Piper was taken aback, thinking it would be only two dollars, but quickly realized the fourteen cents was the state sales tax. What did the state need his money for anyway, those rotten crooks? He handed the cashier the two one-dollar bills, then spent a few seconds rustling through his pockets. He finally came up with a nickel and a dime, handing them to the cashier and getting one cent back in change. He walked from the store and started to feel hunger pains, but with only one penny to his name, he had few options.

CHAPTER 48

Mel was patrolling the Thompson Business Park area when he heard Charles dispatch Cory and Mark to a complaint of a disturbance at the Templeton Ale and Bowl on State Road 76. Charles broadcast over the police radio that the caller thought the man causing the disturbance might have a mental problem. Hearing radio dispatches such as this often made him think of retiring. It wasn't that he didn't enjoy police work, he did, but he was tired of unraveling other people's problems. He was frustrated with wrestling with all the gear on his duty belt while trying to get untangled from the seat belt every time he got in and out of the police car. He was tired of all the nonsense-spewing defense attorneys and belly-aching victims. Was it his fault you left your tools in an unlocked truck in your driveway all night, only to find them gone in the morning? He preferred working late shift, mostly because the department brass wasn't around, but lately, trying to sleep during the day was wearing on him. The one thing he liked about late shift was the solitude of the squad car. While late shift had more serious activity, there was usually less total activity than other shifts, allowing him more alone time in his patrol car. The other officers on the shift would have been surprised to discover Mel spent much of his time on patrol quietly listening to soft instrumental music or audio books narrating classic novels.

Mel wanted to retire, but retiring was a confusing math problem and he hated math. In fact, the only reason he majored in Criminal Justice Studies while in college was that, at the time, it was the only course of study with no math requirement. He smiled, thinking about how his lack of aptitude in mathematics steered him into a career in police work. Unfortunately, the math of retirement was now a requirement. He was 56 years old, and in Indiana, a police officer can retire after 20 years of service and be rewarded with a

50% retirement. Even with those 20 years, an officer would not be able to collect that retirement until he reached his 52nd birthday. But continuing to work after 20 years adds another two percent per year to the retirement payout, topping out at 74 percent after 32 years. Mel talked to a financial planner who added more numbers to the retirement calculation, such as his inability to collect his full social security until he was 67 years old. Still, he could start collecting at a reduced rate at age 62. Then again, he would get a much larger monthly Social Security check if he waited until he was 70 years old. Mel became even more confused when the financial planner talked about mortality rates, the average surviving years after retirement, and assisted living planning. He was to the point of deciding to avoid the entire issue and continue to work for as long as he was able. He sometimes thought about how frustrating police work could be, and if he had a chance to do it all over again, he might choose a different profession. On the other hand, he would not want to give up all the rewarding experiences police work provided him over the years.

Mel was once again mulling his retirement options as he cruised around, patrolling the businesses still open at that late hour. Remembering Lt. Weber had asked for more patrol at VendMate Food Service, he made his way toward the vending company's back lot. As he was shining his spotlight against the building's back doors and windows, his mind drifted to thinking about the dispatch to the bowling alley, which he knew well from numerous previous incidents. The big neon sign on top of the bowling alley read, "Templeton Ale and Bowl." Just under the name, "We Set Them Up, You Knock'em Down," was spelled out in smaller, attention-grabbing bright flashing red letters. He wasn't sure if the slogan referred to the bowling pins or the ale. As he drove around to the back of the VendMate building, his spotlight illuminated a white male reaching into a dumpster near the back door. The man looked homeless and dirty. He had on a black hoodie with a backpack slung over his shoulder.

Mel radioed to dispatch, "Car 30 to control. I'll be checking a person behind VendMate in the Thompson Business Park."

Dispatcher Charles responded, "Car 30, I have you out at VendMate. Do you need any assistance?"

Mel replied, "Control, no assistance now." Mel got out of his police car, and as he walked, he shined his flashlight toward the guy asking, "What's ya doing here?"

CHAPTER 49

It was dark in the VendMate back lot. Piper was standing on an upside-down milk crate, leaning into a dumpster, trying to reach a small box he hoped would contain some snacks. He had learned from his dad, who had worked for VendMate, that the company couldn't sell snacks past their expiration dates even though they were still sealed in their original packages and perfectly edible. Because his dad regularly brought them home from work, he also knew that the snacks still tasted good long after their expiration dates. Straining to reach deep into the dumpster and about to grab the box, he was surprised by a spotlight shining in his direction. "Great, just what I need," he thought as he turned and saw a serious-looking policeman climbing out of a police car.

The policeman asked what he was doing, and Piper figured this time there was no reason to lie, explaining, "Just grabbing some snacks. It's just a dumpster. I didn't think anyone would mind."

The policeman walked to almost an arm's reach of Piper and asked, "Can I see your ID?"

Because his driver's license was suspended, Piper only had an Indiana identification card which he pulled from his front pocket. An occasion like this was why he carried his ID card in his front pocket, never in his wallet. He kept his fake driver's license in his wallet and hoped that keeping his real ID in his pocket would keep him from accidentally pulling that fake driver's license out if he ever got stopped by the police while driving a car. That fake license might keep him from getting locked up for driving with a suspended driver's license. The fake ID was valuable, and he would only use it when absolutely necessary.

Piper was aware of the arrest warrant out of Florida. He also knew Florida wouldn't extradite on that charge, so there was no worry about handing the policeman his real ID. He didn't think he was doing anything that would get him arrested, so he pulled it from his pocket and handed it to the officer, ready to bolt if anything went wrong. After all, he didn't want to get busted with the pistol in his backpack.

Piper heard the policeman talk into his police radio, "Control, check for warrants, one Patrick J Sandpiper." As the policeman began to read Piper's full name and date of birth into his two-way radio, he was distracted thinking about the pistol. He considered where to run if the policeman wanted to search his backpack. That's when he heard some excited yelling come out of the police radio, something about needing assistance.

CHAPTER 50

Mel was standing a safe distance of five feet from Sandpiper while he gave the police dispatcher Sandpiper's personal information needed to check for arrest warrants. If he was clean, Mel planned to chase him off, telling him not to return to the VendMate back lot or get arrested for trespassing if he did.

Suddenly, Mel heard Cory's excited voice calling for assistance over the police radio, "Control, I have a resistor, Templeton Ale and Bowl, need assistance." Immediately, Mel tossed the ID in Piper's direction and, as he trotted back to his police car, yelled to Sandpiper, "Get outta here and don't come back, you hear?"

Surprised at his good luck, Piper didn't bother responding. Before he could utter a word, the policeman was inside his cruiser, racing out the back lot, tires squealing, siren blasting, and the bright red and blue lights lit up.

CHAPTER 51

Cory and Mark arrived at Templeton Ale and Bowl at about the same time and quickly walked in. They were greeted by the manager, who pointed to the back of the bowling alley and said, "He's crazy. Get him outta here. He's running in and out of the pin spotters, acting like a stupid robot or whatever, yelling something crazy about Albuquerque. Just get him outta here and try not to tear anything up, okay? I saw all the damage after you guys caught that burglar in here. Please don't let that happen again, please?"

Mark would have a tough time forgetting what happened in the Templeton Ale and Bowl when it was burglarized last year. On that day, when he and Parker arrived on the scene of the burglary alarm, they found a back door had been forced open. Because it was a large building, for officer safety, they decided to call a K-9 to search the building. They set up a perimeter around the building in case the burglar tried to escape while they waited for the K-9 to arrive. Officer Tonya Meyer arrived with her police dog and assessed the situation. Because of the building's size and wide-open interior, she decided not to enter the building herself. Instead, she released the dog into the building to search for the burglar alone. The dog's name was Dolphus, which is German for Noble Wolf. This female, 78-pound K-9, was known for being crazy and sometimes overly aggressive. This is why every officer on the scene got back into their police cars for their own protection before Tonya got the dog out of her police car.

Tonya pointed to the open back door of the building and released Dolphus, yelling, "Cherche," which any well-trained German Shepherd police dog knows is German for search. Dolphus ran, frantically barking, ten feet into the building, then abruptly stopped. The police dog then excitedly ran twice, in a tight circle, tail stuck straight up in the air with her nose pointed toward the center of her circuit as if she had found something worthy of further investigation. The dog suddenly stopped, walked toward the center of the circled area and sniffed before hunching back into a semi-sitting position, then defecated onto the smooth tile floor. Once that task was completed, Dolphus jumped back into action and ran, barking all the way across the bowling alley into the arcade.

Dolphus located the now petrified burglar hiding behind a Galaga arcade game and before you could say hand me the toilet paper, chomped down on the burglar's left calf. The burglar wrapped his arms around the Galaga arcade game in a tight bear hug, desperately holding on as Dolphus began to drag him away, pulling the Galaga game over and crashing onto the floor in the process. As the burglar was slowly being dragged away, he kicked at the determined dog with his right leg, managing to free himself, then ran toward a life-sized race car simulator, hiding on the far side under the passenger window and out of view. Dolphus, who was now in a fully crazed frenzy, wildly barked as she leaped through the simulator's driver's side window and through the passenger side window in a single bound. She used her enormous jaws to attach herself to the burglar's right arm, causing the burglar to thrash around, trying to pull the crazy dog off his arm. He fell into the Space Invaders game, knocking it over and scattering broken glass and game tokens all over the floor. Falling backward, he stumbled into, oddly enough, the Mortal Kombat video game, breaking off the game player controllers. Unable to steady himself as he tumbled, he tripped and fell back into the ball-catching net of the Pop-A-Shot indoor miniature basketball game. The burglar flailed about trying to escape but was trapped in the loose netting of the game. Dolphus chewed on his kicking legs until Tonya ran up yelling, "Fuss, Fuss," the German command for stop. Dolphus immediately stopped chewing, stepped back, and sat on her haunches as a scoreboard over the Pop-A-Shot indoor miniature basketball game flashed, "GAME OVER."

That night Mark was the shift supervisor, and the time-consuming task of photographing and documenting all the damage fell on him. Tonight, much like the manager, he also hoped they would not do "that thing" again.

Mark and Cory walked into the bowling alley area, followed by the manager. Suddenly, the manager yelled, "There he is!" as he pointed to a very tall, stocky man dressed in camouflage clothing with a red beret perched on his head who was moving quickly from the bowling alley into the arcade.

Cory yelled toward the guy, "Stop!" As if he didn't hear the command, the guy continued moving quickly into the arcade. Cory wondered as he watched the guy, was he walking or marching? The guy was moving fast, using an exaggerated military style of walking or marching, pulling his knees up high as he stepped forward, then lowering his legs in a precise cadence motion. His fists were clenched and arms bent at 90-degree angles moving up and down in rhythm to his marching as if he were one of the King of England's palace guards.

Mark and Cory were closing in on him as he rounded a corner, but rounded wasn't the correct word for what he did. The guy stopped suddenly at the corner, then holding his body erect as he stood tall and straight on the ball of his right foot, then sharply pivoted left, reminding Cory of a cartoon toy soldier in a Rose Bowl Parade marching band. The guy stomped his way to the coin-operated Super Helicopter kiddie ride, which was mounted on a moving pedestal, where he stopped. He stood at attention with palms facing in and arms held tightly against his sides as he waited for the officer.

The huge guy looked ridiculous standing next to the kiddie ride. He raised his right arm and stretched it out straight, and using his forefinger to point at the kiddie helicopter ride, he announced in an emotionless, staccato robotic type voice, "You will put me on this plane, and it will go to Albuquerque." While the officers stared at the guy, he lowered his pointing arm and stood straight up at attention, again holding his arms tightly to each side.

Cory and Mark carefully approached, cautiously watching, and Cory asked, "Is he crazy or something?"

Mark reacted with, "I think both."

The guy continued with the same exaggerated voice and repeated, "You will put me on this plane, and it will go to Albuquerque."

Cory, standing a few feet from the guy and trying to make a connection, looked up into his face and asked, "What's going on buddy?"

Still standing at attention, the guy responded, again with the same emotionless, staccato robotic sounding voice insisting, "You will put me on this plane, and it will go to Albuquerque."

"We're getting nowhere like this," Mark said and asked the guy, "You think maybe you wanna go the hospital and get checked out?"

Undaunted, the guy came back with the same robotic voice and repeated, "You will put me on this plane, and it will go to Albuquerque."

Cory jumped in with, "Ya know, I love Albuquerque too. It's a great place, warm this time of year. But how about we all take a nice little ride to the hospital and see what's bugging you?"

Again, the response was the same strange voice, "You will put me on this plane, and it will go to Albuquerque."

Cory told the guy, "Nope, sorry, you're going to the hospital instead, like it or not. We can all go to Albuquerque when you get out, okay?"

For officer safety, a person being taken to a hospital as a mental case is usually handcuffed. Cory pulled his handcuffs from his duty belt while Mark stood in front of the big guy. Cory moved behind him, grabbing the guy's right wrist to begin the handcuffing process, and that's when the brawl started.

It had been Couples Friday Night Trivia in the restaurant bar of the bowling alley and some of the holdovers were still present as the brawl began. Of course, that crowd made their way to the arcade to watch the action. As any good citizen would, they all had their cell phones out and ready, hoping for the chance to record some exciting turmoil they could post on social media. Most of the bowlers had stopped and moved in closer to watch just as the robot man started to resist the handcuffing.

Cory was struggling, trying to put on the cuffs, but with his hands full, he could barely key his radio and call for assistance as Mark jumped into the fray. The two officers took the big guy to the floor while trying to handcuff him. The guy was strong and, with apparently little effort, stood up with both Mark and Cory hanging all over him, like wet clothes hanging in the wind on a rural clothesline, all while screaming, "ALBUQUERQUE" in that robotesque voice.

Cory thought about dropping off, pulling his taser to give the guy a good steady jolt, but was confused about what he was told in taser training. If he tased this guy, would Mark, who was still hanging on, also feel the Taser effects? If so, that would leave Cory to fight the robot guy alone, which was not an option he preferred. He re-holstered his taser and continued trying to handcuff the guy making a mental note to pay more attention during the upcoming Taser recertification training. Mark and Cory wrestled with the guy for what seemed like forever when Mel made his entrance into the arcade.

Mel arrived at Templeton Ale and Bowl and ran into the bowling alley and was surprised at the crowd surrounding the entrance to the arcade. As he got closer, he could hardly hear Cory yelling, "Stop resisting or I'll tase you," over someone else screaming, "Albuquerque." Mel had to push his way through the gathered crowd of cell phone-pointing spectators, which reminded him more of the pandering celebrity paparazzi than Templeton Friday night trivia lovers.

Once he got to the scuffle, he helped Cory grapple with the stocky guy's arms, trying to pull them around the guy's back for handcuffing, but the guy was just too big and strong. Mel repositioned himself to face the resistor's right side. As trained, he held the subject's right forearm with both hands and used his right knee to kick the guy on the outer thigh, just above the knee, in what is known as a Peroneal Knee Strike. This defensive tactic, while not causing permanent injury, should temporarily disable a resistor by causing a loss of motor control, but in this case, it had no effect. He stepped back and struck the arrestee once more with another knee strike which, again, had no effect.

Even though Mel was big, this guy was bigger, stronger, and much crazier. Later, Mel couldn't remember why, but he stepped in front of Cory and pushed Mark aside. This positioned himself directly behind the crazy guy, then he bellowed, "Ok, you asked for it robot man." Mel then jumped on the guy's back and threw his arms around his shoulders as if riding a wild stallion bareback. He locked his right hand into his left wrist and tried to wrap his legs around the robot man's waist but failed when the guy obviously sensed Mel hanging on his back and began to violently spin around and around in a circle trying to dislodge Mel. The guy spun around faster and faster like a mad Twirling Dervish, with Mel hanging on only by his arms around the guy's chest, looking as if he was the Twirling Dervish's skirt flying high in the air as he twirled furiously around. The robot man must have started to get dizzy and slowed, then slightly stumbled. Sensing a weakness, Mel wrapped his legs around the guy's waist and forced his weight forward into the robot man's back, causing the guy to lose his balance. As the robot man started to fall forward, Mel grabbed hold of the back of his shirt with one hand and a hunk of hair with his other hand, then rode that wild stallion all the way down to the floor like a bad stock market in a mad panic.

The huge guy clumsily belly-flopped on the tile floor with so much force he bounced hard and was left stunned, gasping for air. Mel figured the robot man had the air knocked out of him and needed to move fast before the big guy recovered. The burly man's stout shoulders were so broad it was impossible to bring his hands together behind his back close enough to cuff him with only one pair of handcuffs. Mel grabbed Cory's handcuffs and linked them to his own to make a daisy chain combination long enough to get the huge guy cuffed behind his back. Once he was restrained, Mel jumped to his feet like a champion rodeo cowboy looking for his competition take-down time. Looking around, he was startled to see the trivia lovers all pointing their cell phones at him, recording every second of the dramatic action. Meanwhile, all the bowlers were standing a safe distance away, hooting and hollering while loudly applauding. Cory pulled himself up off the floor, tucked in his loose shirt, used both hands to adjust his duty belt, and stood over the now handcuffed robot man who was lying face down on the floor. Pointing his right index finger directly down at the robot man and in his best Star Trek Borg-like monotone staccato-sounding voice, he boasted, "Resistance is futile."

CHAPTER 52

Piper was relieved when the big policeman left in such a hurry. He figured rushing away as he did, the policeman wouldn't be back soon. As a result, Piper casually disregarded the policeman's order to leave and climbed back on top of the milk crate. He used the flashlight on his cell phone to relocate the package inside the dumpster that he hoped contained a tasty snack. He leaned way over into the dumpster, so far that his feet left contact with the milk crate at about the same time he grabbed the precious white box. Leaning back off the dumpster, regaining traction on the crate, he stepped off to examine the package. He was in luck, a box of six individually packaged Twinkies! A feast for a king! Tucking the treasure under his arm, he trotted to the minivan, which was parked out of sight.

Piper was sitting in the van munching on a Twinkie and thinking about where he would go to siphon some gas. Wouldn't it be a hoot to siphon gas from a police car right there in the police department parking lot? Reason got the best of him and he settled on the Hidden Creek housing edition. This was where he dumped the Malibu, and it might be nice to see if it was still there. He knew that housing edition would have lots of cars parked on the street or in their driveways this time of night. It should be easy pickings, he confidently thought.

While driving to the Hidden Creek edition, he passed the Templeton Ale and Bowl, noticing several police cars parked outside, all with their emergency lights still on. He wondered why policemen did that, leaving their emergency lights on after they had arrived at their destination. Figuring it was probably just a big boy and their toys kinda thing, he dismissed the thought.

Piper arrived at the Hidden Creek housing edition and quickly noticed the blue Malibu was gone. Good, he thought with satisfaction. Some pill freak probably took it. When he gets caught in it, he'll be the one to take the rap. He didn't have to drive far inside the edition before seeing several good prospects for siphoning. He parked the van about half a block away from a pickup truck that looked like a good target. It was parked in a dark driveway and the gas tank lid faced opposite the front door, away from any prying eyes and or doorbell cameras. As he crept up within ten feet of the pickup truck, a security light over the garage door suddenly turned on. Not knowing if someone inside the house was looking out and turning the light on or if it was simply a motion-activated spotlight, he turned on his heels and ran.

A few blocks away, he noticed a Mazda parked in a driveway next to an old Honda Civic. Noting there was no spotlight over the garage door, he quietly approached the Mazda. When he discovered the fuel tank lid and all the car doors were locked, he moved to the Honda and quickly opened the unsecured gas cap lid and removed the cap. Piper slid one end of the plastic tubing inside the opening and down into the fuel tank. Next, he sucked hard on the other end of the tube until he could sense the movement of fluid flowing up. By the time he removed the tube from his mouth and into the empty spring water jug, he could smell and almost taste the unleaded gasoline moving up through the tube. In less than a minute, the jug was almost full, and he stopped the flow of gas by pulling the other end of the tube out of the car's gas tank. Carrying the gallon of gas, he jogged to the stolen minivan and emptied it into the gas tank. He repeated this gas siphoning process five more times before putting the gas cap back on and closing the Honda's fuel tank lid, hoping the owner would not be the wiser about the missing gasoline. Piper was peeved he would have to siphon gas again soon if he didn't come into some cash. A hybrid, why couldn't he have stolen a hybrid car that wouldn't use so much gas?

Driving away, he was thinking about how rough life was in Templeton, particularly in the cold winter months. Didn't his dad consider transferring to the VendMate plant in southern Arizona? Yes, Arizona, where it's warm all year long. Maybe he should go there. He didn't have any warrants for his arrest there. Yes, there were lots of rattlesnakes and scorpions, but there would be no cold winter snows and no Templeton cops to hassle him. Arizona, yes, that sounds about right. He needed an action plan, a way to get there. Right now, he had no money and not much gasoline. An action plan is just what he needed. As he was driving, he began to mull over the options for getting enough money to get him to Arizona. Another robbery, maybe? But where?

CHAPTER 53

After showing the clerk the photo line-up, which included a mugshot of Sandpiper, Pierson drove out of the store parking lot and did a happy fist bump, accidentally hitting the interior ceiling of the unmarked police car. No, most people couldn't appreciate the satisfaction and sometimes thrill of having a criminal investigation fall into place. A little earlier that evening, the clerk at the Imperial Liquor Store took only seconds to look at the photo line-up before pointing to the photo of Sandpiper and announcing with enthusiasm, "That's him, no doubt!"

Afterward, Pierson drove to the Easy Stop to meet with Sandra Knowles, the clerk working the cash register at the time of the robbery. By that time, it was getting late in the evening. To make sure he could connect with robbery victims to show them photo line-ups, he first tried to catch them at work. He entered the store and noticed Knowles behind a cash register. The store wasn't busy, so he approached her and asked a few questions about the robbery. As always in cases such as this, Pierson set out a single sheet of paper with six color photos printed on it, then told Knowles, "The guy who robbed you may or may not be any one of the people in these six photos. If you're sure you see the guy who robbed you in these photos, let me know. If you don't see him, that's okay. These photos aren't all recent so try to concentrate only on things about the robber's appearance that don't change. Things like the shape of his nose and lips, but not the color or length of the hair. And remember, he may not even be pictured in these photos."

Knowles nervously wrapped a lock of her medium-length brown hair around her left forefinger and twisted while moving her right forefinger left to right over the paper, scanning the six photos. Pierson remained silent as Knowles viewed the photos. When showing photo line-ups, he was always careful not to do anything which could be considered prejudicing any choice a witness might make. Knowles scanned back to photo number five, which pictured a white male with an aggravated look on his face. She pointed her finger at the photo of Patrick J Sandpiper and said, "He's the one. That's the guy that robbed me!"

Pierson rarely had a series of robbery cases come together so well and so quickly. As he drove away from the Easy Stop, he reviewed in his head some of the relevant facts relating to the robberies. He was thinking about how to word the probable cause statement he would prepare in order to obtain an arrest warrant while mumbling off the basic facts: "Sandpiper identified at the Imperial Liquor Store. Sandpiper identified at the Easy Stop. Sandpiper's fingerprint matched at the Imperial Liquor Store, and the clerk saw a blue Chevy Malibu leave the scene and, guess what," he smirked, "a few days later, we get Sandpiper's fingerprint identified inside a stolen blue Chevy Malibu." Steering with his left hand, Pierson used his right hand to jot a note in his notebook, which was lying on the seat next to him as he drove, "Arrange an appointment to show photo line-up to Wayne Thompson." After a few minutes of thinking, he also jotted down another note reminding him to put Sandpiper's photo and personal identifiers on the supervisor's roll call clipboard.

On his way back to the police station and starting to get hungry, he noticed his half-eaten chicken sandwich left over from lunch, partially covered by the sandwich wrapping, sitting on his duty bag positioned on the passenger seat. Having left it after a hastily eaten lunch, he picked it up and gave it a cursory smell check. Satisfied it probably wasn't lethal, he finished it on his way to his office.

CHAPTER 54

In the safe confines of his rented garage, Rex approached a small floor model home safe that he had set on his workbench. He slipped an old sock over a thick hockey puck-sized magnet, then placed it against the front of the safe. He leaned over and tilted his head, putting his left ear close to the front of the safe. Listening closely, he slowly slid the sock-covered magnet around the door of the safe, close to the handle, until he heard an almost undetectable click. He moved the magnet around more until he heard a slightly louder click, then pulled the handle down, easily opening the door of the safe. In less than 30 seconds of effort, he had the safe open. Rex would admit that the ease with which he could open these cheap department store home safes was less impressive once you knew how poorly they were made.

He had been in jail when he learned how to open electronic safes using a rare earth magnet and an old sock. Kenny the locksmith happened to be in jail for a violation of child support at the same time Rex was serving time. Kenny, a small and timid-looking man, was looking for a friend as protection in jail and shared a multitude of lock-picking tips with Rex in exchange for his protection services.

Rex wasn't normally a violent guy, but in his profession, you couldn't be too careful. Even though he didn't have, or more accurately, couldn't have, a handgun permit because of a prior felony conviction, he sometimes carried a pistol.

On this occasion, Rex landed in jail as a result of conducting business with a doper who was strung out and too desperate to think straight. After a brief argument over the price of some meth Rex was selling, the doper pulled out what looked to be a pistol but was actually a pellet gun and pointed it at Rex. Taken by surprise,

Rex, thinking it was a real gun, reacted by pulling out an old Smith and Wesson 32 caliber pistol he had concealed under his shirt.

The Mexican standoff must have looked like something from the big screen until the doper pulled the trigger on the pellet gun. Rex felt the pellet bounce off his chest and instinctively fired his real pistol at the doper. He would never admit it, but at the time, he was confused and scared and pointed his handgun at the doper's head, closed his eyes, and pulled the trigger, shooting the doper in the thigh. Of course, he didn't hang around for the cops to show up.

The doper survived and immediately ratted on Rex. When the police found the pellet gun in some weeds near the scene where the doper tossed it before calling the police, the truth came out. Because the doper used what appeared to be a real gun during the confrontation, Rex was only charged with carrying a handgun without a license. The prosecutor's office didn't file any charges against Rex for shooting the doper, determining he was acting in self-defense.

Good thing the cops never found the handgun Rex used that night because, of course, it was stolen. He never felt bad about shooting the doper but, because of his criminal history, was sentenced to three months in jail for possession of the handgun offense. After the court hearing, he overheard his public defender joking with the judge that the incident reminded him of a childhood game, rock-paper-scissors. The doper had scissors, but Rex had rock. The whole thing had ended up working in Rex's favor. As a result of the conviction, he met Kenny the locksmith in jail. More importantly, because of the shooting, he also ended up with some incredibly useful street cred.

He opened the safe door and pulled out some old personal papers, an assortment of photos, a small open box with heirloom-type jewelry, a handful of old coins, and a purple Crown Royal bag with an interesting rattle when shaken and weighed enough to be encouraging. Hopefully, he could get enough money from the old coins to make the purchase of the stolen safe worth the effort. He got the safe from a thief he regularly did business with. The safe had pry marks on the edges of the door, which were left in an unsuccessful attempt at opening it. Rex offered five bucks for the unopened safe and the thief, unable to get it open, gladly accepted. It was a gamble, but at the time, Rex felt it was worth it. You never knew what could be in a home safe. Sometimes you would find cash, other times only personal papers, and once he discovered a stash of quaaludes. He retrieved a magnifying glass from his workbench to examine the coins. He was big and strong, but his eyesight was meager and weak. Disappointed after looking at the assortment of old dimes and buffalo nickels, he moved on to the Crown Royal bag. Immediately upon opening the bag, he was pleased. Rex could see a wad of two-dollar bills and a pound or two of junk silver coins. Junk silver usually consisted of pre-1965 United States coins. Before 1965, the U.S. government used real silver in the coin minting process, making those coins more valuable in today's market, not only to collectors but also to investors of precious metals. Rex had a couple of good contacts he could quickly sell these coins to.

He returned to his workbench, an old kitchen cabinet a neighbor put out for the trash Rex put into service in the rented garage and grabbed a bottle of vinegar and a work rag. After dampening the rag with some vinegar, he used the damp cloth to rub several pieces of the heirloom jewelry. After a few minutes of rubbing, each piece of jewelry revealed a nice shine, convincing him they were made of real gold. Had the jewelry turned dull instead, he would have assumed it to be worthless costume jewelry. He would dump the now empty safe into an unlocked dumpster a few blocks away and try to sell the coins and jewelry to the same fence he used to sell all the stuff he got from Piper. That is everything but the blank check.

Rex used dopers to cash forged checks and was careful not to handle the checks without using latex gloves. He insisted the dopers write out the checks themselves, telling them exactly what to write. Because you couldn't trust a common doper, he would drive the doper to a bank to cash the check while he waited outside. When the doper returned from inside the bank, Rex traded drugs for the cash the doper had just received. He figured the dopers all had a fake IDs, but that was their problem. Even if one got caught and ratted him out, the cops could never prove he was involved. Until the recent past, he often used a doper named Brian but didn't plan to use him anymore, that guy was getting too spaced out, and Rex couldn't trust him not to screw up. The last time he used Brian, after getting about a block from the bank they had just passed a forged check at, Brian remembered he had left his glasses inside and wanted to return to get them. Of course, he was high. Not wanting to be involved with him anymore, Rex refused and dropped him off at a dump Brian called home. It wouldn't be hard to find another desperate doper who would be happy to trade his services for some drugs.

Rex jammed the safe's contents into an old basketball he had modified and used to transport stolen property and drugs. Previously he had carefully cut a slit down a seam of a basketball to conceal stolen property inside. Because most basketballs keep their original shape, even when deflated, it would look normal enough at a casual glance. Once he had all the safe's contents securely tucked away, he simply tossed the basketball into the cargo area of his van. If he got stopped by the cops, they would never suspect the basketball, nor would anyone who might try to rip him off, which was his bigger concern. Because he didn't like keeping stolen stuff around, he tried to convert it into cash as soon as possible. Cash is king and not traceable. And speaking of cash, he had the perfect hiding place for that at home, inside a freezer bag stuffed in the bottom of a giant 143-ounce box full of powdered laundry detergent. No one would look for anything valuable in there.

CHAPTER 55

As he was getting ready to go out into the cold, Gill felt good about tonight. He preferred stealing from mailboxes instead of rummaging inside unlocked cars. He recently met Rex, who would buy pretty much any type of stolen gift card.

Gil wasn't sure what Rex did with the gift cards, but that guy wasn't stupid. Before he bought any of the cards, he used his cell phone to check the card numbers through a website that would give him the up-to-date balance on each card. If he was lucky, Rex would give him ten percent of the remaining gift card balance.

As he crossed the living room of the tiny trailer, Gran was perched in her chair in the living room. As usual, she was chain smoking those nasty brown cigarittos and drinking a mixture of cola with a little bit of Dog Legg Whiskey. Or, more likely, Dog Legg Whiskey mixed with a little bit of cola. She was engrossed in tonight's episode of Gilligan's Island and laughed out loud as Gilligan climbed a palm tree, causing a coconut to fall onto the Skipper's head. Gran laughed as the Skipper danced around, grabbing his head with both hands in obvious pain. He didn't find it unusual Gran would find someone getting injured to be funny. He worked his way through the thick cloud of cigaretto smoke in the living room as he was putting on his coat before walking out the trailer's front door. Navigating his bike through the snow had never been easy, and he really couldn't use it very well while doing mailbox thievery, so tonight, he was on foot. He started walking aimlessly past Wilford's burned-out trailer considering which neighborhoods within walking distance would be good pickings.

CHAPTER 56

"I hate that dog. I don't sleep well thinking about what that mangy mutt's been doing at night while I am at work. I just know he's on the bed doing that two-legged, butt rubbing, dog scoot on my pillow," Cory complained to Thaddeus while waiting for roll call to begin. "And my wife, she always wants me to take the little critter out for a walk. Yeah, right, it ends up more like a stop-and-sniff than a walk. Gee, next thing you know, I am taking it for a drag!" In a mocking voice, he added, "And my wife calls it her little angel."

Thaddeus answered in a sympathetic tone, "Sounds more like Satan's angel to me."

"You may be right, but at this point, when I'm around, it answers to *Get Lost*," Cory said with a snort.

Lt. Weber walked into the roll call room as Cory was finishing and said, "Let's get started before Cory calls Animal Control, okay? I have some interesting information to share, but first, Mel, where did you learn that spider monkey move that you used on that robot guy's back? I've never seen anything like that in any training video."

It was no surprise when Cory jumped in with, "I think at the police academy, it's called the Manual Back Grapple Take Down Maneuver."

Thaddeus added with a satisfied smile, "As opposed to the Mechanical Back Grapple Take Down Maneuver, which normally involves the use of a nightstick."

It was easy to make fun of police training because every defensive tactic, pistol range instruction, or emergency driving action had a long and complicated sounding name requiring at least four, three-syllable words and a dictionary to create the complete training title in an attempt to give it more credibility.

Mel, trying to ignore the good-natured taunts, added, "I heard that robot guy works as a program engineer for a big tech company, and this was his second meltdown."

Mark commented, "I think the guy's flipping nuts. But then, now that I think about it, I figure we all are completely insane. It's just that some of us handle it better than others."

Thaddeus said, "Maybe, but that dude was one potato short of a beef stew."

Cory looked over at Mel and in a serious manner explained, "I think that robot needs his hard drive reprogrammed."

Weber added, "By the way, Mel, you've gone viral." Mel looked over at Weber with a puzzled look as Weber continued, "Yeah, buddy, you're an internet sensation, imagine that! One of the trivia people posted a video online of the whole incident. You already have 310,000 views just since last night, and growing. Very impressive indeed!"

Mark, smiling broadly, jumped in with, "Hey Mel, I hear there's a lonely old widow in Nebraska that likes your moves and wants to meet you!"

Weber announced, "And Cory, your incident report on the arrest, nice job. I think we can safely assume you are the first police officer in the history of all law enforcement to ever use the phrase *staccato robotic sounding voice* in a police report. Enough of all that. Let's move on before we have an alien attack or something. We have lots of ground to cover."

Weber continued, "I have some good news. Detective Pierson cleared up the series of robberies we have been having. It seems he got a fingerprint match from a print lifted from the Imperial Liquor Store glass door. Pierson put that guy's mugshot into a photo line-up and got positive identifications that he was the person who robbed not only the Imperial Liquor Store but also the Easy Stop." Then while glancing at Teresa, he continued, "Oh, and he got another fingerprint match of the same perp from a latent fingerprint lifted from inside a recovered stolen vehicle that matched the description of a car used in one of the robberies." Looking directly at Teresa he continued, "it was that blue Malibu you found and processed the other day. Good work Teresa."

Everyone could hear Teresa quietly congratulating herself with a satisfied sounding, "Yes!"

Weber squinted a little as he read what must have been some fine print, "Oh, and here's our hold-up man's criminal history. Quite an accomplished young outlaw: shoplifting, another shoplifting, business burglary, residence burglary. Ah, no surprise here," he exclaimed as he looked up at the attentive group of police officers while pointing aggressively down at the sheet of paper he was reading from, "A robbery! And it appears there is an open arrest warrant for him for Vehicle Theft out of Florida. Unfortunately, it's marked as a no out-of-state extradition warrant. All this, and he's only 29 years old."

Thaddeus interrupted, "I know what to get this guy for Christmas, some gloves and a mask!"

Cory turned to smile at his friend, saying, "Thaddeus, that's just like you, always thinking about other people."

Weber continued, "And now for the unveiling," and held up an eight by ten color mug shot to show the officers. Mel abruptly sat forward in his seat and looked intently at the photo as Weber read the suspect's name, "One Patrick J. Sandpiper."

Mel immediately jumped up and walked quickly toward Weber, trying to get a better look at the mugshot, saying, "VendMate, that's the guy that was dumpster diving behind VendMate last night!" Mel grabbed the photo with both hands, holding it in front of his face and studied the mugshot. "I was in the process of identifying him and running a warrants check when I got called away to the disturbance with the robot guy." Infuriated, Mel stomped back to his seat while ranting to a mostly sympathetic group, "What's going on here in the U.S. nowadays? With that criminal history, why wasn't he still in jail for any one of those convictions? Instead, he's out here in Templeton, of all places, committing more robberies and who knows what else. And you know what, these rotten thugs, they keep on robbing until they get caught or die. They don't quit on their own." After a brief pause, he sat down and continued the tirade, "I know our politicians want to legalize all kinds of drugs, saying we've lost the war on drugs. Well, I tell you, because of crap like this, we've lost the war on crime!"

As usual, the rookie, Adam, had to look away and hide a grimace. Mel's frequent rants made him uncomfortable. He wanted to engage Mel in a civil discussion about the causes of criminal recidivism, such as biological risk factors, dysfunctional family lives, substance abuse issues, and criminal peers. Being a rookie on the shift, he had low standing in roll call. Anyway, it appeared Mel was so entrenched in his personal philosophies he doubted his educated reasoning would do any good. He had studied all this in college while pursuing his degree in sociology and learned that offender recidivism was a societal problem often entirely out of the offender's control. Once his probationary year is over, he might not be so quiet and submissive when Mel goes off like this. What Adam didn't know and would have surprised him was something Mel would never say out loud. Mel believed differences in political opinion, even extreme ones, were good for our county and protest without harm or damage could be a good tool needed for change.

CHAPTER 57

Not a bad night, Gil thought after another evening of holiday mailbox thievery. He took in another handful of lottery tickets, a $20 Walmart gift card, and two $10 bills. He got back to the trailer at about 3:00 a.m., but as he was climbing the porch steps, he thought it odd the television and the living room light were still on. He opened the front door, entered the trailer, and immediately understood. Gran was flat on her back, stretched out on the kitchen floor with thick dark red blood pooled around her right ear. He started to feel a crippling fear swell up inside him. Then he noticed blood spatter on the pointy corner of the kitchen counter and a beverage glass on the floor next to her with the contents spilled out and reeked of alcohol.

Gil was stunned and stood quietly still, trapped in a paralyzing panic only one step inside the open front door. The cold night air seeped in as he absent-mindedly gaped at the scene in front of him and tried to think. "Oh, no," he muttered without moving. He glanced to the corner of the living room at Gran's chair, where he saw an almost empty bottle of Dog Legg Whiskey sitting on the floor, and it became clear what had happened. Her face was a lifeless pale color, and her mouth was slightly open in an unnatural way. One of her legs was twisted awkwardly underneath her, but her eyes, why were they still wide open? Gil had no idea of time passing as he stood, stared, and thought.

What scared him most was what the police would think. They had been here before, and no, this would not look good for him. He had to get out of there and think. Minutes must have passed before he regained control of his body. He left Gran just as he found her but was careful to turn out all the lights and lock the door to the trailer as he left. Not wanting anyone to see him, Gil walked around to the back of the trailer.

Gran's trailer was in the last row of the trailer park. All the back windows faced a grassy field that sloped sharply down toward a retention pond being constructed as part of the new Rose Garden Villas housing edition. As he was walking around to the back corner of the trailer and into the darkness of their unlit small backyard, he stumbled into one of the fifty-five-gallon barrels Gran used so many years ago as individual swimming pools, knocking it over, then lost his balance before falling over the overturned barrel causing a loud clatter. Gil lay motionless in the snow for several minutes before looking around to see if anyone saw or heard him.

Thinking no one heard the noise, he pulled himself from the ground and sat on the rounded side of the overturned barrel facing the retention pond at the bottom of the hill. He had barely caught his breath while aimlessly gazing into the night in the direction of the pond when an idea came to him. He hoped no one had heard the clatter of him stumbling over the barrel but also hoped no one heard his almost silent snicker as he unconsciously uttered, "Now that's something to *pond*er," emphasizing the word pond.

CHAPTER 58

Jeramy was glad for the slow night, which gave him time to think. So much had happened recently, starting with Carl's death. Not that he'd been particularly close to Carl, no more or less than the other officers on the shift. What scared him was the idea of dying. What happened after death, really? Did Carl suffer when he died? Did he feel the pain of the injuries that caused his death? Why did Carl have to die? Was he in heaven, as the pastor suggested at the funeral, or does our soul, our inner being, die along with our bodies? When our bodies die, is that it, just an abrupt period at the end of our life's sentence?

These questions were hard for Jeramy to take in. And the things he found out about Carl later, about how he had been involved in doing so much good, which, honestly, at the time, Jeramy had not really noticed. Carl had done it all with little or no recognition, and it sure didn't appear he pursued any praise or appreciation. And Carl's family life was a thing to envy. He wondered about Carl's faith. If Carl had been so faithful, why did God take him so young, leaving behind two young daughters?

Jeramy turned these thoughts over in his mind, but it still made little sense to him. What did make sense was the impression Carl left on others in his wake. Finally, after a couple of hours of soul-searching during his silent patrol, Jeramy decided what he should want. He should want what Carl had, a life of service to others and a wonderful family life. But did he want it all, which would include putting his total faith in God? And what would that mean? He wanted to talk to Chaplain Gossett about these things. It occurred to him the chaplain often stopped by Dio's Pancake Palace for breakfast at about 6:00 a.m., so maybe he would drop by this morning before he got off work to see if the chaplain was there.

Sure enough, as Jeramy drove by Dio's Pancake Palace at 6:00 a.m., Gossett's police department-issued car was in the parking lot. Jeramy parked, entered the restaurant, and spotted the chaplain sitting in a booth toward the back. After greeting the chaplain and asking if he could sit and talk, he settled into the booth facing the chaplain.

The two made small talk for a few minutes, only briefly being interrupted by Dio bringing Jeramy a cup of coffee. Jeramy paused to sip his coffee and Gossett, always the direct type, asked, "You don't often join me for breakfast, and you seem a little, well, troubled. What's up?"

Jeramy looked up from his coffee and while not looking directly at the chaplain, said, "Well, plenty has happened lately, what with Carl and other things. I just, well, I was hoping I could talk to you." Jeramy looked down at the coffee cup he was holding with both hands and continued, "It's kinda about Carl, but other stuff too." Gossett sat quietly listening to Jeramy as he continued, "So many things I don't understand, you know, about God."

"Yes," Gossett replied, patiently waiting for more.

"As I said, it's not really about Carl, but it sorta is. Carl was such a good guy. I never really stopped to think about it. I had no idea, nor did I notice he did so many good things and had such faith in God," Jeramy said as Gossett nodded his head in agreement. "Why then, why did he have to die like that?" asked Jeramy, less as a question and more as a plea.

Gossett took a deep breath and replied, "As I have said before, there are so many things I don't have an answer to, so I just have faith that God is in control." Pausing to think, then added, "Control, maybe that's the problem. We try to control everything in our lives, but death is the one thing we can't control. Is that what's bothering you, dying?"

Jeramy looked at Gossett with an almost guilty look as the chaplain continued, "Jeramy, all of us, our lives are significant to God. That's why we have the Ten Commandments and the teachings of Jesus so we can live our best lives here. When you really consider them, these laws and teachings don't put restrictions on our lives, but obeying them, makes our lives better. Believe me, sin makes a mess of things. But as good as life can be here on earth, in the scope of eternity, our earthly lives are like a strobe light that shines brightly here but for a fraction of a second, then quickly fading away. Just know that while earthly life is short, eternity is forever."

Jeramy, distressed, almost pleading, said, "But Carl, the way the accident happened, it could have," pausing to think back on the keys dropping to the floor, then continued, "no, it should have been me that died, not Carl."

Gossett calmly replied, "So, do you believe God is in control or not?" After a brief pause, he said, "You've noticed Carl was a good guy, the things he did with his life? Did you know that he was a part of a group that visited the juvenile detention center once a month to minister to the kids being held there? Oh, and here's another one, he was also involved in a homeless ministry. That one was tough for Carl. He told me he never understood homelessness, what with all the public resources available. And jobs, yes, Carl knew jobs were out there, even some for the ones with criminal histories."

Jeramy listened closely and asked, "But what about the ones with mental illness?"

Gossett responded, "Carl talked about that. He knew many homeless people were mentally ill but figured there were many mentally ill people successfully working and with a place to call home. To Carl's credit, while he didn't understand homelessness, he felt a calling to get involved to see if there was something he could do. He started an annual cookout at the homeless shelter. But this wasn't an ordinary cookout," Gossett smiled as he shook his head side to side, "Oh no, it wasn't. Not only did the residents of the shelter enjoy the cookout, but Carl would assign them all duties to perform, such as grilling the burgers, setting up the tables, and cleaning up afterward. The key to the success of the cookout was inviting all the shelter's donors, the neighbors of the shelter, and local city officials. It only added to the success of the cookout when these stakeholders saw the joy on the faces of the homeless as they served the guests."

Gossett stopped and watched Jeramy before continuing, "Interesting, now that I think about it. Part of how Carl worshipped

God was the way he lived his life. Almost silently but persistently practicing his faith. But now, we know at least one person was affected by it." he hesitated a second, stared straight at Jeramy, and said, "You were. The good things you are now noticing about Carl, the things that are making you stop and think, might move you into action of your own. The way Carl lived his life and interacted with other people were like the seeds of faith Carl was planting. It seems you are just now seeing these signs of the seeds of his great faith. But please understand, and I want to stress Carl is not in Heaven because of all the good things he did. Carl is in Heaven because of his faith. It's as simple as that. His good works resulted from his acceptance of God's grace and faith which drove him to do God's will for his life."

After another pause, Gossett continued, almost matter-of-factly, saying, "You know, I was almost expecting to hear from you. Several weeks before he died, Carl told me he was praying for you. He said he felt God was at work on you. By the way, why did your parents name you Jeramy with the letter "a" instead of the more commonly spelled Jeremy with the letter 'e'?"

"Don't know. I guess they wanted it to be a little different, so it wasn't so common," replied Jeramy.

"Well, here is some food for thought," Gossett continued with a sly smile, "In ancient Hebrew, Jeramy with an 'a' means God will uplift."

Distracted with so much on his mind, Jeramy barely finished breakfast as Gossett politely used his napkin to wipe his lips, then asked, "Jeramy, I gotta get to the office and get to work, but before we leave, do you mind if I say a prayer for you?" After Jeramy nodded in the affirmative, Chaplain Gossett, in a low, clear voice, prayed, "Lord, we thank You for this day and every day You provide for us. I thank You for putting Carl in our lives. I pray that You cause an increase in Jeramy's faith in You. Please draw him close to You. Keep him from evil and teach him to love as You want us all to love. And please, Lord, give him the bravery to face life not only as a Christian but as a faithful Christian policeman. Amen."

Jeramy was used to pastors spouting off long windy, preachy prayers and was surprised at the brevity of this prayer. As the chaplain got up to go, Jeramy stopped him and sheepishly asked, "But one quick question. Are you scared to die?

Gossett dropped a couple of dollar bills on the table as a tip and, in an earnest tone, replied, "Jeramy, let me leave you with this. When a Jewish leader feared for his sick daughter's life, Jesus told him, 'Don't be afraid, just believe.'" After another pause, he added, "I may be frightened of the physical pain of death," then, looking directly at Jeramy, he continued with what looked like a gleam in his eyes, "but I don't think I can be threatened with the prospect of Heaven."

Jeramy finished the remainder of the uneventful shift and was restless as he arrived at his empty home. He searched through his bookshelf looking for a Bible, thinking every house had to contain a Bible, even his, didn't it? Finally, on the far end of the bottom shelf, he pulled out an old Bible, which must have belonged to his mother. He flipped it open and pointed to a verse at random, hoping to find meaning in such an arbitrary verse selection. "Humm, Proverbs 11:1, 'The Lord detests dishonest scales, but accurate weights finds favor with Him,'" Jeramy uttered. "Well, that took me nowhere. How about another spin of the Bible verse roulette wheel," he spoke out loud as he flipped through a couple of hundred pages of the Bible. "Okay, let's try this one, Jeremiah 2:23, 'How can you say, I am not defiled, I have not run after the Baals.'" Nope, Jeramy thought, better try again, this time landing on 1 Corinthians 3:6. He yawned before he read, "I planted the seed, Apollos watered it, but God has been making it grow." Jeramy, now very tired, reasoned he didn't need any farming advice, closed the Bible, and made his way to bed.

CHAPTER 59

Gil pushed the fifty-five-gallon barrel upright, then walked aimlessly around town thinking while avoiding what he knew he must do. He had the barrel, a shovel, and a burial place. What else would he need? There were other things he should probably be considering. Fortunately, there were no other family members who lived close who might bother to care about either Gil or Gran, so no problems there. The last time he had seen any extended family was three years ago when Cousin Earl dropped by trying to borrow money. Gil chased him off and hadn't heard from him since. He wondered if the neighbors would notice Gran was gone. He really wasn't sure, after all, she rarely left the trailer, and he ran most of her errands. Heck, they didn't even have a car anymore.

He was sitting on a bus stop bench, straining to think when it came to him. If anyone bothered to ask, he would say he had to put Gran in the county nursing home. After all, Gran hadn't done much to cultivate friendships, so it was doubtful anyone would think to visit her at the county home. If any suggested they might want to visit, he planned to explain her condition was so bad it prevented her from having visitors. Considering her current circumstances, that would be about the most truthful thing he had said in a long time. He was sure no one would have a problem with the nursing home explanation. He would just let the Social Security people keep depositing that monthly check into Gran's bank account while he used her debit card to withdraw the cash. Lucky thing he had used the ATM for Gran in the past otherwise, he wouldn't know the debit card PIN number.

It was almost daybreak when Gil returned to the trailer and got to work. Gran never got rid of the barrels behind the trailer, so he went to check them out. There were about half a dozen barrels, but he found only one with a lid, which fortunately fit snuggly. It had his cousin's name, Gladys, painted in faded pink on the side. While the barrel wasn't free of rust, it was in good enough condition for the use he had in mind, and anyway, Gladys hadn't cared much for Gran.

The empty barrel was heavier and more awkward to handle than he expected. He had to huff and puff to get it up the back porch steps and through the trailer's back door. He managed to get the barrel into the living room, then gently tipped it down onto its side. Now came the dirty work of getting Gran into the barrel. But first, he looked around to see what needed to be cleaned. The blood next to Gran's head had settled into a disgusting thick dark red mass that looked to be drying. There was blood splatter on the corner of the kitchen counter and other splatters on the floor, but thankfully, not too much to clean. Getting Gran into the barrel would be another matter.

Other than in a funeral home, Gil had never seen a dead body, much less touched one, and he sure didn't want to touch this one. He was pacing the tiny living room, looking down, staring at the threadbare, six-foot by six-foot area rug, when a thought came to him. The rug, he could roll Gran up into the living room rug. The thought of this caused a sly grin to creep up on his face as he unconsciously murmured in a low soft voice, "You know, kinda like a Gran Burrito." He started to snicker, thinking, "Too bad she hated Mexican food."

Gil moved what little furniture there was in the living room that was in his way of dragging the rug into the kitchen next to Gran. As he crouched next to her body, he smelled a foul odor and wondered if it resulted from natural decomposition. Curious, he leaned over close, sniffed deeply, then stood up slowly. Turing his head up at an angle, he considered the odor while in deep thought, much like a professional wine steward when sniffing a fine wine. After a few seconds he shook his head side to side thinking, "Naw, she's always smelled like that."

Wanting to get this nasty chore over, he grabbed Gran's arm and began to pull her onto the area rug. He was surprised at how stiff she was but even more surprised when he turned Gran sideways, and blood gushed out of the gash in the side of her head onto the rug. Gil reacted by quickly rolling Gran over, face down, onto the rug. After tucking one corner of the area rug under her arm before rolling her over a couple more times, completely wrapping her into the rug. He relaxed, exhausted from the effort. It had been a long night, and so far, the morning hadn't been much of a picnic either.

He walked over to the shabby living room sofa, intending to sit for just a few minutes, but as he sat there and stared at the rolled-up rug, he unintentionally faded into a deep slumber.

CHAPTER 60

Derek got to the office early. After checking his email, he was pleased to find one from the county prosecutor's office with an attachment containing the subpoena that would compel Brian Sanders to submit to providing handwriting samples. He figured it was too early to go looking for Sanders, so he finished an assortment of paperwork on different files, then started reviewing a few incident reports recently assigned to him. It was early afternoon before Derek finished the paperwork and decided to look for Sanders. He did an incident report inquiry on Sanders, finding a police report from a few months prior where Sanders and a woman named Yvette Treat were arrested for shoplifting. Derek printed the police report, jammed it into the forgery case file, and set out in search of Sanders.

There was no answer to Derek's knock on the apartment door at the four-plex and he wasn't convinced Sanders still lived there. Addicts tend to move on a regular basis. He thumbed through the case file looking for other recent addresses and pulled out the shoplifting report. He didn't see any information relating to Sanders that would be helpful. He noticed a work phone number for Treat. Derek pulled out his cell phone, masked the call so his number wouldn't be displayed on the receiver's phone, and dialed the number. He wasn't surprised when he got a voicemail recording stating the address and hours of operation for Olivia's Gentleman's Club.

Strip clubs like Olivia's were usually closed during daytime hours. Derek had learned from other investigations some of their employees arrived for work late in the afternoon to prepare for the evening's business. He busied himself with other work as he waited until late in the afternoon when he drove to Olivia's Gentleman's Club and parked in the back lot, close to the rear door. The door was unlocked, so he walked in. Working as a detective, he had learned that if he wore a sports coat and tie while handling himself with a certain air of confidence, he could breeze into most situations and obtain the cooperation he needed. Such was the case when he walked by the men's restroom, which was propped open, and noticed a guy cleaning a toilet. The bathroom looked disturbingly filthy, and Derek had no plans to enter that germ factory. If pressed for a description, he would guess the walls were painted white, but the paint had faded badly or just oddly stained. He didn't know which and didn't care to ask. There were three bathroom sinks on one wall, one of which had an out-of-order sign leaning against the faucet. There were no doors on the toilet stalls, the walls of which were covered in handwriting, except for the areas where the paint was chipped.

The cleaning guy was leaning over, vigorously brushing out a toilet, when he noticed Derek standing in the bathroom doorway. He stopped scrubbing and stood up straight as he turned to look at Derek for a few seconds without saying anything. Derek broke the silence by asking if the manager was around. The guy turned back to the toilet and replied, "Check the bar." Derek, professionally polite to everyone, replied, "Thank you," turned and walked through a doorway and into a large open area.

A stage was built into one side of the room. It was set up about three feet off the main floor and was bare other than a cheap red carpet, a couple of large audio speakers, and two vertical brass poles, six feet apart that extended from the floor to the ceiling, which for a room this large, seemed very low. Stage lights were attached to the ceiling and aimed at the stage. Tables and chairs were scattered all around the big room, and of course, there were chairs pushed up to the edge of the stage for what Derek would, if asked, delicately describe as better viewing. There was another chair at the side of the stage that faced all the other chairs, and he knew that was where a bouncer would sit to monitor the customers. The main entrance was on the opposite wall from where he was standing. A podium with a small flashlight resting on top stood next to the front door and was used by the doorman as he collected cover charges and checked patron identifications. All the overhead lights in the main room were on. Derek knew this would not be the case during regular operating hours when the only illumination would be from the stage lights, a dim light over the bar, and the flashlight the doorman used while checking identifications.

Derek had always thought strip clubs were extremely dark on the inside during regular evening and nighttime operating hours. He never fully realized why until the first time he had the opportunity to visit one during the day while working on another investigation. Of course, there were no windows, but he was surprised to discover all four walls in the main room were painted in a solid flat black. Another thing he hadn't realized was how dirty those black walls were. He was disgusted and uncomfortable in strip clubs. The first time he entered a strip club during the day before operating hours, with all the lights on, well, disgusted couldn't completely describe how he felt. He was always careful never to touch anything while inside any strip club and always felt unclean until after leaving. Of course, he vigorously scrubbed his hands clean with strong soap at his first opportunity.

The bar was across from the stage, and as Derek was looking around, a rotund bald man impatiently yelled at Derek, "You need something mister?"

Not wanting the other employees to know why Derek was there, he walked toward the man and asked, "You the manager?"

"Yeah, what do ya want?" the man replied.

Derek moved his sports jacket aside enough to expose the badge he had clipped to his belt and said, "I'm with the Templeton Police. You gotta dancer here that goes by the name Treat?" He knew this was the tricky part. The manager could always say no, then warn Treat the police were looking for her. Or, and this was often the case, the manager would cooperate, giving Derek the requested information, hoping his cooperation would come in handy if in a pinch somewhere down the road.

The manager turned to face Derek, "Yeah, I do, Yvette Treat. I hope she isn't in some kind of trouble. I need her dancing in here tonight."

Derek assured him, "Oh, no, she's not in any trouble, but I'm looking for a guy named Sanders, Brian Sanders. He might be living with her. You know how I can find him?"

Derek could sense the manager was weighing it over, just how much trouble giving information about Sanders would cause him, compared to the advantage of having a neighborhood cop that might be inclined to be friendly at a time when he was in need. After a few seconds, the guy said, "Yeah, he picks Yvette up after work every night. He drives an old tan Chevy Impala. I don't want no trouble in here. You wanna pick him up, please, please get him before he gets into our parking lot, please!" the manager begged, holding his hands together as if in prayer. "I don't want no trouble in here. Yvette gets off work around three in the morning, and he usually waits for her in the rear parking lot. I would seriously appreciate it if you could catch him someplace other than here." the manager begged.

As Derek listened, he decided to return to Olivia's at about 2:45 a.m. that following morning, knowing Yvette would not be leaving until 3:00 a.m. In Indiana, bars can sell alcohol until 3:00 a.m. When the dancers weren't on stage, they mingled with the crowd trying to hustle liquor sales, of which they earned a commission.

The manager smiled and quickly added, "I'm Ricky Melbourne. Glad to help you."

Knowing what the manager was getting at, Derek smiled while handing Melbourne his police department business card. As he turned to leave, he told Melbourne, "I will do my best. Thanks for the help."

CHAPTER 61

Pierson couldn't figure out why it was so difficult to make contact with a retired piano tuner, but was finally able to reach Wayne Thompson by phone, arranging to meet at Thompson's residence. When he arrived, Thompson answered the door wearing a red t-shirt. The shirt had "In Tune But Strung Out" printed boldly in green on the front with musical notes surrounding a cartoon drawing of an angry-looking long-haired man sitting on a piano stool, pounding furiously on the keys of a grand piano, lid open to show the piano strings vibrating wildly. He assumed this was considered good humor within the piano tuning industry but refused to smile anyway. After the perfunctory introduction of "I'm the detective investigating your case," he got down to business and asked. "Can you identify the guy that robbed you at the ATM?"

Thompson squirmed a bit and said, "I'm not sure, it was dark, and it happened so fast."

Pierson had the impression all along that Thompson wasn't interested in prosecuting the offender or in seeing his robbery cleared. A police report was made, he had a good suspect, and he would investigate this case as well as he could, regardless of the victim's lack of interest. "I'm going to show you some photos," he said and went through the exact same spiel with every photo line-up he conducted. He explained how to view the photos in the photo line-up, with instructions to not pay any attention to things that can change, such as hairstyle or color. He continued instructing, "Concentrate on things that don't change, such as the shape of the face, nose, and lips." If Pierson ever had to testify in court on how he conducted any particular photo line-up, he didn't have to rely on his memory because he performed each one the exact same way. Thompson looked at the photos, but the way he was acting, Pierson knew he wasn't going to identify anyone, even if the hold-up man was one of the persons pictured. Frustrating as it was, it happened often. Some people just didn't want to get involved in court proceedings no matter what, and it appeared Thompson was one of those people.

After Thompson stammered, "Nope, sorry detective, I just can't help you with these photos." Pierson thanked him for his time and returned to his office.

CHAPTER 62

Gil was startled when he woke up, not knowing where he was, and suddenly became fully conscious when he looked down at the rolled-up rug. Jumping up, he moved to the living room window and adjusted the blinds enough to see the sun was going down and realized he had slept all day. He was tempted to pop some dexies to get him through the ordeal ahead but decided against it, reasoning he needed a clear head to finish the job. He planned to get Gran into the barrel, clean up the mess, and dispose of any bloody rags inside the barrel before securing the lid. He would worry about getting it down the hill when the time came.

Gil judged the barrel was almost four feet tall and Gran was just shy of five feet. All he had to do, he figured, was to fold her over once, then squeeze the folded human burrito into the barrel. She was a tiny woman, so it shouldn't be tough. He picked up one end of the rug and was surprised at how little it weighed, but as he lifted it up, there was no bend in the middle as he had expected. He set the rug back on the floor and tried to fold it over from the other end, with the same result. He wondered if she was in what those old police shows called rigid morris or whatever you call it. Aggravated, he gave the situation some serious thought. Then he wondered, a crease, like the creases made in a sheet of paper before being folded into a paper airplane. He needed to make a crease across the middle of the rug, and Gran, to make it easier to fold the mess over long ways. He couldn't put a crease into that rug with his fingers like he had the childhood paper airplanes, but after scanning the living room, his eyes landed on the baseball bat Gran propped by the front door.

Gran had always been scared someone would break into their trailer and try to steal something, as if they possessed anything worthy of thievery. As a precaution, she placed a baseball bat next to the front door. He had no doubt if some idiot tried to break into the trailer through the front door, Gran wouldn't have hesitated to step into the batter's box and take some serious swings at the unfortunate burglar who wandered into that strike zone. Gil moved to the front door, grabbed the bat by the handle, and wasted no time stepping up and furiously swinging toward the middle of the rolled-up rug.

Making contact, he flinched at the cracking noise. Wondering if the bat had cracked, he checked it for damage. Satisfied it was sound, he took a few more strokes before deciding it was time to try to fold the rug over again. On the second attempt at folding the rug over, it gave enough that he heard more cracking when he applied more pressure. The then rug folded down into a size he figured he could shove into the barrel. Gil rolled the open end of the barrel to the folded rug. Refusing to fail, he pushed and shoved the rolled-up and folded-over rug containing Gran until it was all squeezed into the barrel. Relieved that the chore was complete, he then struggled to tip the barrel up on its end. Once upright, he took both ends of the old thinning rug sticking out the top and folded them down, stuffing them into the open top end of the barrel.

At first, he wondered how he would clean the blood from the floor, then grabbed some of Gran's old shirts, figuring they now weren't good for anything else. It wasn't as if Gran had a pantry full of household cleaning products. In fact, the only cleaner in the trailer beside a rarely used bar of hand soap in the bathroom was some seldom used dish soap. He had to remove the mound of dirty dishes from the kitchen sink to use the faucet to dampen one of the old shirts. He added some dish soap and then used the shirt to rub the blood off the corner of the kitchen counter. The blood was dry, so he had to use some elbow grease to get it all off. Next, he wiped up the blood spatters from the linoleum kitchen floor, working his way to the large mass of blood where Gran's head had landed. He wasn't sure if he could get all that blood off the floor with just rags, so he improvised by pulling a dirty spatula out of the kitchen sink and scooping up the blood with several swipes of the spatula. He was surprised at how thick and heavy the mass of blood was but was able to scoop most of it up and onto one of Gran's shirts, which he had spread out on the floor just for this purpose. He dampened another of Gran's old shirts and used it to wipe the remaining blood from the floor. Once done, he tied together the corners of the shirt that held most of the blood and tossed it, the other bloody rags, along with the blood-stained spatula, into the open barrel.

Gil fetched the solid metal lid and placed it onto the top of the barrel, using it like a shield as he pushed the rug and bloody rags protruding from the top down into the barrel far enough to put the lid in place. Using a hammer, he tapped around the edge of the lid, bringing it down tight. Once the lid was properly seated on the barrel rim, he sealed the barrel closed with a metal band that wrapped around the edge of the lid. Next, he pulled the hinged lever, attached to the metal band, over, locking the lid tightly onto the barrel. Hearing the snap of the hinge as it locked into place, he let out a sigh of relief. Now, all that was left to do was wait until the middle of the night to finish the job.

CHAPTER 63

Cory already had a bad day even before he arrived for roll call. One of his kids woke him up early to inform him that the cover to their above-ground swimming pool had blown away, jeopardizing this fall's winterization. The very same pool he dearly hated. Between cleaning it, treating the pool water, maintaining the water pump, staining the deck, and of course, winterizing it, he figured he spent more time working in and around the pool than all his kids put together did playing inside it. According to Cory, if you wanted to punish someone, put a pool in their backyard. To wake him up early to give him the bad news only compounded his already existing grief. Earlier, his wife had shown him a Christmas gift she had purchased for their young daughter. It was a doll playhouse she'd really wanted. It needed to be assembled before Christmas Eve, and it looked like the instructions were written in Korean. Of course, this task would fall to him.

Cory didn't think he was an unhappy man, even though he felt he had all the evidence to prove otherwise. Sadly, deep down, he felt most happy when he was asleep. Considering the totality of his current life, all he really wanted was to be a missing person. To be fair, his wife might also want him to be a missing person. But he wasn't. He was a dutiful husband, a patient father, and a late shift policeman waiting in roll call for his assignment. He dismissed these melancholy thoughts and shifted his attention to Lt. Weber, who was starting roll call.

Weber began by announcing everyone's patrol assignments. He also reminded the officers, "Make sure you check the bulletin board and review the Sandpiper mugshot and personal information before leaving roll call." He shuffled through more papers, then reading from one, "Hastings Repo emailed information on a couple of cars they plan to snatch tonight. Make sure you check this list before you take any vehicle theft reports during the shift." Setting that memo aside, and after scanning the next, Weber said, "And let's get more patrol around the grocery stores. Gordon's Grocers had another purse grab in the parking lot on the evening shift. Maybe a patrol car cruising the area will slow the perps down."

Weber picked up the roll call clipboard and cracked a smile while reading a police report. "Okay," he began, looking at Thaddeus, then Cory, and smiled as he announced, "Seems the evening shift took a medical identity theft report. If I read this correctly, Wanda Milligan, who lives on Jefferson Street, reported she recently received an invoice for, well, let's just say, some elective surgery, which she claims she never received. A check on her credit report indicated that in addition to this medical procedure, there were a couple of unauthorized credit pulls for various department store credit cards."

Mel sat back in his seat and patiently folded his arms across his chest while he slowly and calmly asked, "Okay, lieutenant, tell us exactly what this elective surgery was for?"

Weber cheerfully answered, "Breast augmentation surgery!"

With a serious look on his face, Thaddeus chimed up, "*Undercover* work may be necessary for this investigation."

Cory jumped in, "Yeah, ya think the detectives will set up a *booby* trap for the suspect."

Thaddeus responded in a serious tone, "I think she is hiding out in *Silicone* Valley."

At this point in the exchange, Thaddeus and Cory, who were sitting next to each other, were now face to face launching one bad pun after another. "I bet this investigation is gonna end up with a couple of *big busts*," said Cory.

Thaddeus waved his hands in a dismissive gesture while countering, "Any *melon*-head could clear this case."

Back to Cory, who was rubbing his forehead as if in pain, "This is the kinda incident that sure can get under your skin."

Thaddeus, pointing at Cory, came back with, "You're just making *mountains* outta *molehills* fella."

In a mischievous tone, Cory added, "I bet she had only the *breast* of intentions." There was a slight pause in the exchange as

Thaddeus temporally ran out of relevant bad puns. He was thinking of an appropriate comeback when Cory quipped, "If my *mammary* serves me right, it's your turn."

Teresa couldn't take anymore and, in an expression of exasperation, threw her hands up in the air as if in surrender as she walked out of the roll call room, muttering, "So many men, so few brains!"

CHAPTER 64

Gil decided to wait until between 2:00 a.m. and 3:00 a.m., when all his neighbors would hopefully be in bed and asleep, to roll the barrel down the hill and bury it in the retention pond. It was hard to relax in the trailer with that fifty-five-gallon drum and its contents just sitting in the living room, almost accusingly staring back at him. Pulling back the living room curtain just a bit, he peeked out the front window, then looked back at the barrel and decided he would rather be outside in the cold than inside and warm with that barrel. Maybe he could walk to the Burger Boy and, if it was still open at this time of night, grab a burger. He walked over to Gran's chair where she usually sat, reached down, and grabbed her purse. He pulled out two crisp $20 bills from a billfold and declared, "She won't be needing these," as he stuffed the bills into his pants pocket and then grabbed his coat and walked out of the trailer into the cold, snowy night.

Gil, hands deep in his pockets, trying to keep them warm, looked down while deep in thought as he walked up to State Road 76. He intended to cross the highway, but his mind was racing, wondering how long it would take to dig a hole deep and large enough to bury a fifty-five-gallon barrel and not be noticed. A loud car horn startled him as he stepped off the curb. Thankfully he looked up in time to avoid the car headlights coming straight at him as he was about to walk into the street.

Teresa had just left roll call and was patrolling some low-income residential Templeton neighborhoods. She was driving around on patrol, admiring the outdoor Christmas decorations adorning many of the homes. This was an area where the residents could least afford elaborate decorations. Nonetheless, many apparently splurged. She wondered to herself what the attraction to all the strands of plain tiny white Christmas lights was. What happened to all the colored Christmas lights? She was an old-fashioned girl and preferred the Christmas traditions of her youth, including the classic ceramic, C-9 colored Christmas light bulbs.

There was a fresh, clean coat of white snow covering the ground, which was getting deeper as the snow continued to fall. Teresa noticed a fresh coat of snow on every roof-top in this housing edition except for one, which was completely free of any snow on the northwest corner of the roof. She drove through the alley behind the house and noticed windows below that area of the roof had been blacked out, and an exterior surveillance camera was mounted to the back corner. She noted the address with intentions to forward this information to the Metro Drug Task Force, thinking there was a possibility that underneath that part of the roof may be a space used as a marijuana grow room. Large indoor marijuana grow rooms require many lights, which use a considerable amount of electricity. This could throw off enough heat to warm the roof enough to prevent snow from accumulating. In addition, these same grow rooms require more water than a typical household would use. The task force could check utility records on water and electric usage, comparing it to normal residential usage in that neighborhood. They could also conduct surreptitious trash pulls, hopefully revealing trash related to grow room products. With any luck, all this information could lead to a larger investigation.

Interrupting her patrol, the dispatcher contacted Teresa over the police radio sending her to State Road 76 and Pennington Row to investigate a property damage accident. She was approaching an intersection, traveling in the right-hand lane of the four-lane highway, when she noticed a scraggly-looking guy, maybe homeless, almost stumble into the road in front of her. She honked her car horn at the guy and narrowly avoided him by moving to the inside lane. Disgusted, she thought, "Now there's a bug looking for a windshield," and planned to return and check on him after taking the accident report.

Hearing the car horn, Gil quickly jumped back from the street. He almost tripped over a raised buckle in the sidewalk but looked up in time to notice a police car driving away from him. "That was close," he mumbled out loud. He stood in that one spot for a long minute, still spooked from all the evening's activities.

CHAPTER 65

"What does it take to hire good help nowadays?" Dio asked Carolyn as she waited for him to finish placing the just-cooked omelet and hash browns onto a sturdy serving plate. This was a familiar outburst of Dio's. The last couple of years, he had trouble hiring good cooks for all shifts, much less the midnight shift. Eventually, he began to arrive at the restaurant at about 2:00 a.m., right before it got busy, when the bars started to close at 3:00 a.m. He didn't mind the cooking and guessed he really didn't mind the crazy hours. What bothered him was the lazy people claiming they couldn't find work while he regularly advertised for cooks and waitresses with little response. He was equally bothered by people who suggested that if he just offered to pay the prospective applicants a higher wage, he would be able to find the needed employees. Dio knew those very same people would complain each time he had to increase the prices at his restaurant because of rising costs. What did those people think, that he was getting rich working in the middle of the night?

At least while he was the cook, he could make sure the omelets were prepared to perfection, and the hash browns were crisp and slightly browned. He set a plate full of steak and eggs under the heat lamp on the wide ledge of the window that separated the kitchen from the dining room as he noticed Mel and Cory enter the front door. He smiled and waved broadly at the two, greeting them with a hearty, "Good morning officers! You're early this morning."

Both officers waved fondly back to Dio as they took their usual seats. What the officers didn't know, but could have suspected, was when Dio was younger, he wanted to be a policeman. Unfortunately, that nagging little thing about citizenship kept him from applying for the job. What the officers did know was that before Dio, a tall, stocky, well-built man, started the restaurant, he had been a professional wrestler using the stage name, "The Dio-Stroyer." He retired from wrestling after suffering a careering-ending back injury due to an opponent's over-enthusiastic use of the feared and effective Elevated Double Strut Chicken-Wing Fling. Dio liked almost every Templeton officer he had met, but it was the big officer named Mel he admired most.

Dio was particularly impressed when Mel was inside Dio's one early morning, drinking coffee and eating breakfast. A drunk sitting a few tables away, unbeknownst to almost everyone else in the diner, began to choke on an oversized sausage and biscuit sandwich. Mel spotted the trouble immediately and calmly walked the few steps to the drunk, who, with a terrified look on his face, was now holding his neck with both hands while leaning over his food. Dio watched in amazement as Mel literally picked the drunk up from behind and held him off the ground, the drunk's feet dangling loosely, as he performed the Heimlich maneuver. After three vigorous abdominal thrusts, a chunk of partially chewed sausage spewed from the drunk's open mouth, bouncing onto the table. As Dio remembered the incident, it appeared the drunk immediately realized the big policeman had just saved his life and was turning to thank him, but paused, put a hand to his mouth, then puked brownish-yellow stomach contents all over the big policeman's right pants leg. The drunk sheepishly tried to apologize as Mel dispassionately looked down at his vomit-covered leg, then picked up a couple of napkins from the drunk's table and, without expression, slowly wiped the biggest of the chunks of vomit off his pants and onto the tile floor. He then dropped the puke-covered napkins onto the drunk's plate, then, without ever speaking a word, returned to his table. Mel calmly and quietly resumed eating his breakfast, ignoring the dining room patrons that had finally noticed the incident as it was in progress and started to cheer and clap.

There was another early morning the big policeman and his partner were in Dio's. Two drunks sitting across from each other at one table got into a loud argument. Dio hoped it wouldn't lead to a fight when the big policeman stood up. The dining room went completely silent as the policeman slowly, yet confidently, strode toward the table where the arguing drunks were sitting. He was an imposing site standing arm's length in front of the two drunks, again, not saying a word, just glaring down at them. As Dio watched the big policeman, he thought Mel looked like a giant Mexican prairie rat about to go so loco no one would dare to cross him. Obviously scared, a third drunk at the table held up his cell phone to show the big policeman and asked, "Can I just call a cab for the three of us?" After silently glaring at the three for what seemed like minutes, the big policeman slowly nodded his head in the affirmative. The confident way he handled himself was a physical warning to the drunks. After the quick phone call to arrange a cab, without ever having said a word, the big policeman returned to his table and quietly stared in the direction of the drunks as he quaffed down the rest of his pancakes. As Dio watched, Mel never quit staring at the drunks until a cab pulled up in front of the restaurant. The three drunks quickly scampered out the front door and into the waiting cab. Dio was in absolute awe of how the big policeman could control a situation with only his posture and demeanor.

This morning Mel took his usual seat at his customary table, and Cory plopped down across from him. Carolyn hurried over with two coffee cups and a fresh pot of hot coffee. She grinned as she served Mel first, saying, "You're early tonight."

With a soft smile, Mel looked up at Carolyn and replied, "Sorry to upset the schedule, but we just finished up a domestic report and thought an early breakfast might be nice." Mel's heart warmed as he watched the pretty smile she flashed his way.

Cory, unaware of the moment occurring between the two, was intent on ordering his breakfast and, while staring at the menu, told Carolyn, "I think I'll have the Denver Omelet, hash browns, and sourdough toast. Oh, and, ah, some ranch dressing for the hash browns."

Mel glanced at Cory with a questioning look. Cory tapped the table slightly with the handle end of his fork as he defended himself with, "Ranch dressing, didn't ya know, it's the new ketchup!"

"What about your diet?" Mel protested.

"I don't need that anymore," Cory said as he stood up next to the table, legs shoulder length apart, setting his palms on his hips with his elbows extended in a quasi-Superman pose. "Haven't you noticed? My body's a weapon."

"Yeah, maybe like a suicide bomber!" Mel chuckled, then turned back to Carolyn and ordered his breakfast.

The officers were talking and sipping their coffee while waiting for their food when Cory asked Mel, "So you stopped that hold-up guy, Sandpiper, the other night, eh?"

"Yeah," Mel replied, "Wish I'd known then what I know now. Woulda locked him up for trespassing or something. You know, he looked homeless. I just can't understand why someone would choose to live that way. Seems to me that being homeless might require more effort than simply working for a living."

Carolyn appeared with their food just as Mel was finishing his sentence. As she was setting their food on the table, Cory looked toward a large group seated at the other end of the restaurant that had just been served their food. When everyone in that group bowed their heads for prayer, Cory asked Carolyn, "Where are they from?"

Carolyn answered, "That's a church group from Tennessee. They are a nice bunch of folks. They're headed home after a week of mission work in eastern Michigan. Because of delays caused by road construction work in northern Indiana, the Federal DOT regulations required the bus driver to stop because he was timed out. They all came in to eat during the wait."

Cory looked at Carolyn as if he didn't understand.

Mel turned in his seat to get a good look at the group. As the group sat and prayed, Mel added, "They were probably helping some poor families fix up their houses or something."

"Oh," responded Cory, satisfied with the response.

The sight of the group and the fact that they would take the time and effort, probably at their own expense, to travel and help others who were less fortunate than themselves caused Mel to stop and think.

Still deep in thought, Mel turned back in his seat and noticed Carolyn reaching into a pocket of her apron. She fumbled around until she pulled out a small handsome jewelry box and handed it to a surprised Mel, saying, "It would mean a lot to me if you would carry this with you while you are on duty." She looked down bashfully and continued, "I worry about you sometimes."

Mel looked intently at the small box he now held in his big hand as he said, "I don't know what to say." Carolyn patiently waited as he opened the box to reveal a silver-colored, small Saint Michael's necklace. The pendant was in the shape of a police badge, complete with Mel's badge number 30 custom engraved at the bottom. Touched by the gift, it took Mel a few seconds to take it all in. Then, still seated, he looked up at the standing Carolyn and, in his most sincere voice and matching facial expression, added, "No, I'm sorry, I do know what to say. Carolyn, thank you so very much."

Carolyn set her hand on Mel's shoulder and smiled while she replied, "You're welcome," then turned and walked to a table where a young couple had just been seated.

Mel was still looking at the pendant he held in his hand while Cory leaned over the table to get a better look and asked, "What's that?"

Eyes still locked on the pendant, Mel explained, "It is a Saint Michael's necklace."

Cory stared blankly, so Mel continued, "Okay, as a good Catholic boy, we learned this stuff in Catholic school. See, Saint Michael is an Archangel, and his job is to defend the church. But he also protects people from evil." As he was talking, Mel was surprised he remembered such a thing from school. He looked at Cory, who appeared to be confused, then added, "It may be a Catholic thing, but lots of policemen wear a Saint Michael's necklace on duty, you know, kinda for good luck." As Mel continued to look at the pendant affectionately, he continued, "But understand, it's more than a luck thing. For many people, it is a faith thing."

Cory asked, "You a Catholic?"

Looking straight at Cory, Mel, in his sober deep voice, explained, "I will take strength from anything God provides."

Cory asked, "So you went to Catholic school when you were little?"

Mel replied, "Well, my mom was a Baptist, but there weren't any Baptist schools around, so for elementary school, my mother sent me to a Catholic school. Later, she told me she figured I would get better discipline there than in public school. She also said she wanted me to get a good grounding in religion." He looked at Cory, who appeared content with the explanation, then stole a glance over at Carolyn as she was attending to the young couple. He slipped the necklace over his head, briefly running his fingers over the pendant before tucking it under his uniform shirt.

Cory was surprised to hear all this talk about God and religion from a tough guy like Mel and couldn't wait to tell Thaddeus about the gift Carolyn gave him. Looking in Carolyn's direction with a child-like puzzled expression on his face, Cory naively asked, "Why is she so nice to you?"

Mel winked at Cory, who had begun to wolf down his omelet, and in a confident voice, suggested, "Maybe I'm some kind of nice eye candy, eh?"

Cory almost choked on his food at the thought and shot back with, "Yeah, right, like a sour apple sucker!" After clearing his throat with a big swallow, he continued with that goofy smile of his, "You know Mel, you're just like a fine wine," dragging out the word fine while holding his right hand up with this thumb and forefinger pinched together much like an orchestra conductor would do when holding a note, then after a strategic pause continued with, "You just keep aging!"

CHAPTER 66

Detective Pierson was the kind of policeman who, while he didn't always like it, did what had to be done. He didn't enjoy working cases late at night, but tonight he needed to look for Patrick Sandpiper. After reviewing incident histories, it appeared Sandpiper was most criminally active between 1:00 a.m. and 4:00 a.m. He planned to use his unmarked patrol car to cruise between all the Templeton late-night establishments that handled cash and were open during those hours. This was a detail he should not have been conducting alone, but Pierson figured he wasn't likely to find Sandpiper and didn't want to bother the other detectives. No matter, he preferred to work alone. If he spotted Sandpiper, he planned to call for backup, then wait for help to arrive before making a move on him. He stopped at the Easy Stop store for a large coffee to keep him company. Afterward, he began a slow regular patrol between businesses, checking the surrounding areas for any vehicle which might look out of place. He sipped the coffee slowly, thinking it could be a long night.

CHAPTER 67

"Why do those policemen all drive so crazy?" Gil thought to himself. He was still a little shaken up by the near miss with the police car, but after a few minutes, with senses now sharpened, he decided to finish the job. He had to get back to the trailer and bury Gran.

He spent the time walking home thinking back on his life. Gran took him in when he needed a place to live. She could be a cranky old coot and no doubt hard to get along with, but there were some good times when he was a kid. He did love the camping trips and those individual swimming pools on hot summer days.

By the time he had returned to the trailer, he had reconciled himself to the fact that Gran had lived a good and full life, so why should he feel guilty about what he was about to do? He thought, "After all, I didn't kill her. It was an accident, and I'm giving her the good burial she deserves. What's the difference between this and a crummy plot at the county cemetery where no one would ever go to visit?" Gil stopped to think, "This is better than the county cemetery. At least she'll be close to home and in a pretty spot," he reasoned.

Back in the trailer's living room, Gil faced a dilemma. Looking out the back window toward the retention pond, he wondered, even at this early hour, how he would get that heavy barrel down the hill and to the pond without anyone noticing. He peeked out each trailer window checking for any signs of any human activity. He saw it was starting to snow again but was pleased the coast seemed to be clear.

The trailer's weak floor creaked as Gil rolled the heavy barrel on its side to the back door. Stepping outside, he looked around. Seeing no activity, he tipped the barrel upright to get it through the door. He pushed it over the back-door threshold onto the flimsy wooden back porch, where he sat it next to the porch railing. He turned and walked back through the back door, intending to turn off the kitchen light when a rotted wooden floor brace that was situated beneath the porch floor directly under the barrel gave way. As the corner of the porch started to crack and collapse, the barrel tipped sideways through the porch railing, slamming on its side with a noisy splat onto the snow-covered ground. Surprised, he crouched Ninja-like, low on the porch, looking around to see if anyone had been disturbed by the sudden noise.

Scared out of what few wits he had left, he stayed in the crouched position, not moving for several minutes until he was brave enough to duck-walk toward the trailer's back door. He stood up with his back against the door, trying to blend into the wall and be invisible. Gil waited as he watched and listened for any activity that might indicate someone heard the porch collapse, but the only thing he noticed was the snow coming down heavier than before. Lucky for him that most of the nearby residents were old pensioners with bad hearing.

Ten to fifteen minutes passed before Gil thought it safe to finish the job. Relieved he didn't have to figure a way to get the barrel down the four rotted porch steps and onto the ground, he stepped off the porch and walked to the barrel. He wondered how he would get it down the hill and stood next to the barrel, trying to come up with a solution to this problem. He glanced behind him and was surprised to see the footprints he had just left in the heavy snow on top of the rolling impression the barrel made. Standing next to the overturned barrel, he looked down the hill toward the pond, thinking, "How am I going to get this thing down the hill without it looking like a snowplow drove through here?" Again, he looked around, making sure no one was watching. Satisfied there were no spectators, as an experimental test run, he pushed the barrel the short distance through his backyard to the crest of the hill overlooking the pond. Disappointment sunk in as he stared back and noticed the track-mark impression the heavy rolling barrel made in the fresh snow.

Disgusted, Gil sat down on the round side of the now snow-covered barrel, holding his chin with both hands, elbows on his knees, and back to the pond, trying to think. Within seconds he accidentally slid down and off the slick barrel. His body weight inadvertently pushed the barrel away from him, causing it to begin rolling down the slope toward the retention pond. Panicked, Gil jumped into action and chased the speeding barrel down the snow-covered hill. He ended up only a horrified spectator after he slipped and fell face-first into the snow. From this prone position, he could clearly see the barrel recklessly careen toward the pond, bouncing like an unbalanced wheel and picking up speed along the way. As it approached the pond, he watched in surreal amazement as the speeding barrel crested the slightly raised edge of the pond and lifted into the air as if launched off a ski ramp. At its apex, it seemed to pause in midair before dropping straight down like a heavy stone through a few inches of icy snow that covered the bottom of the unfinished pond, landing with a loud thud.

Panic couldn't describe what Gil was now feeling. In fact, his meager vocabulary didn't include any words that could describe his state of mind as he lay in the snow looking at the partially submerged barrel sticking up from the pond, ten feet from the edge. Still in the prone position, he flattened himself out as much as possible. He was practically hugging the ground, hoping to stay out of sight of any old codgers living in the trailer park who might peek out a window. Frazzled, he wondered, "Could this night get any worse?"

CHAPTER 68

After watching the 10:00 p.m. local news, Derek completed his bedtime routine, then climbed into bed promptly at 10:15 p.m., much as he always did. He woke to his alarm at 1:45 a.m., allowing him enough time to throw on some clothes and get to Olivia's by 2:30 a.m. He planned to set up surveillance from the used car lot across the street from the club. Once he saw Sanders' Chevy Impala approach, he planned to contact the dispatcher and ask for assistance with approaching Sanders in Olivia's back lot.

CHAPTER 69

Gil wasn't sure how long he lay prone in the snow on the side of the hill. Since the barrel crashed into the snowy pond, he had not heard anything to make him believe anyone had been disturbed by the barrel rollicking on its wild ride down the hill and into the pond. He stood up and made his way back to the top of the hill, intent on retrieving Grandpa's round-point shovel out of the mini barn. Of course, he might also need the flat transfer shovel to move the layer of icy snow more easily. Also, the long blade of the trench spade might be helpful to turn and loosen the dirt faster.

Gil had shoveling tool options. Much like some women are clothes hounds, his grandpa had been a tool hound. The mini barn was still loaded with tools galore left after Grandpa died. Too cheap and poor to buy these tools new, he acquired them from garage sales, thrift stores, and pawn shops. Grandpa always said that a man had to have the right tool for every job, and he did his best to equip himself. The odd thing about this situation was that while Gil was definitely lazy, with no intention of ever working an honest job, as a child, he often helped his grandpa when using his precious tools and somehow absorbed some of his grandpa's tool-handling talents.

He quickly grabbed the round-point shovel and the trench spade, but when he turned to exit the mini barn, his eyes locked on the steel-handled tamper plate. The tamper plate was basically a 3/8-inch-thick, ten-inch by ten-inch square plate of steel with a pole connected to the center at a right angle. It was used to tamp down and smooth out small asphalt patches manually. Using this tool required some strenuous effort, but as Gil considered this tool, he decided that once he had the barrel buried and finished shoveling the dirt back on top, it would make the job of leveling and packing together the loose soil covering the hole easier. He grabbed the steel-handled tamper plate and the two shovels and started toward the pond. To his pleasant surprise, his footprints in the snow and the barrel tracks leading down the hill were already beginning to disappear under new falling snow.

Gil, digging tools in hand, walked down the hill to the pond, making his way through the mushy, almost frozen snow which covered the pond to the barrel. The barrel was on its side with one end partially sticking up above the snow. Leaning on the shovels, he took one last look around, checking for witnesses before he got to work. Trees surrounded the pond on the side facing the trailer park, and from his position, he could only see one trailer, Gran's trailer. "This'll be a good spot for you, Gran. Close to home where I can keep a watch on ya," Gil whispered as he leaned over and used his right hand to affectionately pat the barrel. He looked at the area around the barrel and decided to start by using the flat transfer shovel to move the snow.

Not used to manual labor, he was surprised at how heavy the snow was, but there was no time to complain. Once he had moved the snow aside and reached the ground level of the pond, he used the long blade trench spade to thrust down several times. At the end of each downward thrust, he would turn the blade as he pulled it out of the ground, loosening the dirt. After several minutes of this aggressive spade action, Gil stopped and used the round-point shovel to remove the loose dirt. After tossing it aside, he repeated the process over and over until he hoped the hole was deep enough for the barrel to fit inside. He wasn't sure why there wasn't much water at the bottom of the pond but thought it must have something to do with the new housing edition's drainage system not flowing into it yet. He wasn't going to look a gift horse in the mouth because he had thought he would have to contend with a lot of mucky water during the dig.

After a considerable amount of digging and moving dirt, he stood at the edge of the hole. He shoved the handle end of the shovel to the bottom of the hole, trying to gauge how deep it was. Using the same shovel, he measured the height of the barrel as it lay on its side and, with some disappointment, concluded he needed to dig deeper. He shoveled another 20 minutes and stepped back to assess his progress. Concerned it still wasn't deep enough and wanting to ensure his work would be concealed, he continued digging another two feet deep. He was tired but reasoned this was not a job where he could cut corners. He wouldn't have a second chance to get it right.

Before he started digging, he knew it would be a strenuous job but didn't really understand just how strenuous. The continuously falling snow made it difficult to get traction as he worked with the shovel. He was exhausted from the difficult work, and the heavy cold air didn't help. After a short break, he concluded the hole was big enough and ready for use.

Gil pushed the barrel into the hole, gratified it fit. He used the shovel to push dirt into the hole and around the barrel. He occasionally stopped to use the tamper plate to pack down the loose dirt. He was getting close to having the barrel covered with dirt when he realized there would be a lot of dirt left over. He had not considered the size of the barrel would displace some of the dirt he removed when digging the hole. He had to move more snow out of the way to spread the extra dirt evenly. He used the tamper plate to pound the excess dirt flat into the ground to make the bottom of the pond appear untouched. Gil was annoyed the snow continued to fall, hampering his efforts. But on the other hand, he was happy that it was covering up his dirty work.

CHAPTER 70

Pierson parked his unmarked police car among other cars parked in a body shop parking lot across the street from the Templeton Bank and Trust. This spot gave him a good view of the bank's outdoor twenty-four-hour ATM. At 2:30 a.m., he heard Derek on the police radio informing Templeton dispatch he also was on duty and conducting surveillance close to Olivia's Gentleman's Club. He wasn't sure what case Derek was working on and wasn't too curious, thinking he would find out the next day in the office. He was concentrating on clearing the robberies. He had Sandpiper's latest mugshot, which included his most recent physical description, clipped to the side of his car's floor-mounted laptop. With the Christmas robbery season in full swing and Christmas Eve around the corner, he was starting to feel like it was a good night to look for Piper.

CHAPTER 71

Piper didn't care what the big policeman said. He was headed back to the VendMate dumpster to get some travel food for his road trip to Arizona. He parked the stolen minivan a few blocks from VendMate, grabbed his backpack, and began the walk toward the dumpster. He hoped to shove enough prepackaged snacks, donuts, and sandwiches into his backpack and coat pockets to last him most of the way to Arizona. Food for the trip would be nice, but he would also need some cash. Maybe he would snatch some snacks from the dumpster, then hit the road and do a few roadside robberies on his way to Arizona.

CHAPTER 72

Derek arrived at the used car lot across from Olivia's at exactly 2:30 a.m. and parked his unmarked police car in a used car lot behind the front row of cars, close to the street. The spot provided a good view of both directions of travel on State Road 76 and would allow him to exit the lot quickly. As his habit, even in cold weather, he lowered both his driver's side window and the front passenger side window enough to be aware of his surroundings. He hoped to snag Sanders and serve the subpoena commanding him to provide handwriting samples. This meant that this morning's detail could last several hours.

Derek had planned to ask for backup from on-duty officers once he spotted Sanders, then wait until they arrived. It was best for a uniformed officer in a marked police car to make the first contact in an investigation such as this. Because of this, he planned to have the uniform officers make the first approach to Sanders.

There had been several occasions when Derek, while in plain clothes, confronted a suspect who didn't believe he was a real police officer. On other occasions where, because of his somewhat "soft" appearance, other suspects questioned his authority and challenged him. Although he was uncomfortable when challenged or confronted, he had always been able to work his way out of such situations. Nonetheless, his already slim confidence in his ability to handle himself had been shaken during those encounters. When faced with such situations, Derek wasn't sure if he was scared or merely just untested. He wondered how it was with officers like Mel. It seemed they could walk into any situation without fear of harm or failure, confident they could handle whatever was placed in front of them. He wanted a swagger and unflagging confidence like Mel.

Derek knew he wasn't the first person whose bravery had been questioned, which explained how his Geronimo plaque hanging in his office came about. Legend had it that in 1940, at Fort Benning, Alabama, the United States Army tested a new type of parachute. Some of the young troops involved were nervous about the testing the next day. To relax, they went as a group to a movie theater and watched the recent release of, "Geronimo." After the viewing, some of the troops joked with one of the next day's parachuters, who seemed particularly nervous about the jump, suggesting he would be too scared to remember his own name when he jumped. Having his courage called into question, this parachuter responded by bragging to his buddies that the next day, as he jumped out of the plane, instead of his own name, he would scream "Geronimo." To his credit, that's exactly what he did. Next thing you know, all the other jumpers followed suit screaming "Geronimo" as each jumped from the plane, establishing a new and enduring parachuting tradition. This story was such an encouragement to Derek that he had the Geronimo plaque made for his office to remind him that bravery was not in the talking, but in the doing.

CHAPTER 73

While on patrol and doing security checks on businesses in his assigned district, Mel thought about Carolyn and how he should get her something nice as a Christmas gift. It was only a few days until Christmas, but the time felt right to move things along in this relationship. At the thought of Carolyn, he pulled the Saint Michael's pendant by the chain out from under his shirt and gently rubbed it between his forefinger and thumb, thinking how sweet she was and what a nice, thoughtful, and most important, meaningful gift she had given him. He turned his squad car into the VendMate parking lot, drove toward the rear of the building, and turned on the car's spotlight, shining it toward the loading dock.

The spotlight beam crossed over a figure leaning into the dumpster next to the loading dock. The figure was wearing a black pullover sweatshirt with a backpack slung over his shoulder. Mel immediately recognized him as Sandpiper. Releasing the pendant, he grabbed the steering wheel and punched the accelerator of the squad car, pointing it toward the dumpster. While in motion, he unbuckled his seat belt expecting to bail out in a foot pursuit. He turned on his bright headlights hoping to blind Sandpiper. Using his police radio to call for assistance, he informed other officers of his location and that he had Sandpiper in sight. Mel slid his police car to a stop with the passenger side door facing Sandpiper, using the car body as cover. After opening the driver's door and jumping out, he grabbed his flashlight with his left hand while gripping the handle of his holstered pistol with his right hand. Using a loud commanding voice, he yelled at Sandpiper, "Stop and throw your hands in the air!"

Derek didn't have to wait long before he saw an old Chevy Impala traveling eastbound on State Road 76. It slowed down and, without using a turn signal, turned left into the Olivia's Gentleman's

Club parking lot, moving toward the back lot. The turn signal violation was enough justification to stop the car. He put his police car in gear, but as he was reaching for his police radio to call for backup, he heard Mel's excited voice over the police radio's speaker, "Dispatch, start me a back up to the VendMate loading dock. I have Sandpiper!" Derek froze for a second, then recognized the name Sandpiper from the robbery intelligence bulletin Pierson distributed that prior afternoon.

Teresa was assisting Jeramy on a traffic stop, and both were standing behind the passenger side of the traffic violator's car. They were about to contact the police dispatcher to run a check on the driver's operator's license when they heard Mel over the police radio saying he located Sandpiper at VendMate. Teresa looked at Jeramy and said, "You got this. I'm heading over there," then turned and trotted to her squad car.

Knowing apprehending Sandpiper was far more important than this routine traffic stop, Jeramy ran to the driver's side of the stopped car. He tossed the driver's ID and vehicle registration through the open window onto the surprised driver's lap. As he turned to run back to his squad car, he yelled toward the driver, "You're good to go." Jeramy jumped into his police car, emergency lights already on, activated his siren and started for VendMate.

CHAPTER 74

"Why is it the best snacks are always way in the back of the dumpster?" Piper mumbled as he was standing awkwardly balancing on the tippy-toe of one leg while on top of an empty milk crate, leaning over and partially into the VendMate dumpster. He was using the hooked end of a broken umbrella he found in the parking lot, trying to move a package of glazed donuts close enough to reach when he saw a spotlight move toward him. He turned to look in the direction of the light, stumbled, and fell off the milk crate, but not before he noticed a police car roar up next to the dumpster. Getting his bearings, he picked himself up off the ground, but it didn't take a rocket scientist to see he was in trouble. When he saw the big policeman get out of the police car, Piper decided it was time to go. He scurried toward a privacy fence bordering three sides of the VendMate back parking lot. He jumped on the hood of an old Honda Civic, which was parked next to the six-foot privacy fence and threw himself up to the top, balanced on one hand as he fell sideways over the fence, landing on the other side.

As he chased Sandpiper toward a privacy fence, Mel was sorry he had not kept himself in better shape. He was impressed when Sandpiper jumped onto the hood of the Honda, then scampered over the fence. Knowing the immediate area better than Sandpiper, Mel skipped the privacy fence-jumping heroics and ran to the far side of the Honda and opened the unlocked privacy fence gate before running through in time to see Piper galloping across the VendMate front parking lot and toward State Road 76. He yelled at Sandpiper to stop, but to no avail. He radioed dispatch that he was in foot pursuit, giving his location and direction of travel, along with a clothing description of Sandpiper. As he continued to chase Sandpiper, he began to hear the approaching sirens over his labored breathing and the clitter-clatter of all his uniform police gear being jostled as he ran.

Jeramy was approaching VendMate in a four-lane section of State Road 76 while listening closely to the updates Mel was broadcasting over the police radio and trying to guess where Sandpiper might run. Much like Mel had done a few seconds earlier, Jeramy, while driving his police car and anticipating a confrontation, started the process of using one hand to unfasten his seatbelt to get ready to jump from his cruiser. He then noticed Teresa's police car slide to a stop in the outside travel lane just in front of him.

Piper had surprised himself by scaling the privacy fence so easily but couldn't believe it when he looked back and saw that big dumb policeman still chasing him. Somehow, the big oaf had gotten over the fence, and that fact scared him. He ran as fast as he could, which wasn't easy in the snow-covered parking lot. If he could somehow circle around and get to where he had parked the stolen minivan, he might be able to escape. As he was running, he looked back to see where the big policeman was, and his heart jumped when he realized the big policeman was gaining ground on him. Trying to run faster, he slipped and tumbled head over heels. Getting up, he ran toward the street. That's when he remembered the Glock in his backpack.

CHAPTER 75

Gil looked down on his handy work and had, at least for him, the unusual feeling of satisfaction from a job well done. Being chilled from the cold sweat of exertion, he rested. As he leaned on the tamper plate, he felt nostalgia for his younger days before Grandpa died and Gran started drinking heavily. After all, she took him in when both parents abandoned him, providing him with a place to stay. Looking at the burial site, which was quickly being covered with snow, he eased his conscience by telling himself Gran was in a better place now, or so he convinced himself. After a few moments of quiet reflection, he cautiously looked around. Feeling confident he had not been watched, he carried the tamper plate and both shovels out of the retention pond, up the hill, and returned them to the mini barn. He then walked back to the crest of the hill and looked down toward the retention pond, pleased he could hardly see any evidence of his recent work under the fresh snow. Turning to enter the trailer, he heard lots of sirens in the distance. He reversed himself, walking away, thinking it best to get some distance from the area for a while, just in case.

CHAPTER 76

Pierson reached the front VendMate parking lot, but as he was trying to turn in, his police car slid into a ditch bordering the street, getting stuck in the deep snow. He hopelessly gunned the car's engine, trying to back it out with no luck. Giving up quickly, he got out of the car, and even though he was still some distance away, he started to run straight for Sandpiper. From his vantage point, he could see the entire field of action. He could see Mel running toward Sandpiper and closing in, then saw Sandpiper slip and fall. While Sandpiper was getting up, it looked like he was reaching into his backpack. He heard sirens, then Teresa and Jeramy drove to the edge of the parking lot and stopped. Sandpiper got to his feet and, while he was looking back, probably at Mel, started to run toward the street bordering one side of the parking lot. Sandpiper was clearly concentrating on evading Mel. At the same time, unaware he was running in the direction where Teresa and Jeramy were setting up, cars side by side in the street. As Pierson was running through the parking lot, he noticed Sandpiper had something in his hand.

Over the police radio, Jeramy heard Mel yell, "He's running through the parking lot toward State Road 76." Jeramy followed Teresa to the scene, and when she stopped her police car in front of the VendMate parking lot, he drove up next to her, stopping in the inside lane of the four-lane road. Scanning the area, he saw a man in a black hoodie run into the street 30 feet in front of him. The man stopped in the middle of the road, and when he turned to see Jeramy, he appeared startled. Jeramy tried to jump from his police car but lost a fraction of a second when his loose seatbelt got tangled with the grip of his pistol. He quickly untangled the seat belt, but as he got out of the car, he saw the man raise his right arm, shoulder high, holding a pistol. Without time to react, a flash of light erupted from the end of the gun. Jeramy was still standing, and it had not registered yet in the pain centers of his brain that he had just been struck in the upper left leg by a 9mm bullet when he saw another flash of light burst from the end of the pistol. This time the impact of the bullet entering his lower stomach, just under the reach of his ballistic vest, picked him up off his feet and propelled him backward and flat onto his back.

As Teresa approached VendMate, she could see Mel on foot chasing Sandpiper through the VendMate parking lot. Sandpiper ran into the road about 30 to 40 feet in front of her with a pistol in his right hand. She stopped her car and was unbuckling her seatbelt when she noticed Jeramy stop his police car next to hers. Jeramy was trying but having trouble getting out of his car. At the same time, she was reporting on the police radio Sandpiper's location and that he had a gun. She saw Sandpiper raise his right arm and quickly fire two gunshots in Jeramy's direction. Getting out of her car in a flash, she remembered from training that inexperienced gunmen generally tended to jerk their finger while pulling the pistol's trigger, causing them to shoot high. As a result, Teresa, while drawing her pistol, crouched low behind her open car door, using it as a barricade. Holding her pistol with both hands in a low ready position, she slid sideways around her car door. She raised her pistol into the ready position, quickly putting Sandpiper's chest in her front sites, and confidently squeezed the trigger in a smooth motion. Even with the lighting from the headlights of the police cars and streetlights shining down, it was still partially dark, and she was momentarily distracted by the long, bright flash of flame issuing from the barrel of her pistol. Immediately she could see a puff of red start to spread from Sandpiper's left shoulder and his knees buckled slightly. He twisted to his left, trying to locate where the attack came from. His left arm was now hanging loosely at his side, but he was able to stay on his feet. Right arm still outstretched, he turned enough to point his pistol in Teresa's direction. After the recoil of her first shot, Teresa was already calmly and smoothly bringing her pistol down level. She was putting Sandpiper's center mass back into her sites, intending to fire another shot, when she was distracted by the roar of a car engine and the peculiar sound of someone screaming loudly.

As Piper picked himself up, he reached into his backpack and pulled out the Glock as he ran from the parking lot into the street. He stopped in the middle of the street when to his surprise, he was confronted by two police cars, tactically parked side by side in front of him. He was now acting on pure adrenaline and not thinking about what he was doing, and if he had, he surely would have decided to surrender. Instead, like a crazed animal, he instinctually reacted to the situation, raising his arm and firing two quick shots at the policeman who was getting out of a police car. For a brief moment, he was strangely fascinated, staring at the policeman as he stumbled and fell backward. Standing tall, Piper was overcome with a mighty conqueror's sense of power when out of the corner of his eye, he noticed a tiny policewoman hiding behind the door of the other police car just as she fired a shot at him. Piper felt an incredibly sharp pain as the 180-grain, 40-caliber hollow point bullet pierced his left shoulder, severing and shattering bone, muscle, and tendon. Looking down at his shoulder, which was now in intense pain, his rage swelled as he could almost taste the anger he felt. That policewoman attacked him, and he was going to kill her for that. Still feeling invincible and reveling in his direct hits on the policeman, he turned slightly in the policewoman's direction. Smiling wickedly, he aimed at his new target, but before he could fire, he was distracted by a loud noise.

Pierson could hardly take it all in as everything was happening in front of him. As he was running toward Sandpiper, he could only watch as Teresa and Jeramy drove up, surprising Sandpiper in the middle of the street. Horrified, he saw the gunfight unfold. First, he saw Jeramy get out of his police car, and it looked like Jeramy was going to engage Sandpiper. Pierson was momentarily stunned when Sandpiper fired two quick shots at Jeramy, knocking him down and out of the fight. That's when Teresa joined the fray, firing at Sandpiper. Sandpiper staggered for a second, and he felt sure Teresa's shot had landed true, but Sandpiper stayed on his feet and was turning his pistol in Teresa's direction when it happened.

CHAPTER 77

Derek hated missing the opportunity to take Sanders in for handwriting samples. He had worked hard on the investigation and wanted that forgery arrest. The urgent tone of Mel's voice over the police radio prompted him to assist the other officers. Derek was close to VendMate and wheeled his unmarked police car out of the parking lot, quickly moving in that direction. In all the excitement, he forgot to roll up his car windows or activate his emergency equipment.

Driving toward the scene, Derek listened to the police radio, hearing updates of the ongoing action. Not long after Mel reported locating Sandpiper behind VendMate, Mel was back on the radio reporting he was in foot pursuit. During the foot pursuit, he heard Teresa yell over the radio, "Gun!" But the most distressing part was after she said gun, and while her radio microphone was still keyed in the open position and still transmitting, Derek could hear two quick gunshots echo over the radio. He was seconds away from VendMate when he next heard Pierson yell over the police radio, "Shots fired!"

Before this day, Derek would have thought that sensory overload of this magnitude would cripple him. As he barreled toward the scene from about a block away, he heard Mel huffing and puffing as if running hard, trying to yell over the police radio, "Officer down, start medics!" It wasn't that things were moving in slow motion. That wasn't it. It was that Derek's senses were on high alert, absorbing everything as he acted deliberately, yet unconsciously, without concern for his personal safety. As he approached the scene, he saw two police cars parked in the street in tactical positions with emergency lights flashing. Teresa was barricaded in a combat position behind her police car's driver's door and pointing her pistol in the direction of a guy standing in the middle of the street. That guy was pointing a pistol back at Teresa. In the corner of his eye, Derek also saw Mel, still in the parking lot, running fast toward the guy standing in the street. As he ran, Mel yelled and pointed his pistol at the guy with the gun.

As in emergency driving training, Derek had his hands positioned at ten o'clock and two o'clock, firmly grasping the steering wheel with elbows extended outward. He was completely unaware his right foot was pushed hard, down on the police car's accelerator pedal all the way to the floorboard as the unmarked police car roared through the snow-covered street and into the scene.

There was no fear or hesitation. In Derek's mind, his mission was clear, eliminate the threat as quickly as possible, in any way feasible. He took a deep breath as he swerved his police car into the empty oncoming lane of traffic to get around the two stopped police cars in front of him. Passing the two cars, he noticed Jeramy lying on his back next to the open door of his police car, blood pooling around his leg. He saw Teresa, pistol up, ready to fire at the man in the street, who, in turn, was pointing a pistol back at her.

Sandpiper stood firm as Derek's car raced towards him and deliberately turned his body toward Derek's approaching car as if in defiance. Derek saw the evil in Sandpiper's eyes as he stood straight and pointed his pistol at the windshield of Derek's car. This was Derek's moment. Piper and Derek's eyes locked, then with a determined grimace on his face, Derek leaned forward in his seat, hunching over the steering wheel as if aggressively advancing on an adversary. Mouth wide open, he began a long and loud scream of "Geronimo!!!" as he aimed his police car directly at Sandpiper.

He was so focused on Sandpiper he could clearly see Sandpiper's forefinger pull the pistol's trigger. Without lifting his foot from the accelerator, Derek saw a flash shoot from the end of the pistol just before feeling a hard thump at the front of his car. The windshield glass shattered, part of which fell on him in a heap. He could see Sandpiper awkwardly somersault in the air over the hood of his police car. Then a blood-streaked right arm punched through what was left of the shattered passenger-side windshield. Sandpiper's pistol rattled as it slid across the hood of the police car. Derek could see Sandpiper's limp body draped over the car's hood but couldn't see much else out of the broken windshield of his still-speeding police car. He then felt a bump and the car sharply changed direction to the right before coming to a painfully jolting stop.

CHAPTER 78

As he was running to the scene, Pierson watched the entire incident, all of which couldn't have lasted more than 15 to 20 seconds. Derek didn't have any emergency lights or sirens on, so Pierson didn't notice him approaching until hearing the roar of the racing engine of the unmarked police car. Derek's car careened past Teresa and Jeramy's police cars, then Pierson saw Sandpiper's body, arms spread out like a jagged scarecrow, cartwheel through the air and into Derek's windshield. After striking Sandpiper, Derek's speeding car hit the curb and swerved sharply without slowing down, then, with heavy impact, struck a telephone pole. The telephone pole cracked and wobbled and would have fallen to the ground if not for the tightly strung electrical wires supporting it by the connecting poles on either side of the downed pole.

Smoke and steam were streaming from the front of Derek's car, and Pierson couldn't see anything moving inside. Seeing Mel and Teresa move toward Jeramy, he decided to check on Derek and ran to the wrecked car. As he approached, among the smell of burnt wires and radiator fluid, he was surprised to catch a faint whiff of discharged gunpowder. The frame of the mangled police car was buckled and bent, and one front tire was lifted off the ground, still spinning. Sandpiper was lying motionless astride the hood of Derek's car with one arm almost severed and extending through the broken passenger's side windshield. Pierson quickly checked on Sandpiper's torn body, determined he was surely dead, then moved to Derek.

Try as he might, Pierson couldn't get the damaged driver's side door open, so he ran to the passenger side door, forcing it open, in the process bending some of the car body's thin sheet metal. Looking into the car, he saw Derek's motionless body pushed back into the seat. The frame of the driver's seat was obviously broken and pushed backward, sandwiching Derek between the seat and the inflated airbag protruding from the steering wheel. The car's dashboard had been bent down, causing the bottom of the steering wheel to press down on Derek's legs, trapping him in the car. Part of the shattered windshield was lying on Derek's head and face, and blood seeped down from his right ear, cheek, and nose.

Pierson didn't know how badly Derek was injured, but it was clear that the fire department would have to cut him out of the car. He crawled through the passenger side door of the wrecked police car over the crushed glass particles and had to push Sandpiper's dangling arm aside to make his way through. He had to move broken interior car parts and the scattered contents of the car out of his way to get close to Derek's face. He put his left hand on Derek's right shoulder and, looking into his face, asked, "You okay buddy?"

Derek grimaced as he turned his head slightly, trying but unable to face Pierson, and coarsely asked, "Threat eliminated?"

"Yeah, buddy, threat eliminated," Pierson replied with a smile. He used his right forefinger to point through the windshield at the limp body lying on the hood of Derek's car, glad Derek was coherent enough to ask. When he pulled his left hand back from Derek's shoulder, he saw blood on his hand. Looking back at Derek's pinned and bloodied body and after looking closely, he noticed the very top of Derek's right ear was missing. Looking closer, behind Derek's head, punched into the right side of the driver's seat headrest, was a matching blood-stained bullet hole.

CHAPTER 79

Mel got to Jeramy first and holstered his weapon. Kneeling on both knees, and placed his first two fingers on the right side of Jeramy's neck, checking the carotid artery for a pulse. Not finding one, he held his face sideways close to Jeramy's face while looking down at his chest, not only to see if Jeramy's chest was expanding, moving up and down in a breathing motion, but also listening, trying to hear the faintest of breaths. Finding no pulse, no chest motion, and no breathing, he positioned his knees next to Jeramy's chest and spoke calmly into his police radio, announcing, "Starting CPR." Still on his knees, he bent over at his waist while straightening his back and arms. He clasped his hands together flat and used the combined palms of both hands to press into Jeramy's chest just above the sternum. Mel rhythmically repeated the motion fifteen times, then stopped. He put his left hand under Jeramy's neck, raising it slightly to allow air to pass as he placed his open mouth over Jeramy's, forcing air into his lungs. As he returned to performing chest compressions, he urgently murmured, "Breath, Jeramy, breathe!"

Teresa popped open the trunk of her police car, retrieved her first aid kit, and ran to Jeramy. Mel was already with Jeramy checking for a pulse as she quickly scanned Jeramy for injuries, seeing a large mass of blood pooling under and around his upper left leg. As Mel began CPR, she noticed a small tear covered with blood in Jeramy's upper left pants leg. Opening her first aid kit, she grabbed the bandage scissors. After cutting the pants leg open, she immediately noticed a perfectly round bullet hole in the front of Jeramy's thigh, and blood was gushing out of the hole with each chest compression. Acting quickly, she retrieved the tactical tourniquet from her first aid kit. She gently lifted Jeramy's injured leg at the knee with her left hand as she used her right hand to wrap the tourniquet around his upper left thigh just above the bullet hole. Using the tourniquet's fasteners to secure it, she turned a tightening rod until it was snug, stopping blood flow. She then scanned Jeramy for other injuries. He was flat on his back and had not moved since hitting the ground. His eyes were open, and she thought they were moving, almost twitching. She knew these eye movements were probably involuntary reactions caused by the physical trauma because Jeramy didn't move or respond in any other way. She noticed blood on Jeramy's lower stomach, just above his duty belt. In an impatient voice, she reported over the radio, "Advise medics, officer down, has two gunshot wounds, one to the abdomen and one to his left thigh with possible arterial damage." Glancing over at Derek's wrecked unmarked police car, she added, "Also, start two more medics, one for another injured officer and one for the suspect." She turned her attention back to Jeramy as Mel was doing chest compressions. Teresa, realizing there was nothing to be done about the stomach injury, moved to the opposite side of Jeramy, knelt near his face, then said, "Two-person CPR. Ready for breaths."

Mel was already exhausted. He had just chased Sandpiper flat out through heavy snow over a couple of hundred yards, and now he had been doing CPR for only a few minutes and getting very tired. It had been a while since Mel had done CPR and had forgotten how tiring it could be, down on your knees, back straight, rocking up and down, doing chest compressions over and over. Teresa was in place to give breaths in two-person CPR, and he was glad for the few seconds of rest while she helped by giving the breathing part of CPR. She put her left hand under Jeramy's neck, raising it slightly to allow air to pass. At the same time, she put her right palm against Jeramy's forehead, keeping his head steady as she sealed her lips completely around the outside of Jeramy's lips tight so air could not escape. After she blew two successive steady breaths into his lungs, Mel restarted the rhythmic chest compressions, counting out loud, "One, and two, and ....," all the way to 15 when he paused. Teresa, still kneeling, bent over and gave two more quick breaths. The Saint Michael's necklace Mel wore had escaped from under his shirt and was hanging loosely from the chain around his neck. He grabbed the pendant, briefly held it in his palm as he looked down at it, then quickly tucked it back under his shirt before reaching up and checking Jeramy for a pulse. Finding none, Mel resumed CPR.

Teresa watched Mel closely as he counted through another 15 chest compressions, waiting for her turn to perform more rescue breaths. Her mind was so involved with administering live-saving maneuvers that she wasn't conscious of what she might be feeling, that was until she glanced at Mel's face. Mel was doing chest compressions and was starting to tear up as he turned his head and looked into Jeramy's face. With emotion she had never seen or heard from Mel before, she heard him plead, "Come on Jeramy, don't die on me. Lord, please don't let him die," as he continued with the chest compressions.

CHAPTER 80

Jeramy tried but couldn't move his legs, his arms, or any part of his body. He couldn't talk or respond in any way to all that was happening around him. He could think well enough and was aware of the activity surrounding him. He was grateful he didn't feel pain even though he knew he had been shot in the leg and stomach, thinking the one gunshot must have severed his spine. He knew Mel and Teresa were working hard to save his life. He never gave it much thought before, but he loved them both. Not just for trying to save him, but he loved them for who they were, his friends, his coworkers, and fine police officers. They were working so hard and well as a team, so professional. He was proud of them, but then what did he expect? This is how they always performed. He had worked with them for years, and they were more than co-workers and friends. They were his family, his police family. He wondered if they knew he loved them and sincerely hoped they did. Out of the corner of his eye, he noticed something shiny in Mel's hand. Mel tucked the object under his shirt just before begging him not to die. Was that a tear in Mel's eyes? And Teresa, she was so intent on breathing life into his still body. Did anyone else know how amazing these friends were?

Jeramy lay motionless on his back as he gazed into a snow-flecked sky and marveled at the endlessness of outer space. He never understood how outer space could go on forever without end any more than he could understand gravity and how that worked. Even though he couldn't see or understand these things, he took it all on faith. Jeramy thought about the Bible verse Chaplain Gossett last left with him, "Don't be afraid, just believe." He never understood God, that is until now. Staring into that magnificent and boundless sky, it became clear and so obvious to him. The way the earth was created so perfectly for God's creations to occupy, this was no cosmic accident. How the human body was formed and how all the parts work together was simply beyond amazing. There was nothing the creator of heaven and earth could not do. Jeramy believed now. He believed with all of his heart, a belief and faith mixed with total amazement. He wondered if anyone would know he had become a believer. He hadn't told anyone, but then it really didn't all come together completely for him until right here, in the street, lying on his back.

Jeramy still didn't know why God took Carl so young, but he knew Carl had been an instrument God used to draw him close. He wondered, how many other people in his short life did Carl touch? He wished Carl's wife and family knew the effect Carl had on his and probably others' lives. If not here and now, he was sure they would know someday. What a wonder, how God used the horrific death of a good and faithful man like Carl to plant the signs of the seeds of faith in his life and certainly others.

Jeramy knew he was dying, but to his great surprise, he was okay with that. He was no longer afraid to die, and in fact, he now welcomed what would follow. That previous morning, reading that Bible verse, it was now so clear to him about the Apostle Paul planting seeds and Apollos watering those seeds. Carl planted the seeds of faith that Chaplain Gossett watered. Had God sent others to him in the past to plant seeds, he wondered? Surely, He had. After all, his mother had always encouraged him to live a faithful life, and there must have been others. But at the time, those seeds had fallen on the unwilling soil of Jeramy's soul. Now, in the last few moments of his brief earthly life, like the thief on the cross, in his last moments, Jeramy accepted his salvation. He felt a calming peace amid the chaos surrounding him, maybe even happiness, knowing this was not the end, but the beginning.

Feeling his earthly body fade, Jeramy tried, but couldn't focus on Mel or Teresa. It wasn't because things were going dark. Quite the contrary, everything around him was getting brighter as if exploding in all the colors of the rainbow. He felt indescribable joy as he silently prayed, "Lord, forgive me for all those wasted years of disobedience to You. I am finally ready."

CHAPTER 81

Gil walked and walked until he couldn't hear the police sirens anymore. Once the sirens went silent, he waited a little longer, then thought it safe to return to his, yes, now his, trailer. He planned to return home by walking through the Rose Garden Villa housing edition to get one last look at the retention pond before he got some shuteye. He walked next to the snow-covered empty retention pond and stopped to admire his work. "A nice tree would look good there. Right next to Gran. Maybe a pine tree, like that one Grandpa burnt down. Yes," he thought to himself as he looked toward the edge of the retention pond just beyond the burial spot, "Gran would like a nice big pine tree right there next to her."

"And the City has no need of sun or moon to shine on it, for the glory of God gives it light, and its lamp is the Lamb."
Revelation 12:23, (EVS)

"In the same way, let your light shine before others, that they may see your deeds and glorify your Father in Heaven."
Matthew 5:16, (NIV)

"The heavens declare the glory of God;
the skies proclaim the work of his hands."
Psalm 19:1, (NIV)

Made in the USA
Columbia, SC
14 December 2022